STARGAZER

Also by Claudia Gray

Evernight

CLAUDIA GRAY

HarperCollins *Children's Books*

First published in hardback in the USA by HarperCollins Inc. in 2009
Published in paperback in the UK by HarperCollins Children's Books in 2010
HarperCollins Children's Books is a division of HarperCollinsPublishers Ltd,
77-85 Fulham Palace Road, Hammersmith, London W6 8JB

The HarperCollins website address is
www.harpercollins.co.uk

ISBN 978 0 00 735532 7

Stargazer
Copyright © 2009 by Amy Vincent

Printed and bound in England by Clays Ltd, St Ives plc

Typography by Andrea Vandergrift
1

FSC is a non-profit international organisation established to promote the
responsible management of the world's forests. Products carrying the FSC
label are independently certified to assure consumers that they come
from forests that are managed to meet the social, economic and
ecological needs of present and future generations.

Find out more about HarperCollins and the environment at
www.harpercollins.co.uk/green

Prologue

FROST BEGAN TO CREEP UP THE WALLS.

Transfixed, I watched lines of frost lace their way across the stone of the north tower's records room. The pattern swept up from the floor, covering the wall, even icing the ceiling with something flaky and white. A few small, silvery crystals of snow hung in the air.

It was all delicate and ethereal—and completely unnatural. The room's chill cut deeper than my skin, down to my marrow. If only I hadn't been alone. If somebody else could have been there to see it, I might have been able to believe it was real. I might have been able to believe I was safe.

The ice crackled so loudly, I jumped. As I watched, my eyes wide and breath coming in thin, quick gasps, the frost etching its way across the window obscured the view of the night sky outside, blocking the moonlight, but somehow I could still see. The room possessed its own light now. All the many lines of frost on the window broke this way and that, not at random but in an eerie pattern, creating a recognizable shape.

A face.

The frost man stared back at me. His dark, angry eyes were so detailed that it seemed as though he were looking back at me. The face in the frost was the most vivid image I'd ever seen.

Then the cold stabbed into my heart as I realized: He really *was* looking back at me.

Once, I hadn't believed in ghosts—

Chapter One

AT MIDNIGHT, THE STORM ARRIVED.

Dark clouds scudded across the sky, blotting out the stars. The quickening wind chilled me as strands of my red hair blew across my forehead and cheeks. I pulled up the hood of my black raincoat and tucked my messenger bag beneath it.

Despite the gathering storm, the grounds of Evernight still weren't completely dark. Nothing less than total darkness would do. Evernight Academy's teachers could see in the night and hear through the wind. All vampires could.

Of course, at Evernight, the teachers weren't the only vampires. When the school year began in a couple of days, the students would arrive, most of them as powerful, ancient, and undead as the professors.

I wasn't powerful or ancient, and I was still very much alive. But I was a vampire, in a way—born to two vampires, destined to become one myself eventually, and with my own appetite for blood. I'd slipped past the teachers before, trusting in my own powers to help me, as well as some dumb luck. But tonight I waited for that darkness. I wanted as much cover as possible.

I guess I was nervous about my first burglary.

The word *burglary* makes it sound sort of cheap, like I was just going to barge into Mrs. Bethany's carriage house and ransack the place for money or jewelry or something. I had more important reasons.

Raindrops began to patter down as the sky darkened further. I ran across the grounds, casting a few glances toward the school's stone towers as I went. As I skidded through the rain-slick grass to Mrs. Bethany's copper-roofed carriage house, I felt the queasy pull of hesitation. *Seriously? You're going to break into her house? Break into anyone's house? You don't even download music you haven't paid for.* It was kind of surreal, reaching into my bag and pulling out my laminated library card for a use other than checking out books. But I was determined. I would do this. Mrs. Bethany left the school maybe three nights a year, which meant tonight was my chance. I slid the card between door and doorjamb and started jimmying the lock.

Five minutes later, I was still uselessly wiggling the library card around, my hands now cold, wet, and clumsy. On TV, this part always looked so easy. Real criminals could probably do this in about ten seconds flat. However, it was becoming more obvious by the second that I wasn't much of a criminal.

Giving up on plan A, I started searching for another option. At first the windows didn't look much more promising than the door. Sure, I could have broken the glass and opened any of them instantly, but that would have defeated the *don't-get-caught* part of my plan.

As I rounded a corner, I saw to my surprise that Mrs. Bethany had left one window open—just a crack. That was all I needed.

As I slowly slid the window up, I saw a row of African violets in little clay pots, sitting on the sill. Mrs. Bethany had left them where they would get fresh air and perhaps some rain. It was weird to think about Mrs. Bethany caring for any living thing. I carefully pushed the pots to one side so I would have room to hoist myself through the window.

Getting in through an open window? *Also* much harder than it looks on TV.

Mrs. Bethany's windows were pretty high off the ground, which meant I had to kind of jump to get started. Panting, I began to pull myself through, and it was difficult not to just fall flat on the floor inside. I was trying to come down feet-first. But I'd gone through the window headfirst, and I couldn't exactly turn around halfway through. One of my muddy shoes hit a windowpane hard, and I gasped, but the glass didn't break. I managed to lower myself the rest of the way and flop onto the floor.

"Okay," I whispered as I lay on Mrs. Bethany's braided rug, my legs still up above my head, braced against the windowsill and sopping wet from the rain. "So much for the easy part."

Mrs. Bethany's house looked like her, felt like her, even smelled like her—strong and sharp with lavender. I realized I was in her bedroom, which somehow made me feel like even more of an intruder. Though I knew that Mrs. Bethany had traveled to Boston to meet "prospective students," I couldn't help feeling as though she might catch me at any second. I was terrified of getting caught. Already I was shutting down, withdrawing deep into myself the way I did when I was afraid.

But then I thought of Lucas, the guy I loved—and had lost.

Lucas wouldn't want to see me being scared. He'd want me to stay strong. The memory of him gave me courage, and I pushed myself up to get to work.

First things first: I took off my muddy shoes, so I wouldn't track any more muck into the house. I also hung my raincoat on a nearby doorknob so it wouldn't drip water everywhere. Then I went to the bathroom and grabbed a handful of tissues that I used to clean up the mess I'd already made, plus my shoes. I tucked the tissues in my raincoat pocket, so I could throw them away somewhere else. If anyone was paranoid enough to go through her own trash can to find evidence of an intruder, it was Mrs. Bethany.

It was surprising that she chose to live here, I thought. Evernight Academy was grand, even grandiose, all stone towers and gargoyles—very much her style. This place was hardly more than a cottage. Then again, here she had privacy. I could believe that Mrs. Bethany might treasure that above anything else.

Her writing desk in the corner looked like the place to begin. I sat in the hard-backed wooden chair, put aside a silver-framed silhouette of a nineteenth-century man, and started rifling through the papers I found there.

Dear Mr. Reed,

 We have reviewed your son Mitch's application with great interest. Although he is obviously an exceptional student and a fine young man, we regret to inform you—

A human student who wanted to come here—one Mrs. Bethany had rejected. Why did she allow some humans to attend Evernight Academy but not others? Why did she allow *any* humans in one of the few vampire strongholds left?

Dear Mr. and Mrs. Nichols,

 We have reviewed your daughter Clementine's application with great interest. She is obviously an exceptional student and a fine young lady, and so we are pleased to—

What was the difference between Mitch and Clementine? Fortunately, Mrs. Bethany's organized filing system led me straight to their applications, but studying those didn't offer any answers. Both of them had scary-high GPAs and tons of extracurricular activities. Reviewing their lists of accomplishments made me feel like the world's biggest slacker. Their pictures made them both look pretty normal—not gorgeous, not ugly, not fat, not thin, just regular. They were both from Virginia—Mitch lived in an apartment building in Arlington, and Clementine in an old house in the country—but I knew that they both had to be rich as sin to even think about going to school here.

As far as I could tell, the only difference between Mitch

and Clementine was that Mitch was the lucky one. His parents would send him to a regular high-class boarding school on the East Coast, where he would mingle with other megarich kids and play lacrosse or go yachting or whatever they did at those places. Clementine, meanwhile, would be surrounded by vampires every second. Even though she would never know that, she would sense that something here was terribly wrong. She would never feel safe. Even I never felt safe at Evernight Academy, and I would become a vampire—someday.

Lightning brightened the windows, thunder following only a few seconds later. The storm would get harder soon; it was time for me to get back. Disappointment settled heavily upon me as I refolded the letters and put them back where they'd come from. I'd been so sure I would get answers tonight, but instead I hadn't learned a thing.

Not true, I told myself as I slipped on my raincoat and glanced at the flowerpots. *You learned Mrs. Bethany likes African violets. That's going to be REALLY useful.*

I straightened the violets on the windowsill just the way they'd been and left by the front door, which luckily locked automatically. How like Mrs. Bethany to not leave even that to chance.

The wind whipped the rain against my cheeks so that they stung as I ran back toward Evernight Academy. A few windows of the faculty apartments still glowed golden, but it was late enough now that I wasn't worried about anyone seeing me. I put my shoulder to the heavy oak door, and it swung open obediently without even so much as a creak. Shutting it behind me, I figured I was home free.

Until I realized I wasn't alone.

My ears pricked, and I peered into the darkness of the great hall. It was a vast open space, with no nooks to hide in or columns to duck behind, so I should've been able to see who it was. But I couldn't see anyone. I shivered; it suddenly felt much colder to me, more as though I were in a dank, forbidding cave than within Evernight's walls.

Classes wouldn't start for another two days, so the only ones at the school were the teachers and me. But any of the teachers would've immediately started scolding me for being out on the grounds so late in the middle of a thunderstorm. They wouldn't spy on me in the dark.

Would they?

Hesitantly I stepped forward. "Who's there?" I whispered.

Nobody answered.

Maybe I was imagining things. Now that I thought about it, I hadn't actually heard anything. I'd just *felt* it, that weird sense you sometimes have that somebody is watching. I had been worrying about people watching me all night, so maybe the worry was catching up with me.

Then I saw something move. I realized that a girl was standing outside the great hall looking in. She stood, draped in a long shawl, on the other side of one of the windows, the only window in the hall that was clear instead of stained glass. Probably she was my age. Though it was now pouring outside, she looked completely dry.

"Who are you?" I took another couple of steps toward her. "Are you a student? What are you—?"

She was gone. She didn't run, she didn't hide—she didn't even move. One second she was there, the next she wasn't.

Blinking, I stared at the window for a couple of seconds, like she would magically reappear in the same place. She didn't. I walked forward to try to get a better view, saw a flicker of motion, and jumped, startled—but I realized it was my own reflection in the glass.

Well, that was stupid. You just panicked at the sight of your own face.

That wasn't my face.

But it had to have been. If any new students had arrived today, I would've known, and Evernight was so isolated that it was impossible to imagine any stranger wandering by. My overactive imagination had gotten the better of me again; it must have been my reflection. It wasn't even that cold in here, once I thought about it.

Once I'd stopped shaking, I crept upstairs into the small apartment my parents and I shared over the summer, at the very top of Evernight's south tower. Fortunately, they were sound asleep; I could hear Mom's snoring as I tiptoed down the hallway. If Dad could sleep through that, he could sleep through a hurricane.

I still felt creeped out by what I'd seen downstairs, and being soaked to the skin didn't improve my mood. None of that bothered me as much as the fact that I'd failed. My big bad burglary attempt had come to nothing.

It wasn't like I could do anything about the human students at Evernight. Mrs. Bethany wasn't going to stop admitting them just because I said so. Besides, I had to admit that she'd protected them, policing the vampire students to ensure they didn't take even one sip of blood.

But knowing Lucas had made me aware of how little I understood the existence of vampires, even though I'd been born into that world. He'd made me see everything in a different way, made me more likely to ask questions and need answers. Even if I never saw Lucas again, I knew he'd given me a gift by awakening me to the larger, darker reality. No longer would I take anything around me for granted.

After I stripped off my wet clothes and curled up beneath the covers, I closed my eyes and remembered my favorite picture, Klimt's *The Kiss*. I tried to imagine that the lovers in the painting were Lucas and I, that it was his face so close to mine, and that I could feel his breath on my cheek. Lucas and I hadn't seen each other in almost six months.

That was when he'd been forced to escape Evernight because his true identity—as a Black Cross hunter of vampires—had been revealed.

I still didn't know how to handle the fact that Lucas belonged to a group of people dedicated to destroying my kind. Nor was I sure how Lucas felt about the fact that I was a vampire, something he hadn't realized until after we'd fallen in love. Neither of us had chosen what we were. In retrospect, it seemed inevitable that we would be torn apart. And yet I still believed, down deep, that we were destined to be together.

Hugging my pillow to my chest, I told myself, *At least soon you won't have so much time to miss him. Soon school will start again, and then you'll be busier.*

Wait. Am I reduced to HOPING for school to start?

Somehow, I have discovered a whole new level of pathetic.

Chapter Two

ON THE FIRST DAY OF SCHOOL, NOT LONG AFTER dawn, the procession began.

The first few students arrived on foot. They stepped out of the woods, simply dressed, usually with just a single bag slung over one shoulder. I think some of them had walked all night. Their eyes searched the school hungrily as they came closer, as though hoping they would immediately be granted the answers they sought. Even before I saw the first familiar face—Ranulf, who was more than a thousand years old and didn't understand the modern era a bit—I knew who the students in this group were. These were the lost ones, the oldest vampires. They didn't make trouble for anyone; they sank into the background, studying, listening, trying to compensate for the centuries they'd missed.

Lucas had slipped in among these last year. I remembered the way he'd appeared from the fog in his long black coat. Even though I knew better, I kept searching the face of each student who arrived on foot, wishing I could see his face again.

At breakfast time, the cars started to arrive. I was watching from the hallway of the classroom area, just a couple of stories up, so I could see the ornaments on the hoods: Jaguar, Lexus, Bentley. There were little Italian sports cars and SUVs big enough for the sports cars to park in. I could tell that these were the human students, because none of them came alone. Most of them had their parents with them, with a few younger brothers and sisters along for the ride. I even recognized Clementine Nichols, who had a light-brown ponytail and freckles across her nose. To my surprise, Mrs. Bethany met most of them in the courtyard, holding out her hand as graciously as a queen receiving courtiers. She seemed to want to talk to the parents, and she smiled warmly at them as though they were making friends for life. I knew she was faking it, but I had to hand it to her—she was good. As for the human students, the longer they hung out in the courtyard and stared up at Evernight Academy's forbidding stone towers, the more their smiles faded.

"There you are."

I turned from the scene below to see my father, who had pried himself out of bed early for the occasion. He wore a suit and tie, like a professor should, but his rumpled, dark red hair revealed more of his true personality. "Yeah," I said, smiling at him. "I just wanted to see what was going on, I guess."

"Looking for your friends?" My father's eyes twinkled as he stood by my side and peered out the window. "Or scoping out new guys?"

"*Dad.*"

"Backing off as requested." He held up his hands. "You seem a little happier about this than you did last year."

"I'd almost have to, wouldn't I?"

"Guess you would," Dad said, and we both laughed. Last year, I'd been so anti-Evernight that I'd tried to run away the day the students arrived—it seemed like a lifetime ago. "Hey, if you want some breakfast, I think your mother's got the waffle iron fired up and ready to go."

Even though they usually stuck to drinking blood from the clandestine shipments the school provided, my parents always made sure that I ate the real food I still needed. "I'll be up in a sec, okay?"

"Okay." His hand rested on my shoulder for a moment before he turned to leave.

I took one last look at the courtyard. A few families continued milling around or dragging in suitcases, but the third and final wave of students had begun to arrive.

They each came alone, in rented cars. There were a couple of taxicabs, but most of the cars were hired sedans or limousines. When the students emerged, they were already dressed in their tailored uniforms, their hair slicked back and shining. None of them had suitcases; these were the ones who had sent their many possessions on ahead in the boxes and trunks that had been arriving at Evernight for two weeks now. To my displeasure, I saw Courtney, one of my least favorite people, waving airily to some of the other girls. She was one of the many who wore dark sunglasses. That meant they were sensitive to sunlight, which in turn meant they hadn't drunk blood in a while. Dieting, probably, so that they'd look thinner and fiercer.

These were the vampires who needed help with the twenty-first century but weren't yet totally lost in the changes of time. These were the ones who still had their power—and weren't going to let anyone else at this school forget. I always thought of them the same way.

They were "the Evernight type."

By the time I'd finished my waffles and gone downstairs, the great hall was crammed with a throng of laughing, talking students. For a couple minutes, I was jostled around, feeling small, until I heard one voice shout out above the din, "Bianca!"

"Balthazar!" I smiled and raised my hand above my head, waving to him excitedly. He was a big guy, so tall and so muscular that he could've seemed intimidating as he pushed through the crowd toward me, if it weren't for the kindness in his eyes and the friendly smile on his face.

I went on tiptoe to hug him tightly. "How was your summer?"

"It was great. I worked the night shift at a dockyard in Baltimore." He said this with the same kind of relish that anybody else would use to describe a dream vacation in Cancun. "The guys and I made friends, hung out in bars a lot. I learned how to shoot pool. Started smoking again, too."

"I guess your lungs can take it." We grinned at each other, unable to complete the joke while the human students milled around nearby. "Do you need help getting your paper together?"

"Already done and on Mrs. Bethany's desk." All the vampires had to spend the summer months "engaged in the modern world," as the assignment stated, and were required to submit reports on their experiences at the top of every school year. It was sort of the "What I Did on My Summer Vacation" essay from hell. Balthazar glanced around. "Is Patrice here?"

"She's spending some time in Scandinavia instead." I'd received a postcard of the fjords a month before. "Says she'll finish up in a year or two. I think she met a guy."

"Too bad," Balthazar said. "I was looking forward to seeing a few more familiar faces. Besides the one approaching fast from four o'clock, I mean."

"What do you mean?" I tried to figure out where four o'clock was, but then her voice cut through the murmuring like fingernails on a chalkboard.

"Balthazar." Courtney held out a hand to him, as though she expected him to kiss it. He shook it once, then let it drop. Her lipstick-bright smile never wavered. "Did you have a wonderful summer? I was in Miami, hitting the club scene. Totally awesome. You should check it out with somebody who knows the hot places to go."

"I'm surprised to see you here," I said. *Surprised* seemed like a nicer way of putting it than *disappointed*. "You didn't seem to enjoy it much last year."

She shrugged. "I thought about ditching, but the first night

I was out in Miami, I realized I was wearing last season's dress. And my shoes were, like, three years old. *Major* faux pas! Obviously I needed a little more catching up, so I figured I could deal with a few more months at Evernight." Already her gaze was focused on Balthazar again. "Besides, I always enjoy spending more time with old friends."

I said, "If I wanted to learn about fashion, I wouldn't go someplace where everybody wears uniforms."

Balthazar's mouth twitched. Courtney narrowed her eyes, but her smile only grew wider as she glanced at my boxy, untailored sweater and plaid skirt. "And you've never had any interest in learning about fashion. *Clearly.*" She patted Balthazar on the shoulder. "We'll catch up later." Courtney sauntered off, long blond ponytail swinging from side to side as she went.

"I meant to try to get along with her better this year," I muttered. "I guess I haven't changed as much as I thought I had."

"Don't try to change. You're wonderful the way you are."

I glanced away shyly. Part of me thought, *Oh, no, now I have to let Balthazar down again.* The other part couldn't help liking that he'd said that to me. I'd been so lonely all summer—without Lucas, without anybody—and knowing that somebody right here cared about me was like being given a warm blanket after months of cold.

Before I could think of the best way to respond, a hush fell over the crowd. We all turned instinctively to the podium at the far end of the great hall. Mrs. Bethany was about to speak.

She had on a slim gray suit, more like twenty-first-century

clothes than she normally wore, but it suited her severe beauty. Mrs. Bethany's dark hair was swept up into an elegant twist, and black pearls shone in her ears. Instead of looking at the students, her dark eyes looked slightly above us, as though we were hardly visible to her.

"Welcome to Evernight." Her voice rang throughout the great hall. Everyone stood up straighter. "Some of you have been with us before. Others will have heard about Evernight Academy for years, perhaps from your families, and wondered if you would ever join our school."

This was the same speech she had given the year before, but I heard it differently this time. I heard the lies inside every careful phrase, the way she was speaking to the vampires in the room who had been here twenty years ago or two hundred.

As if she'd read my thoughts, she glanced at me, her hawk-like gaze piercing through the crowd. I tensed, half expecting her to accuse me of breaking into her home while she'd been gone.

But she did something even more surprising. She abandoned her script.

"Evernight Academy means something different for every person who comes here," Mrs. Bethany began. "It is a place of learning, a place of tradition, and for some a place of sanctuary."

Only if you're a bloodsucking creature of the night, I thought. *Otherwise? Not so much with the sanctuary.*

With one hand she gestured toward some of the new students, her long fingernails glinting red in the light that flowed through the stained-glass windows. To my astonishment, she was pointing out the human students—though of course they couldn't have understood why. "In order to get the most from your time at Evernight, you need to learn what this school means to your classmates. That's why I urge those of you with more experience to reach out to the new students among us. Take them under your wings. Find out about their lives, their interests, and their pasts. Only in this way can Evernight Academy accomplish its true goals."

A few people clapped uncertainly—humans who didn't know any better. "Okay, that was odd," Balthazar muttered beneath the slight applause. "If I didn't know any better, I'd think I'd heard Mrs. Bethany ask everyone to be friendly."

I nodded. My mind was racing. Why did Mrs. Bethany want the vampires to get closer to the human students? If she didn't want any humans hurt—and I still thought she didn't—then what was she really after?

"Classes begin tomorrow." The familiar, superior smile had returned to Mrs. Bethany's face. "Take this day to get to know your fellow students, particularly those who are new here. We are glad to have you—all of you—and we hope that you will make the most of your time at Evernight."

"Do you think she's gone soft on us?" Balthazar turned to me as people began to mingle again.

"Mrs. Bethany? Hardly." For a moment I considered asking Balthazar what he thought about the whole "admissions policy" mystery. He was smart, and even though he respected

Mrs. Bethany, he didn't take her word as gospel. Besides, he'd been around for more than three centuries; he'd probably have enough perspective to see my question in a different light and perhaps come up with a fresh answer. But Balthazar might also have the perspective to understand that I was asking because of my relationship with Lucas—something he wouldn't like to be reminded of.

Just then, Balthazar grinned and waved at somebody else—no telling who in that crowd, especially given that he was friends with nearly everybody. "I'll catch you later, okay?" I called after him as he started walking off.

"Definitely."

For a moment, I felt lonely without him. I was surrounded by vampires—real vampires, powerful and sensual and strong, with centuries of experience behind their beautiful, young faces. I wasn't yet a full vampire, and the distance between us hadn't closed much during my first year at Evernight. Next to them, I was still small, naive, and awkward.

All the more reason to head upstairs right away, I decided. I would have a different roommate this year, and I couldn't wait to say hello.

When I walked into my dorm room, Raquel sighed. "Welcome back—to hell."

She was flopped across her bare mattress, arms splayed out. Her duffel bag lay crumpled on the floor, as if deflated, and her clothes and art supplies were strewn around. It looked like she'd shaken the bag out and left her unpacking at that.

"Good to see you, too." I sat on the edge of my own bed. "I thought you'd at least be happy that we could be roommates this year."

"Trust me, you're the only reason I can stand the thought of being here again. Did your parents, like, bribe Mrs. Bethany or something? If so, I owe them big-time."

"No, just the luck of the draw." That was almost a lie. My parents hadn't asked Mrs. Bethany for any favors, but apparently there had been an odd number of humans and vampires admitted this year—both boys and girls. Since I still ate regular food more than I drank blood, I was considered the female vampire most likely to be able to hide the truth from a human when we dined in our rooms, as everyone did at Evernight.

Getting Raquel, though—that had been luck. That, and the fact that nearly every other human girl who had come here for her sophomore year had made sure to go somewhere else for her junior year. I couldn't blame them.

"So," I said, trying to keep my voice playful, "besides spending more time in my fascinating company, why did you come back? I know that's not what you'd planned."

"No offense, but even your fascinating company wasn't enough to change my mind." Raquel rolled over onto her belly, so that we were facing each other again. Her dark hair was cut even shorter than last year; at least she'd had a barber do it so that it looked good, even a little bit punk. "I told my parents I wanted to try somewhere else. Maybe live with my grandparents in Houston, go to school there. They didn't want to hear it.

Evernight's 'private' and 'exclusive,' and that should be enough for me, they said."

"Even learning about—about Erich—"

Raquel's mouth twisted into a scowl. "They said he was probably just trying to flirt with me. They said I was too stand-offish with guys, and I had to learn to 'like somebody back.'"

I stared at her, aghast. Erich hadn't been some overzealous would-be boyfriend. He had been a vampire intent on stalking and killing her. Raquel didn't know that, but she'd understood that he was dangerous. If I'd told my parents that somebody had scared me half as badly as Erich had scared her, my father would have held me tightly until I felt safe again, and my mother would've probably taken a baseball bat to whomever had dared threaten her little girl. Raquel's parents had laughed at her and sent her back to this place she hated.

"I'm sorry," I said.

She shrugged one shoulder. "I should've realized they wouldn't listen. They never have. Even when I—"

"When what?"

Raquel didn't answer. Instead, she shoved herself into a sitting position and pointed accusingly at the wall behind me. "So, are we stuck with the Klimt?"

I'd hung my print above my bed. *The Kiss* was so important to me that I'd forgotten Raquel had never seen it before. "What? You don't like it?"

"Bianca, that picture is so cliché. You can get it, like, on fridge magnets and coffee mugs and stuff."

"I don't care." Maybe it's stupid to like something just because everyone else likes it, but if you ask me, it's even stupider to dislike something because everyone else likes it. "It's beautiful, and it's one of my favorite things, and it's in my half of the room. So nyah."

"I might paint my side of the room black," Raquel threatened.

"That wouldn't be too bad." I imagined putting glow-in-the-dark stars upon the walls and ceiling, just the way my room had been when I was little. "That would be great, actually. Too bad Mrs. Bethany wouldn't let us get away with it."

"Who says she'd object? They've done everything else to make this place as creepy as possible. Why not black paint all over everything?"

I got the mental picture of the school's stone towers in shining black—which was pretty much all it needed to go straight to Dracula's castle territory. "Even the bathrooms. Even the gargoyles. I didn't think we could make Evernight any scarier, but we could, couldn't we?"

"It would still be better than being home." Raquel's eyes were strange as she said this—so weary that for a moment she looked older in spirit than the vampires who had surrounded us at the assembly.

I wanted to ask her more about what had happened with her parents, but I didn't know how. As I tried to find the words, Raquel briskly said, "C'mon and help me put away this crap."

"What crap?"

"My stuff."

"Oh," I said, nodding as we got to our feet and headed toward her boxes and duffel bag in the corner. "That crap."

After we'd gotten her bed made and her few things situated, Raquel wanted to take a nap. Her parents weren't wealthy, like most of the families of human students at Evernight; instead of being driven to the front door in a luxury sedan, she'd had to catch a bus from Boston before dawn, make a couple of transfers, and then wait for a cab to bring her up here. She was completely wiped and had fallen asleep even before I'd gotten done lacing up my shoes to go outside.

Raquel is here on scholarship, I thought. *That means Mrs. Bethany is actually paying for her to attend this school. Why would she do that?*

All the human students are here for a reason, and Raquel proves it's not money. But what is it? Is Raquel somehow even more important than the rest?

More questions, still no answers.

I strolled onto the grounds to see how much Evernight had changed, now that the other students were here. The humans were talking to one another eagerly, making new friends, while the vampires watched them, languid and disdainful.

My stomach growled. It was nearly lunchtime. I hoped I was the only vampire thinking about food while we were looking at the humans, but I probably wasn't.

"Yo, Binks!"

Nobody had ever called me "Binks" before in my life, but I knew who it had to be even before I recognized the voice. "Vic!"

Vic was loping toward me across the grounds, a big grin on his face. As usual, he'd made a few adjustments to the Evernight uniform; instead of the school colors, his tie was decorated with a hand-painted hula girl, and his beloved Phillies cap was on his head. We ran into each other's arms, laughing, and he spun me around so that my feet didn't touch the ground.

By the time he dropped me, I was dizzy but still smiling. "Did you have a good summer? I got your pictures from Buenos Aires, but then I didn't hear from you."

"After all the seaside fun, I was put to work. Woodson Enterprises has a summer internship program, and Dad was all, You need to learn the ropes of the family business. But when you're an intern? You're not learning any ropes. You're learning how people like their coffee. I spent the rest of the summer trying to remember who wanted a hot chai soy latte. Seriously lame. Were you stuck here the whole time?"

"We spent the Fourth of July in D.C. Mostly my mother dragged us around to monuments and stuff. But the Natural History Museum was pretty cool—they had some meteorites on display that you could actually touch—"

Vic's hand stole toward the pocket of my skirt. I pretended not to notice the envelope he held. My heart started beating faster.

"Well, it was fun. At least I got to be away from this place for one week of the summer, because as boring as it is during the year, it's even worse when you're here practically all alone." I was babbling, paying no attention to what I was saying. "I went down to Riverton on the weekends sometimes but that's pretty much it. Um, yeah."

"We gotta catch up later." Vic obviously understood that I couldn't think about anything right now besides the item he'd just tucked into my pocket. "You want to meet up after dinner? You can meet my new roommate. He seems pretty cool."

"Okay, sure." I would've agreed if Vic suggested we get together to shave our heads. Adrenaline coursed through me, making me giddy. "Meet up right here?"

"You got it."

Without another word, I ran away from him, heading straight for the cast-iron gazebo at the edge of the grounds. Fortunately, none of the other students were in there yet, which meant I still had it to myself.

I went up the steps and settled onto one of the benches. The thick canopy of ivy leaves overhead sheltered me from the sunlight as I reached into my pocket and withdrew what Vic had tucked there—a small white envelope, addressed only with my name.

For the first second, I couldn't open it. I could only stare down at the handwriting I remembered so well. The letter had been sent to me through Vic, by Vic's roommate from the year before.

Lucas.

Chapter Three

BIANCA,

I know it's been way too long. I hope you haven't been checking your e-mail all this time hoping to hear from me; my Evernight account got yanked, obviously, and they police our computer use pretty tightly in Black Cross. Besides, I figure they're monitoring your Evernight account.

But it doesn't feel like it's been so long since we talked. Sometimes I feel like I'm talking to you all the time, every second, and I have to remind myself that you aren't there to hear me, no matter how bad I wish you were.

Hasn't been much of a summer, to tell you the truth. We went down to Mexico for a couple of months, but it wasn't beach volleyball and Coronas by a long shot. In fact, half the time I ended up sleeping in the back of the pickup truck. Swear to God, I can still feel the metal ridges against my spine. Not fun.

Lucas didn't explain why he was in Mexico, or who "they" were who had gone with him. He didn't because he didn't have to; I already knew. Black Cross had traveled there on a vampire hunt.

Most of the time, I did a pretty good job of not remembering that the guy I loved was a member of Black Cross. Still, though, it was there, the hard fact that separated the world into two halves: mine and his.

Lucas's mother had become a member of Black Cross before he was born, and he'd been raised in the group—the only family he'd ever known. He'd been taught since childhood that all vampires were evil, and that killing them was the right thing to do.

But Lucas had learned things weren't that simple. Although he had fallen for me before he'd learned that I was born to vampire parents, or that I would become a vampire myself someday, learning the truth hadn't changed his feelings. Nothing had ever surprised or moved me more than the moment Lucas said he still wanted to be with me, that he still trusted me. Even though I had drunk his blood.

If you're reading this, that means the vampires aren't searching Vic's stuff. Obviously, Vic doesn't know what's really going on at Evernight or that he's actually dealing with vampires. That means it's not fair to keep putting him in danger. A couple of notes every once in a while—that we could probably get away with. But I know that's not enough for you or for me.

Oh, no. I sat upright, clutching the pages between my fingers so hard they crumpled. Was Lucas about to say that it was too risky for us to stay in touch? That we couldn't ever see each other again?

> *If I were a better guy, I'd break it off with you. I know I'm asking you to go against your parents, and with Mrs. Bethany breathing down your neck, even reading this puts you in danger. I ought to be strong and walk away.*
>
> *But I can't do it, Bianca. I've been trying to talk myself into it for weeks now, and I just can't. I have to see you again somehow. Soon, I hope, because I don't think I can stand this much longer.*
>
> *We're headed back to Massachusetts soon—not far from Riverton, as it turns out. Looks like a few of us are going to be scouting around Amherst near the end of September. I don't know how long we'll be there, but I figure it will be a while.*
>
> *Is there any way you could get to Amherst the first weekend of October? If so, I'll meet you at midnight at the Amherst train station—Friday or Saturday night, whichever you could make it. I'll wait both nights just in case.*
>
> *I realize that I might be off base here. It's been a long time since we've seen each other or been able to talk, and maybe you don't feel the same way anymore. Your parents have had a while to work on you about what a bad influence I am, and if Black Cross freaks you out, I don't guess*

I can blame you. Besides, a beautiful girl isn't going to be left alone for long. Maybe you're with somebody else now, like that Balthazar guy.

Remembering Balthazar's gentle flirtation that morning—and the warmth I'd felt in response—made me embarrassed all of a sudden, like Lucas had been eavesdropping and had overheard more than I'd meant to reveal.

If that's how things are, then—I can't say I'd be happy for you, because "happy" is not how I'd be feeling. I'd understand, though. I promise you that. Just send word to me in Amherst somehow so I know.

But I feel the same way. I still love you, Bianca. I think I love you more than I did when we said good-bye, and I didn't even think that was possible. If there's any chance you still feel it, too, then I have to try.

Okay, I keep reading this letter and feeling like it doesn't say everything I meant to say. I'm not so good with words. I guess you know that by now, huh? If you come to Amherst, I swear I'll find the right words to say. Or maybe we won't need words at all.

I love you.

Lucas

I blinked fast, trying to clear my swimming eyes. The letter shook in my trembling fingers, and my heart felt like a drumbeat beneath my skin. At that moment I could have taken off running toward Amherst, down the roads and over the hills, and been there in minutes—no, seconds—if I'd only known how, maybe I could have shut my eyes and just willed myself there. I wanted it that badly.

Instead, the tie between us was fragile; we were connected only by smuggled sheets of paper and a promise to meet. That was all we could have, because probably Lucas was right about the e-mail monitoring. For all her prim, old-fashioned ways, Mrs. Bethany stayed on top of every technological development that might help her remain in total control of the school. No doubt Mr. Yee had set it up so the headmistress could read every e-mail in the school accounts.

Even being connected only through the mail seemed miraculous now, as I held Lucas's letter in my hand. He had folded the pages within a greeting card, an unusual one—no message inside, and the photo on the cover was one of the constellation Andromeda. Lucas would've had to buy this someplace like a science museum or a planetarium. He remembered how I loved the stars.

Laughter across the grounds made me look up. Courtney and a few of her friends were strolling together at the edge of the lawn, snickering at some of the new human students. She made sure to point. Last year, I had been so intimidated by her. Now she seemed as insignificant as a buzzing fly at a picnic.

However, her presence reminded me that most of the vampires at Evernight knew about Black Cross and about Lucas. The card I held in my hands was evidence that I was communicating with "the enemy." I would have to destroy it, and soon.

At least Lucas had chosen an image that I could always see for myself, one that nobody could take away.

"That's Andromeda," I said to Raquel, pointing up at the night sky.

We were hanging out on the grounds after dinner—our regular dinner, that was. We'd made tuna fish sandwiches in our dorm room; after Raquel was in bed, I'd have to find a way to take a few swigs of the blood I had in a thermos in my dresser. Day one, and my mealtime situation was already complicated, but I'd just have to figure it out.

"Andromeda?" Raquel squinted upward. She had on the same faded black sweater that she'd worn threadbare last year. "That's from Greek mythology, right? I remember the name, but I don't remember anything about her."

"Sacrificial victim, Perseus to the rescue, Medusa head, yada yada." Vic walked up, hands in his pockets. "Hey, do you guys know my roommate?"

My eyes went wide as I turned my head from the stars to focus on the figure by Vic's side. "Ranulf?"

Ranulf held up one hand in a sheepish wave. His soft brown hair was still in the same bowl cut it had been in the year before— and, probably, the thousand years before that. Modernity was a very foreign concept to him; every single class was a challenge for him to even comprehend, much less absorb. And *Ranulf* was the male vampire chosen to have a human roommate? What could Mrs. Bethany have been thinking?

"Hey, Ranulf." Raquel didn't stand and offer a hand to shake, but for Raquel, even speaking to a stranger was being pretty friendly. "I remember seeing you around last year. You seem okay. You know—nonferal. Not like Courtney and her bitch patrol."

Clearly Ranulf didn't quite know what to make of that. After a moment's hesitation, he simply nodded. At least he'd learned how to bluff.

"Checking out the stars, huh? Vic flopped down beside us on the grass, his usual lopsided grin on his face. "I forgot you were into that."

"If you'd ever seen my telescope, you'd never forget."

"Big?" he asked.

"Huge," I said with relish. My telescope was one of my proudest possessions. "I kind of wish I'd hauled it down here tonight. The sky's incredibly clear."

Vic lifted one finger to the sky as if painting a little squiggle. "And that's Andromeda, right?" I nodded. "You see it, Ranulf?"

"Shapes in the sky?" Ranulf ventured as he hesitantly sat down with us.

"Yeah, the constellations. You need us to point them out to you?"

"When I look at the sky, I do not see shapes," Ranulf explained patiently. "I see the spirits of those who died before us, watching over us for all time."

I tensed, expecting the others to freak out or start asking Ranulf questions he couldn't answer. But Raquel merely rolled her eyes, and Vic nodded slowly as he took it in. "That's deep, man."

Ranulf had to pause to think up an appropriate reply. "You are 'deep' also, Vic."

"Thanks, dude." Vic punched Ranulf's shoulder.

Fighting back laughter, I rolled onto my back to look up at the stars. Mrs. Bethany hadn't chosen Ranulf to room with a human; she'd chosen Vic to live with a vampire. Apparently she'd realized that Vic didn't sweat the small stuff and so would simply blow off any of his roommate's weird habits.

Once again, she'd proven how insightful she was—and how well she understood all of us, even Vic. It made me glad that I'd already destroyed Lucas's card and letter. I'd wanted to hang on to them forever, but it was too dangerous. Besides, I still had the stars.

I traced the image of Andromeda over and over again in the night sky. October seemed a thousand years away; it could never have been near enough.

Chapter Four

AFTER THE FIRST RUSH OF EXHILARATION PASSED, I had to ask myself—How was I going to get to Amherst?

Students weren't permitted to keep vehicles at Evernight Academy. Not that I had one to keep here in the first place, but I couldn't borrow a ride from a friend either.

"Why aren't the students allowed to have cars?" I asked Balthazar in a low voice as he walked me to my English class on one of the first days of school. "A lot of people here have been driving cars as long as there have been cars to drive. You'd think Mrs. Bethany would trust them behind the wheel."

"You're forgetting that Evernight was around even before the automobile." Balthazar glanced down at me, in one of those odd moments that reminded me he was almost a foot taller than I was. "When the school was founded, everyone would've had horses and carriages, which are a lot more trouble to store than cars. Horses have to be fed, and their stalls have to be mucked out."

"We have horses in the stables."

"We have six horses. Not three hundred. It's a big difference when it comes to feed—"

"And mucking out stalls," I finished for him, making a face.

"Exactly. Not to mention that there were a lot of hurt feelings when people got hungry and snacked on other people's transportation."

"I bet." Poor horses. "Still, it's not like anybody would be in danger of chowing down on a Toyota. And there's plenty of room around here where people could park. So why hasn't Mrs. Bethany changed the rules?"

"Mrs. Bethany? Change a rule?"

"Good point."

Mrs. Bethany presided over her classroom like a judge presided over a courtroom: peering down at everyone around her, dressed in black and unquestionably in charge. "Shakespeare," she said, her voice ringing throughout the room. Each of us had a leather-bound edition of Shakespeare's complete works in front of us. "Even the least educated of you will have studied his plays in some context before now."

Was I imagining things, or had Mrs. Bethany looked at me when she said "least educated"? Given the smirk on Courtney's face, maybe I wasn't imagining. I shrank down in my desk and stared at the book's cover.

"As you are all familiar with Shakespeare already, you might justifiably ask—why here? Why again?" Mrs. Bethany gestured as she spoke, and her long, thick, grooved fingernails reminded me of claws. "First of all, a deep understanding of Shakespeare has been one of the foundations of Western cultural knowledge for centuries now. We can expect it will remain so for centuries to come."

Education at Evernight wasn't for college prep, or even just to make you smarter or happier. It was meant to carry its students through the impossibly long lives of the undead. That lifespan was something I'd tried to imagine ever since I was a little girl and first learned how I was different from the other kids in kindergarten.

"Second, these plays have been interpreted in a number of different ways since they were first written. Shakespeare was a popular entertainer in his own time. Then he was a poet and artist whose works were meant to be read by scholars, not enjoyed by the masses. In the past one hundred fifty years, Shakespeare's plays have reemerged as drama. Even as their language becomes more foreign to the modern ear, the themes speak to us strongly today—sometimes in ways Shakespeare himself could perhaps not have guessed."

Although Mrs. Bethany's voice always set my nerves on edge, I couldn't help feeling encouraged that we were going to concentrate on Shakespeare this year. My parents were huge Shakespeare buffs; they had named me after a character in *The Taming of the Shrew*, telling me that they'd been certain any name from Shakespeare would be familiar for hundreds of years to come. Dad had even gone to see him act in a few plays, back in the days when William Shakespeare was just one playwright among many fighting for audiences in London. So I'd memorized the dirge from *Cymbeline* before my tenth birthday, seen Baz Luhrmann's *Romeo + Juliet* on DVD about twenty times, and kept the sonnets on my shelf. Mrs. Bethany might give me a hard time this year, too, but at least I'd be prepared for anything she could throw my way.

Again, she seemed to have overheard my thoughts. Strolling beside my desk, where I could smell the lavender scent that always seemed to surround her, Mrs. Bethany said, "Prepare to have any preexisting assumptions you may hold about Shakespeare's works challenged. Those of you who think you can learn all about it from modern film adaptations would be well advised to think again."

I mulled the potential need to reread *Hamlet* until class was dismissed. As we all filed out of the classroom, I saw Courtney sidle up to Mrs. Bethany, saying something in a low voice, obviously hoping she wouldn't be overheard.

Mrs. Bethany wasn't having it. "I will not reconsider. You must resubmit your report, Miss Briganti, as yours was inadequate."

"Inadequate?" Courtney's mouth was a perfect O of outrage. "Finding out how to get into the best clubs in Miami—that's, like, really important!"

"Under some dubious standard of importance, I suppose that may be true. You may not, however, submit your report in the form of phone numbers scrawled on cocktail napkins." With that, Mrs. Bethany swept out of the room.

Courtney stomped after her in a huff. "Great. Now I have to *type*."

I wished I could've told the story to Raquel, who loathed Courtney as much as I did and would probably be in a crummy mood after our first day at the school she hated so much. Instead, we just hung out in our dorm room that evening, talking about pretty much anything except what had happened in classes.

Unfortunately, that whole night, Raquel only left the room once. Her bathroom trip gave me enough time to gulp down about two swallows of blood, not nearly enough. I became hungrier and hungrier, and finally I insisted that Raquel turn off the lights early.

Once she finally seemed to have fallen asleep, I kicked off the covers and slipped out of bed. Raquel didn't stir. Carefully I withdrew the thermos of blood from its hiding place. Tiptoeing into the hallway, I glanced around to make sure nobody else was up either. The coast was clear.

I considered my options before I hurried down the hall toward the stairwell. The stone stairs were chilly at night, particularly considering that I was only wearing boxer shorts and a cotton camisole. But the cold was one reason nobody was likely to come that way in the dead of night and find me drinking blood.

Lukewarm, I thought with distaste as I took the first swallow. I'd nuked it earlier that day, but even the thermos couldn't keep it piping hot forever. Didn't matter. Every coppery mouthful flowed into me like electric power. Yet it wasn't quite enough.

I wish the blood were hotter. I wish it were alive.

Last year, Patrice used to sneak out all the time to catch squirrels on the grounds. Could I do that? Just, like, chomp into a squirrel? I'd always thought I couldn't. Every time I'd pictured it, I'd thought about the fur getting stuck in my teeth. Blech.

When I thought about it now, it felt different. I didn't think about the fur or the squeak or anything like that. Instead, I thought about that tiny heart beating so very fast, as though I could feel that *thrum-thrum-thrum* against the tip of my tongue. And it would sound so good when I bit down and all those little bones snapped, like popcorn popping in the microwave—

Did I just think that? That's disgusting!

That is, I thought it was disgusting—but it didn't *feel* disgusting. It still felt like a live squirrel would be just about the most delicious thing on earth, short of human blood.

Closing my eyes, I remembered what it had been like to drink Lucas's blood while he lay beneath me, clutching me in his arms. Nothing could compare to that.

Something crackled down in the stairwell.

"Who's there?" I said, startled. My words echoed. More quietly, I repeated, "Who's there? Anybody?"

Once again, I thought I heard it: a strange crackling sound, like breaking ice. The crackling came closer, as though it were traveling up the stairs. Hurriedly I screwed the lid back on my thermos, so that no human student would see me drinking blood. I ducked into the hallway and tried to figure out what could be causing that sound.

Had a girl sneaked out of the dorms for a snack, just like I had? The sound was a little like the popping noise ice cubes made after they were dropped into water. Then I stifled a giggle when I wondered if it was a guy instead, sneaking up here to visit the girl he liked. Maybe it wasn't even a person. It could just be an old building reacting to the deepening autumn cold.

The crackling came closer. The air around me instantly went colder, as if I'd just opened a freezer door. My hair stood on end, and goose bumps appeared on my arms. My breath looked foggy, and once again I sensed that somebody was watching me.

Farther down the stairwell, I saw a wavering light. It flickered like a candle, but the light was a brilliant blue green, the color of a swimming pool. Ribbons of illumination rippled across the stones. It looked eerily like Evernight was under water.

By now I was shaking from cold, and I lost my grip on the thermos. The moment it clattered to the floor, the lights vanished. The air around me warmed again instantly.

That was not a reflection, I thought. *That was not my imagination.*

So what the hell was it?

The door nearest the stairwell swung open. Courtney stood there in a hot-pink nightshirt, her blond hair messy around her face. "What is your damage?"

"Sorry," I mumbled as I ducked down to grab my thermos. "I had to sneak out to eat. I—I guess I lost my grip."

Eventually I would have to tell somebody what I'd just seen, but Courtney was the last person I would take into my confidence. Even admitting that I'd done something as simple as dropping a thermos made her roll her eyes.

"God, just catch mice like a normal person, okay?" But instead of slamming her door, she shifted from foot to foot, then said, "I guess that does suck."

"—dropping my thermos?"

Courtney scowled. "Sneaking out to eat. You drew the short straw when it came to roommates."

"Raquel is not the short straw!"

"Be that way." Then she slammed her door.

Wait, did Courtney just try to sympathize with me?

I shook my head. The idea of Courtney trying to be sort of friendly was almost weird enough to make me forget what I'd seen in the stairwell. But not quite.

When I told my parents I would be camping out that Friday night for the meteor shower, they didn't bother worrying about me out in the woods; the school grounds were extremely safe, at least if you were a vampire. I knew they wouldn't double-check whether there really was any meteor shower—a good thing, because there wasn't. But they asked a whole lot of other questions, and in my paranoia, I wondered why.

"It seems like you could get some friends together to go with you," Mom said as we sat down to Sunday dinner: lasagna for me, big glasses of blood for us all. Billie Holiday sang from the stereo, warning about a lover she had believed in once upon a time. "Maybe Archana. She seems like a nice girl."

"Uh, yeah, I guess." Archana was an Indian vampire, about six centuries old; I'd met her in history class last year, but we had hardly said ten words to each other. "I don't know her that well, though. If I were going to ask anybody, I'd ask Raquel, but she couldn't care less about astronomy."

"You're spending a lot of time with Raquel." Dad took a deep swallow of his glass of blood. "Wouldn't it be good to have other friends, too?"

"Vampire friends, you mean. You always told me not to be a snob, that we're more like humans than most vampires claim. What happened to that?"

"I meant every word of it. But that's not what I'm talking about," Dad said gently. "The fact remains that you're going to be a vampire. In a hundred years, Raquel will be dead, and your life will only have just begun. Who's going to be with you then? We brought you here to make friends you can keep, Bianca."

Mom gently laid one hand on my forearm. "We'll always be here for you, sweetheart. But you don't want to hang out with your parents forever, right?"

"That wouldn't be so bad." I meant it—but not the same way I would have once. Last year, I had wanted nothing except to hide out from the world forever in our cozy home, only the three of us; now I wanted so much more.

Balthazar stepped to the edge of the fencing area, his mask still tucked under one arm. He looked incredibly dashing in his white fencer's garb, which outlined his powerful body like he was roughly carved of marble.

Me? I glanced in the mirror along one side of the room and sighed. Dashing was not the word for me. I looked like the lost white Teletubby Pasty. Also, I had no idea how to handle a sword. But there was no way I could claim I needed a second year of Modern Technology class, and fencing was the only other elective that fit my schedule.

"You look terrified," Balthazar said. "You won't actually be dueling for your life in here, you know."

"I get that, but still—sword fighting. I don't know."

"First of all, the actual fighting won't come for a really long time. Neither will the actual swords. Not until you know how to move. Second, I'll fix it so we're partners, at least at first. That way I can make sure you're comfortable."

"You mean, you'd rather fence with somebody you can beat."

"Maybe." He grinned, then tugged the mask down over his face. "Ready?"

"Give me a second." I busied myself with the mask, which to my surprise I could see out of perfectly well.

Sure enough, we didn't start fighting right away. In fact, most of the first day was spent learning how to stand. Sound easy? It's not. We had to hold our legs just so, tensing this muscle but not that one, and position our arms in this incredibly formal, stylized way. I hadn't realized it was possible to exhaust every single muscle in my body just by trying to stand still, but before the hour was up, I was trembling all over and sore from my shoulders to my calves.

"You'll be all right," Balthazar said encouragingly as he adjusted one of my elbows. Our teacher, Professor Carlyle, had already designated him as one of her assistants for the course. "You have good balance, and that's the main thing."

"I would think the main thing would be not getting hit with a sword."

"Trust me. Balance. That's what it all comes down to."

The bell rang. Sighing with relief, I stumbled to the nearest wall and sagged against it. I pulled off the fencing mask so that I could breathe more deeply. My cheeks felt hot, and my hair was damp with sweat. "At least I'll lose weight this year."

"You don't need to lose weight." Balthazar hesitated as he tucked his mask beneath his arm. "You know, if you want to work on this extra, outside of class—we could meet up tomorrow, maybe. Get a little practice in."

"I can't this weekend." If I'd been any less exhausted, would Balthazar have seen the nervous anticipation in my eyes? "Can I take a rain check?"

"Sure." He grinned at me as he headed for the door. All at once, I wondered if Balthazar hadn't meant his offer as a way to get close to me. If so, I'd have to figure a way out of it.

I'd worry about all that later. It was the first Friday in October, and that meant I was only a few hours away from being with Lucas again.

First I hurried back to the dorm so that I could shower. No way was I going to meet up with Lucas smelling like sweaty old socks. I didn't fix my hair or carefully apply makeup, so I wouldn't tip Raquel off to my plans. I imagined my ultrafeminine former roommate, Patrice, gasping in horror as I simply pulled my hair back into a sloppy bun.

Raquel noticed anyway. "Why are you getting dressed up to lounge around in the woods?"

"It's hardly like I got out the fur coat and tiara." I wore jeans and a plain sweater.

She shrugged. "Whatever." Raquel sat cross-legged on the floor, in the middle of another of her art projects; this collage looked fairly depressing, with a lot of black and a prominently displayed etching of a guillotine. All that mattered to me was that she paid no attention as I finished getting dressed. Ideally I would've gone to see Lucas in my prettiest outfit, but there was no way I could believably wear anything dressy. I reached deep into the back of my underwear drawer for a tiny bundle wrapped in a scarf, which I tucked into my backpack along with a thermos that would've looked innocent to Raquel.

"See you tomorrow night, okay?" My voice sounded strange—taut and unnatural, as though it might break.

I put one hand on the doorknob, thinking I was all but home free, when Raquel idly asked, "Aren't you taking your telescope?"

Oh, no. If I were going to watch the meteor shower, of course I would bring my telescope with me—it was heavy, and it had to be handled with care, but I could get it onto the school grounds. What I couldn't do was lug that thing all the way to Amherst.

I thought I'd gone over every detail of my getaway plan. How could I have forgotten something so basic?

"I have another one," I lied, making it up as I went. "Telescope, I mean. It's not quite as good as this one, but it's a lot lighter. So I thought I'd get it from my parents' apartment instead."

"Makes sense." Raquel looked up from her scissors, so that we could see each other's faces. She looked a little sad; maybe Raquel would never admit that she would miss me over the weekend, but I thought she would. "Tomorrow, then."

"Tomorrow." Guiltily, I promised, "We'll hang out next weekend. Figure out something fun to do."

"Here? Yeah, right." She buried herself in her work again, and I was free to go.

As I walked out onto the grounds, twilight was descending over the school. Dusk was one of my favorite times of day; to me it felt as much like a beginning as the sunrise. The sky was a milky violet-gray as I walked to the far end of the grounds and made my way into the woods. My ears pricked up in response to the night sounds: my own footsteps on soft pine needles, the hooting of a faraway owl and—very distant—a girl laughing in a drowsy kind of way that made me think she must be out there with a guy.

I continued on my way, realizing as I went how much sharper my hearing was than it had been last year. Perhaps I'd become so accustomed to the din of Evernight Academy that I didn't sense the difference so much, but out in the woods, it was obvious.

The flapping of birds' wings, traffic whirring along the nearest road—all of that was clear and distinct. It wouldn't have been, before.

I wouldn't have been thinking about how good one of those birds' blood would taste, either.

The vampire in me was closer to the surface. And being with Lucas always brought the vampire—the predator, the hungry one—to life in me more powerfully than before. Maybe I wasn't the only one taking a risk with this meeting tonight.

I'll take care of Lucas. I would never hurt him.

(If I bite him again and drink deeply enough, he becomes a vampire, and then the two of us could be together forever.)

I shook my head, refusing to get ahead of myself. Instead, I kept going until I reached the road. Then it was just a short stroll to the lone intersection in the area, a four-way stop. I took my place on the road that led to nearby Riverton and waited.

Five cars and a motorcycle came by; those were useless to me. From my hiding place in the nearby bushes, I sighed in frustration.

But lucky number seven was the one I'd been waiting for all this time: the laundry service that came to Evernight once a week for the school linens. As always, the driver had his music playing full blast. He would just have left the school, which meant he was headed back—and the sign on the side of the truck confirmed my recollection that the laundry service was based in Amherst.

The truck stopped at the sign. I ran to the back of the truck, which, luckily, was unlocked. As the metal clicked, I flinched, but fortunately the loud music in the cab must have covered it. Quickly I hopped inside among the bundles of laundry and pulled the doors shut behind me as the truck took off again.

See? That was simple! I was both so nervous and so elated that I had to fight not to start giggling. Instead, I curled down among the laundry bags, just one more bundle if he happened to glance back here. Everything smelled a little musty, but not unpleasant, and with all the cushioning around me, my ride promised to be pretty comfortable.

It took approximately an hour to drive to Amherst. Around then, I'd start risking a few peeks out of the small window in the back. Once we reached Amherst, I'd take advantage of another stop to get out—again without being seen, I hoped. After that, I could catch a cab or walk or whatever I had to do in order to reach the train station.

By midnight, I would be in Lucas's arms again.

Chapter Five

"WOOHOO! BAY-BEEEEE!"

The car zipped past me, going way too fast in the Amherst town square. A couple of frat guys were hanging out of the windows and yelling at every girl they saw.

I'd thought that, by this hour, the streets would be pretty much deserted. What I hadn't considered was that Amherst was a college town, with something like three or four universities crowded up against the city boundaries. The town didn't slow down at midnight; the kids around me were just getting the party started.

Kids. These people were up to five years older than me. Their faces and bodies were more mature than those of the students at Evernight. It was strange to think that they'd already lived longer than Balthazar ever did. But when I was at Evernight, I could sense the experience, worldliness, and strength of my classmates; their faces were young, but their centuries showed in their eyes. Compared to them, the cigarette-smoking college students jostling one another on the sidewalk around me were only children.

What did that make me?

I couldn't worry about that for very long. At that moment, I felt too happy to worry about anything—the lies I'd told, the rules I was breaking, or consequences that might follow. All that mattered was that I was about to see Lucas again.

"Excuse me." A girl wove her way through the crowd toward me. Her fair, curly hair was pulled up into a knot from which a few strands dangled. "Can I walk with you?"

I began to tell her that she had me confused with someone else, but the moment our eyes first met, every word I might've said was replaced by only one: *vampire*.

It wasn't that she looked so dissimilar from the other people around me, at least not in any obvious way. But to me, she stood out from the crowd as brilliantly as a bonfire. I'd been able to tell vampires from humans on sight all my life. The thing was, even for a vampire, this girl was different. She was the youngest-looking vampire I'd ever seen. Her heart-shaped face still had the roundness of the baby fat I saw in my own mirror, and she had wide-set, soft brown eyes. Her smile was almost shy. A port-wine birthmark mottled her neck near the jugular vein, probably almost exactly where she would have been bitten. I felt immediately protective, like it was my job to look after her—this lost young girl in clothes that didn't match, a ragged sweater over a skirt with a torn hem.

"Wait." Her expression was like the ones painted onto porcelain dolls, innocent and mischievous at the same time. "There's something about you that's—you're not quite—oh. You're a baby. One of our babies, I mean."

I was impressed that she'd managed to figure that out so swiftly, given that most vampires never met a vampire like me, one born rather than made. "Yeah. I mean, yes, that's what I am, and, yes, you can walk with me for a bit."

"Thank you." She slipped her arm into mine as though we were lifelong pals. Her body trembled, and I wasn't sure whether it was from fear or cold. "This fellow won't leave me alone tonight. Perhaps I'll have better luck if he thinks I've run into a friend."

"I'm actually going to meet somebody." No sooner had I said the words than her smile wavered, revealing a glimpse of loneliness beneath. I remembered Ranulf and the handful of other lost ones at Evernight Academy, and I took pity on her. "But I can get you out of the town square, at least."

"Oh, could you? Thank you so much. What a relief. Did I startle you? I didn't mean to. If I did, I'm sorry."

"It's okay." There was something genuinely childlike about her, so much so that it was surprising to realize she was several inches taller than I was, nearly as tall as Balthazar. "Are you all right? Is there somebody we could call?"

"Fine. I'm fine. I'm alone tonight."

I looked down at my forearm, where her hand rested. Her threadbare sweater was long enough that the only part of her hands visible beneath the sleeves were her fingers. Her nails were filthy and jagged—almost as though she'd been digging through dirt. All at once, I knew that this girl was the single loneliest person I'd ever met.

At first she simply followed me without comment or, apparently, will of her own. We pushed our way through a huge crowd of students that had congregated outside a pizza place. It must have been the most popular place to grab a slice, because more than a hundred kids jostled around outside, holding cardboard pizza boxes and plastic cups of beer. A couple of guys stared at us—at the fair-haired vampire more than me. Despite her youth and disheveled appearance, she had an ethereal, innocent kind of beauty, and her brown eyes searched the crowds as if longing for someone, anyone, to take care of her. I could see how some guys might find that appealing.

Only after we emerged from that crowd did she say, "Where are you going?"

"To the train station."

"That's only a few blocks away." The vampire cast a worried glance over her shoulder. How she could make out anything in that throng of people, I didn't know, but she tensed up. "I think he's still back there. Let me walk with you to the train station. Won't you, please? It's darker around there, and I can slip away, I just know it."

Selfishly, I wanted to refuse; Lucas would be coming any second, and I didn't want any company around for our reunion. Lucas wouldn't exactly be thrilled to see another vampire, because I was the only one he trusted. There was a chance he wouldn't recognize her as a vampire, but given his Black Cross training, I doubted it. Yet she looked so timid that I didn't have the heart to refuse. "Okay, sure. Let's go."

We continued through the square, arm in arm. Music blared from each bar so loudly that the various drumbeats seemed to crash into one another.

"Let me guess." She cast a shy glance in my direction. "Evernight, right?"

"Yeah. Did you go there?"

"I tried once. But the headmistress—oh, she didn't like me. Mrs. Bethany was her name. Is she still there?"

"Like she would ever leave her kingdom," I muttered.

"So true. Well, she didn't care for me a bit. It made things very unpleasant."

"Mrs. Bethany doesn't care for me either. I think she hates most people who aren't—well, her."

"Have you run away from school, too? That's what I did."

I smiled. "Only for the weekend."

"I could never go back, I don't think. Not unless—" Her gaze became distant, but then she shook her head. "It doesn't matter."

As we walked away from the main square toward the train station, a breeze gusted past us and I could smell a definite whiff of body odor. That alone didn't gross me out—I guessed everybody got sweaty sometimes—but along with everything else, it made me feel sorry for her. She hardly seemed able to take care of herself. How terrible it would have to be, living forever alone like this, getting more and more out of sync with civilization.

For the first time, I understood—really understood—why

vampires needed an Evernight Academy. I'd always known that we had a tendency to lose track of the ever-changing now, and my parents had cautioned me about how easy it was to look up and realize your clothes were a couple decades out of date, or that you not only didn't know what was happening in the world but also didn't care. But I'd never really comprehended how that would look—how it would feel, being so alienated. Looking at this girl, I finally got it.

The train station lay only a few blocks away from the main square, but the walk seemed longer. It had something to do with the contrast between the noise and bustle of the student-filled square and the dead silence of the nearby neighborhood. With fewer streetlights around, it was darker, too. My new companion had nothing else to say. She apparently was content just to hang on to me.

I checked my watch. 11:55.

The fair-haired vampire pulled open the train station's door with trepidation, like it might be booby-trapped. Hardly likely for a one-room train station that was basically a hut beside the tracks. "Nobody's home. Your young man hasn't arrived yet."

"I don't guess so." I peered at the station in dismay. I'd hoped it would be pretty or at least cozy; I knew a train station couldn't possibly be romantic enough for our reunion, but it could've been better than this. Scuffed linoleum floor, dim fluorescent lights hanging from above, and a few hard wooden benches bolted to the walls: not exactly my dream setting.

Then again, what did that matter? What would any of it

matter? I knew that I would be with Lucas again soon—within minutes—and once we saw each other, I knew I wouldn't be able to pay attention to anything else.

What if it's not the same for him? His letter was so amazing, but, still, we haven't seen each other in months. What if things have changed between us? What if it's awkward? What if he doesn't feel the way he used to?

"You must be so very happy." The vampire was curled up on a bench, her knees hugged to her chest. She drummed her jagged fingernails against the pale flesh of her calves. The sole was peeling away from the bottom of one of her shoes. "So very happy not to be alone anymore. Sometimes I think I'd die if I had to be alone all the time."

Now I felt awkward saying this, but I had to: "If you don't mind, I'd sort of like some privacy. We haven't seen each other in a while."

"Private time." Her smile was shy and a little bit sad. I wanted to apologize for leaving her so alone, but what else could I do? The only alternative I could offer was her coming with me back to Evernight, and she'd made her feelings about that plain. Who could blame her for loathing Mrs. Bethany? As if she sensed my guilt, she said, "I understand, I do. I'd meant to wait awhile, see if he wouldn't move on, but—okay."

I heard footsteps on the gravel outside and whirled toward the door as Lucas walked in.

He wore a denim jacket, black T-shirt, and jeans. His dark-gold hair had grown slightly longer, but other than that he was the same. Looking at him felt like diving into a sun-warmed pool, filled with light.

"Lucas?" I took one step forward. I wanted to throw myself into his arms, and yet it felt like I could hardly move. "You made it. We both made it."

But he wasn't looking at me. He was looking past me—at the vampire.

"Get the hell away from Bianca," he growled.

"Oh, no." The vampire began scrambling backward, trying to wedge herself into a corner. "No, no, no—"

"Lucas, it's okay. She's harmless."

"The hell she is."

The vampire cried, "I told you, I told you, he's after me, he's after us both!"

This was who she'd been afraid of. She'd been running from *Lucas.*

Lucas's hand closed around mine—the first touch in so long. He was trying to tug me toward the door. "Bianca, you gotta get out of here."

"Wait, stop. Both of you." I looked from one to the other, but they weren't listening to me. They were both shifting into battle mode, ready to fight.

I didn't know what to do or what to think, not for that first split second—and that was one second too long. The vampire launched herself at us, pouncing like a tiger, and Lucas shoved me out of the way so hard that I stumbled and fell on my hands and knees, smacking into the concrete floor. Behind me I heard the sound of shattering wood.

Scrambling back to my feet, hands stinging, I saw to my horror that the vampire had knocked Lucas through the door of the train station. Despite her girlish behavior and appearance, she was obviously a powerful vampire—more powerful than I'd realized. She and Lucas grappled in the doorway for a second, their desperate struggle silhouetted by the glare of the nearby streetlight. Then the vampire threw Lucas into the railing of the station porch. He fell onto the railroad tracks.

"Lucas!" I shouted. He didn't rise to his feet, and he blinked like he couldn't make sense of what he saw. Clearly, being tossed through the door had stunned him.

"You shouldn't be allowed to scare young girls." The vampire tugged at the curls of her hair that had escaped from her bun, just like a nervous child. "You should be stopped. I should stop you."

She's scared enough to kill him, I realized. I had to help Lucas, but how? I was stronger than any human being, but not nearly as strong as a full vampire, no matter how childlike she might appear. Then I realized that when the door had splintered, pieces of wood had been scattered all over the train station's floor. One next to me was the perfect size and shape to be used as a stake.

Staking doesn't kill vampires, not permanently anyway. If the stake goes through the heart, the vampire falls down as if dead—but if the stake is pulled out, then it's just like it never happened. So I should've slammed the stake into the vampire's back without hesitation.

But staking that poor girl—I couldn't do it.

I grabbed a much larger piece of wood from the floor, something almost like a two-by-four, and inched forward, one foot, then the other.

"You shouldn't have followed me." She leaned over Lucas, every muscle in her skinny body tense and her hands curved so that her fingernails seemed like claws. "You'll be sorry."

With all my strength, I swung the board into her head. The vampire went flying a few feet from us—I'd gotten stronger than I realized—and rolled along the ground, over and over. Before she stopped, I dropped the board and grabbed Lucas's hand. "Can you run?"

"Gonna find out." He panted, struggling to his feet.

I pulled him in the direction of the town square, thinking that we'd stand a better chance of losing her in a crowd. But Lucas tugged back to steer us in the opposite direction, so that we were running into the quiet residential section nearby. "Nobody's around, Lucas. We'll be all alone!"

"That means nobody else gets hurt!"

"But—"

"I've got you, Bianca. Trust me."

We ran onto a small street lined with large, classic New England houses. Comfortable family cars and SUVs were parked in every driveway, and front windows glowed and flickered with the lights from television screens. With every step, I longed to scream for help, but I knew doing that would only put the people inside at risk. If they came outside to investigate, there was every chance they would get caught up in a dangerous fight that now seemed inevitable. Lucas and I were on our own.

"He's not who you think!" a thin, quivering voice called, not nearly far enough behind us. "He's Black Cross! You've got to get away!"

Oh, crap. I realized, *She's chasing us to try and save me.*

"Lucas, we don't have to do this!" I could hardly breathe. We could both run almost supernaturally fast, and farther than most humans could, but the vampire was faster. "Just let me talk to her!"

"She's not going to stop at talking!"

Lucas still assumed all vampires were dangerous—but in this case, he might be right. This vampire was powerful; worse, she was scared. People could do terrible things when they were scared. If she hurt Lucas on my behalf, I knew I'd never forgive myself.

We veered around a corner as Lucas pulled me to the right, and I figured he was trying to lose the vampire. It didn't work; her footsteps pounded behind us on the pavement, closer and closer. Sweat rolled down my back.

"I'm going to draw her off." Lucas squeezed my hand tighter. "Count of three, you're going to dive behind the nearest car. Got it?"

"Lucas, I'm not leaving you!"

"I can get help. You have to be safe. One, two—"

No time to argue. He swung his arm around, flinging me toward the side of the road; I dived for cover. Skidding to the ground scraped my palms and knees, but I was able to roll behind a large truck and curl beside one of the tires.

For a few seconds, there was only silence. *Get help,* I remembered Lucas saying. Black Cross was here on a hunt. That meant he had plenty of support nearby. Without me, he stood a chance. I began to calm down and take comfort in the knowledge that he was safe—until the vampire dived behind the truck, too.

Maybe I should've screamed for Lucas, but I didn't want to give her away.

She didn't attack; I'd known she wouldn't. Instead she held out her hand with its jagged, dirty nails. "We have to go," she said. "You don't know what he is."

"I know he's Black Cross. He won't hurt me, but he's coming back with others. Get out of here!"

She shook her head at me in horror. "You're mad. He's the enemy."

"I'm fine!" I insisted. "You're the one in danger!"

She let her hand drop and stared at me, head tilted to one side. In that pose, she looked like a broken toy, and I had the weird but undeniable sense that I'd hurt her feelings. After one long, strange second, she leaped up and ran, vanishing so quickly that I didn't hear even a footstep.

As soon as I was sure she was gone, I called out, "Lucas?" No response. "Lucas?"

I heard footsteps farther down the road. Rising to my feet, I saw Lucas running toward me. He motioned for me to duck down again, but I ignored that.

"She's gone," I promised. "We're safe, okay?"

Lucas slowed to a walk, then took another couple of heavy steps and leaned forward, bracing his hands against his knees. I still felt shaky myself, and I'd had a couple of minutes to get my breath. "You sure?"

"Pretty sure. Are you all right?"

"As long as you are." Lucas straightened up again and brushed back his sweaty hair with the back of one hand. "God, Bianca—if she had come after you—"

"She wasn't dangerous. Not until she got scared."

"What? Are you sure?"

"Yeah." It hit me: For the first time in more than six months, Lucas and I were alone together. I threw my arms around him, and he held me so tightly that I could hardly breathe.

"I missed you," I whispered into his hair. "I missed you so much."

"Me, too." He laughed softly. "I can hardly believe this is real."

"I'll convince you." I took his face in my hands, and we leaned closer to kiss—until headlights swept over us and made us both jump.

The van sped toward us, screeching to a halt only a few feet away. In the brilliant light, I could barely make out that there were apparently several people crowded inside.

Lucas groaned, "Oh, no." When one of the van doors opened, he yelled, "Crisis over. Way to take too long, guys."

"It hasn't been five minutes since your page." The woman emerging from the van sounded familiar. Even before I could see her features, I realized it was Kate, Lucas's mother.

Then the passenger door swung open to reveal a tall, heavy-set black girl with braided hair. I searched my memory for her name: *Dana*. As we looked up at her, Dana's expression shifted from concern to a broad smile.

"Look who we have here." She leaned against the hood and gestured toward us with a crossbow she apparently no longer intended to use. "Lucas, didn't anyone tell you the emergency number isn't to alert us to your booty calls?"

Kate folded her arms. "Now I see why you insisted on joining the Amherst hunt."

"Okay, you found me out," he said lightly, refusing to be cowed. "Can we get Bianca someplace safe? The vampire just scared the hell out of her."

"I realize that," Kate said, more kindly. She liked me, mostly because she believed I'd saved Lucas's life once. The people in the van were nodding and murmuring welcome. "Come on and get yourself cleaned up. Don't worry; you're safe now."

Safe with Black Cross? I was safe only as long as they didn't realize I was "the enemy." Just the thought of turning myself over to a gang of vampire hunters made me feel cold and frightened inside. They'd been kind to me last time we'd met—but the last time had nearly ended in disaster. This time, if they learned the truth, it could get a lot worse.

Lucas and I shared a look, and I knew he understood how I felt. But there was nothing to do but smile, say thanks, and climb in the van.

Chapter Six

LUCAS'S HAND CLOSED AROUND MINE AS THE VAN drove into an industrial park—one that had seen better days, to judge by the fact that half the buildings seemed to be vacant. My head still whirled from the suddenness of the vampire's attack and our escape; I don't think I'd even fully processed the fact that Lucas and I were together again.

Or maybe, I thought as we stole sideways glances at each other, *it's just that it feels like we've never really been apart.*

"I don't guess you kids met up at random." Kate glanced toward us, and her eyes narrowed as she glared at Lucas. She wore olive cargo pants and a black shirt with a lot of pockets; her dark-gold hair was slicked back into a no-nonsense ponytail. "Lucas, don't tell me you went back to that place."

"I didn't go to Evernight," Lucas said. "I asked Bianca to meet me here. But if I have to return to the school again to see her, I will."

"It's too dangerous."

"Can you tell me where in the world we aren't in danger, Mom? Because I just had a closer call than I ever had at Evernight Academy."

Lucas was exaggerating somewhat, given how my father and Balthazar had pursued him last year, but I didn't want to undermine him while he was defending his decision to meet up with me.

Kate sighed, then shook her head. She looked at me next—not gently, because nothing about her was gentle, but in a way that made it clear she didn't blame me for the danger Lucas and I had been in. "Glad to see you're okay, Bianca. I didn't trust the bloodsuckers to keep their word last year."

Those bloodsuckers are my parents, I wanted to retort, but instead I replied, "They did. I'm back in school and we all sort of—pretend it didn't happen."

Lucas helped me out. "Probably they figure even if you did tell, nobody would believe you." I hoped our explanation sounded convincing.

"That was a brave thing you did, giving yourself up to save us from the fire," said an elderly man who sat in the back beside Dana. He'd told me his name—Mr. Watanabe, I remembered. "I think you saved us all."

"Yeah, Bianca, that was pretty badass of you." Dana slapped her hands on my shoulders and gave them a hearty squeeze. "Seriously, you've got guts."

"It wasn't badass. I don't really do badass." That made the half-dozen or so people in the van laugh, even though I hadn't actually been making a joke. Still, my tension eased a little.

Last year, when Lucas had been discovered as a member of Black Cross, he'd been forced to escape from Evernight Academy; I'd fled with him. Together we'd reached Kate and Eduardo's cell, and safety—at least as long as Black Cross remained ignorant that I was a sort of vampire, too. But Mrs. Bethany, my parents, and several other vampires had tracked us down. When I'd gone back with my parents, I'd not only escaped that confrontation, I'd gotten away before Black Cross found out what I really was. They still believed me to be a human child kidnapped and raised by vampire parents—something I needed them to keep on believing.

We drove to one of the abandoned buildings around back. Kate flicked the van's headlights: off, on; bright, off, bright. A metal door, like for a loading dock, started to open, revealing a driveway that sloped down sharply. We drove into an underground parking garage that looked pretty much like any other, except that it was illuminated by lanterns hung on the walls or the concrete pillars. As Kate pulled around a corner into a spot, I saw that a few partitions had been set up—walls of boxes or just tarps hanging over a stretched cord—to carve rooms out of this dank space.

I couldn't keep the surprise from my voice as I said, "*This* is Black Cross headquarters?"

Everyone laughed. Lucas squeezed my hand, reassuring me that the laughter wasn't meant to be unkind. "We don't have an HQ. We go where we need to go, find places to crash.

This is secure. We're safe here."

To me it looked incredibly bleak. Had Lucas grown up in miserable places like this? The air still smelled like exhaust and oil.

As our crew got out of the van, another half-dozen people walked up to us, including a tall, forbidding man with twin scars across one cheek. I recognized Eduardo, Lucas's stepfather and quite possibly his least favorite person. His dark gaze embodied everything that frightened me about Black Cross. "I see this is the big emergency," he said, staring at me.

"You'd prefer another kind of emergency?" Kate said it like she was teasing, but she wasn't. I could hear the real message in her words: *Lay off my kid.*

Either Eduardo didn't hear that message, or he didn't care. "The vampire got away? Again?"

Lucas's jaw clenched at that *again*, but he said only, "Yeah. She's fast."

"Did you see her gang?" Kate shook her head, and I thought, *What gang?* I knew the lonely girl I'd seen tonight didn't have any friends, much less a gang.

"You go to school with vampires for a year and can't figure out why they've admitted humans, then you luck into a shot at this vampire and completely lose her while you're hanging out with your girlfriend." In the lantern's light, Eduardo seemed to have been roughly carved from weathered wood. "This isn't what we trained you for, Lucas."

"What *did* you train me for? To shut up and follow your orders no matter what?"

"Discipline matters. You've never understood that."

"So does having a life."

"That's enough," Kate interjected, stepping between her husband and her son. "Maybe you two aren't sick of this argument yet, but the rest of us are."

They're still freaking out about the human students at Evernight, I thought. *If I figure that out and tell Lucas, we'd show Eduardo.* Seeing how dismissively he treated Lucas made me want to take Eduardo down a notch or two. Or ten.

"Bianca looks really winded," Dana said. "Lucas, you better get her to the first aid room and make sure she's all right."

"Oh, I feel—" I realized what Dana was doing and stopped myself. "That might be a good idea."

Kate didn't say *Kids*, but I knew she was thinking it. She waved us off. Eduardo looked as if he might object, but he didn't.

The murmur of conversation welled up behind us as Lucas led me toward a side door. I realized that this led to the room the parking lot attendant had sat in when this was a garage. "Are they talking about us?" I murmured.

"Probably talking about that damn vampire. But as soon as they get done with that, yeah, they'll start talking about us."

"Who was that vampire?"

"I was kinda hoping you could tell us something," Lucas said as we went up the short stairway to what was now the first aid room, "seeing as how you guys were hanging out."

"She just sort of came up to me. I never met a vampire on

the street before—I was curious."

"Seriously, Bianca, you've got to be more careful."

Before I could say anything else, Lucas turned on the small electric lantern in the first aid room. The area was hardly bigger than the one cot that was pushed against the wall. Dark gray carpet covered the floor, and this room was small enough for the lantern to fill with soft light. This was almost cozy, and definitely private. Lucas shut the door behind us. I felt a river of warmth flow through me as I realized that we were alone together at last, really alone.

Lucas grabbed me and pushed me hard against the wall. I gasped and he kissed my open lips, then kissed me again harder, as I started to respond. My arms slipped around his neck, and his body was pressed against mine from our knees to our mouths, and I could breathe in the scent of him, the one that reminded me of the dark woods near Evernight.

Mine, I thought. *Mine.*

We kissed frantically, like we'd been starved for each other the way people can be starved for food or water or air. The way a vampire can be starved for blood. I cupped his face in my hands and felt the stubble of his beard against my palms. His knee pushed slowly between mine, so that both my thighs straddled one of his, and one hand came up against the small of my back, beneath my shirt. The touch of his skin against mine made me dizzy but not weak. I felt stronger than I ever had in my life.

"I missed you," he whispered against my neck. "God, I missed you."

"Lucas." I couldn't think of anything else to say but his name. It was like there was nothing else worth saying.

I kissed him again, more slowly this time, and that only intensified the kiss. Both his hands pressed against my back now, and we held each other tighter, and I started to wonder how much closer we could get—and then I remembered what it had felt like when I drank his blood.

"Wait." I turned my head away. My breath came in shaky gasps, and I couldn't quite look directly at him. "We have to slow down."

Lucas closed his eyes tightly, then nodded. "Mom is outside." He was saying it to himself, not to me. "Mom. Outside. Mom. Outside. Okay, that kinda sobers me up."

Our eyes met, and then we started to laugh really hard. Lucas stepped away from me, enough that I could breathe normally again, but he clasped both my hands tightly. "You look gorgeous."

"I just got chased down the street. I probably look like a train wreck." I knew my hair was mussed every which way, and my jeans were dusty.

"You gotta learn how to take a compliment, because I'm not going to stop making them." Lucas lifted one of my hands to his mouth. His lips were soft against my knuckles. Outside I heard the conversation between the others in Black Cross getting louder. "How long can you stay?"

"Until tomorrow afternoon."

"Almost a whole day?" He brightened so much that I couldn't

help but blush happily. "That's amazing."

"Yeah, it is." By next week, I knew, this short time would seem like nothing. But for now it stretched out before me as infinite as a sky full of stars, and I didn't want to think about what would come after. That would ruin it. What mattered was here and now.

I sat down on the corner of the cot, and Lucas sat beside me, laying his head on my shoulder. His arms circled my waist. I ran my fingers through his scruffy hair.

His voice was muffled against my shoulder as he said, "There were times I thought I'd never see you again. Sometimes I told myself that would be the best thing for both of us. But I couldn't accept it."

"Don't ever believe that." I kissed his cheek. "Not ever."

The noise from downstairs grew louder yet, and I realized that it was an argument. I tensed, but Lucas sat up and sighed. "Eduardo's mad as hell."

"That girl—the one from tonight—she's the one you guys are here to hunt?"

"That's the whole reason we're in Amherst. There have been reports in this area for a few months now. This vampire—we think she's part of a gang that's been causing trouble more and more often."

"Reports? Like, in newspapers?"

"Sometimes, though of course the papers don't know what they're reporting. But we hear from people—people who know what's really going on in the world, who know about us. Every once in a while, we even get info from vampires. They'll try to buy us off by telling us there's somebody more dangerous around the corner. Sometimes they're telling the truth. The word we got was that this gang is killing about once a week—and that's a lot, even for the deadliest vamps out there."

I tried to think of that as encouraging. Even Black Cross hunters could talk to vampires rationally sometimes. "The girl we saw tonight can't be part of any deadly gang. Lucas, she was scared to death."

Lucas looked over at me again, and in his dark-green eyes I saw that he was wary. We'd had this discussion before, but it never ended well. Quietly he said, "Some vampires really are dangerous, Bianca."

"Some really aren't," I said, just as quietly.

"I know that now." Lucas leaned his head back against the wall, and I could glimpse a kind of tiredness in his eyes. He was three years older than me, an age difference I hadn't really been able to see last year, but his maturity was more visible now. "There are bad vampires who ought to be stopped. We stop them. So I tell myself that what I'm doing here with Black Cross is the right thing to do. But if we were wrong about this girl tonight—if we're ever wrong, even once—I don't know how to deal with that. And I don't know how to tell what's true about the vampires we hunt."

I wanted to provide some answer for him, but I didn't know what that answer could possibly be.

Footsteps echoed on the floor outside, coming closer.

"Incoming!" Dana called before she opened the door. When she did peer inside the first aid room, she frowned. "Oh, man, I thought I was going to interrupt some crazy monkey sex in here. Figured at least I'd get flashed for my trouble."

I blushed bright purple. Lucas rolled his eyes. "We've been alone for *five minutes*, Dana."

"You gotta learn to strike while the iron is hot. Because privacy and this place do not go together." Dana braced her arms against the doorjamb. "We're about to head back out. Kate and Eduardo want to resume the hunt before the vampire's gone too far away."

Resume the hunt? Oh, no.

"They said no patrol tonight." Lucas scowled. "The equipment's not ready, half of us aren't even dressed—"

"That's why we train to get ready fast, buddy." Dana grinned at me, and the overlapping tooth in the front somehow made her look almost sweet. "Bianca can stay safe and warm here. But you and me and everybody else in the crew, we're heading out."

"Dana." Lucas gave her his most melting, pleading look. "I haven't seen Bianca in months. Come on."

That look would've been more than enough to dissolve me into a puddle, but it didn't seem to do much for Dana. "You know I don't care, but Kate and Eduardo don't want to hear it. You're lucky they even let her get a look at this place. Hell, when you sent that distress page in, Eduardo was this close to putting us into lockdown."

Lucas sighed as he looked at me. "Basically, we're screwed.

But only for a little while, okay? We'll be back before too long."

"Whatever we can have. It's enough."

"You gotta move, Lucas." Dana started edging out the door. "Like, in about two minutes, when I come back into this room to get our med supplies ready."

"Thanks," Lucas said. I gave Dana a quick smile as she went.

As soon as the door shut, he kissed me very gently, with his lips closed, but then more roughly as our mouths began to part. That warm tide of feeling inside me started to flow again, so that I wanted to pull him closer, but neither of us could forget that Dana was just outside. Instead, Lucas leaned his forehead against mine and cradled my cheeks in his hands. "I love you."

"I love you, too."

Lucas kissed me once more. After that he let go of me, stood up, and yelled, "All yours, Dana!"

"I don't want your girlfriend!" she called back. "Just the damn first aid kit!" A few people outside laughed, but it was a kind laugh. Maybe Eduardo saw me as a nuisance, but everybody else in Black Cross seemed happy for Lucas and me. I could never get over how a bunch of vampire hunters could seem so—well—*nice.*

We'll be okay, I told myself. *I can make it through this.* Already I was hungry, but I knew that if anybody in Black Cross caught me drinking blood, they'd attack first and ask questions later. Tomorrow, maybe, I'd have a chance to eat in private, or at least to pour the blood in my thermos down the drain. I could hang on until Saturday night if I needed to.

Lucas edged past Dana on the narrow stairs. Although she was smiling as she set to work, she never looked at me; instead she was focused on her task, hurriedly stuffing bandages and gauze into a small plastic box. "You doing okay, Bianca?"

"I guess," I said. "How often do you do this? Go out on hunts like these?"

"You say 'go out' like we had some big mothership we all return to when our work is done. We mostly travel from place to place. Go where we're needed. Some people have their own homes they go back to from time to time, but a lot of us don't. I don't." After a short pause, she added, "Lucas doesn't either. I guess he didn't tell you that."

"He hasn't really had a chance."

"I keep forgetting that you haven't hardly gotten to talk to each other since that whole scene went down last spring. That has to be rough."

"I guess it is."

"He's a good guy." She closed the plastic box and looked at me, serious for once. "Lucas doesn't wear his heart on his sleeve. I've known him since we were about twelve, and you're the only girl he's ever acted like this about. Just in case you were wondering."

"Thanks." Though that was pretty amazing to hear, I was thinking about larger concerns than my love life. Instead, I kept remembering the vampire, with her broken nails and uncertain smile. Black Cross might not be an immediate threat to me, but she remained in danger. She had been so lost and alone, another person made to feel small by Mrs. Bethany.

Was that the way I might end up someday? I shivered. *Never. I'll always have my parents and my friends—and maybe even Lucas.*

That didn't change the fact that the girl I'd met earlier was in desperate danger from Lucas's family and friends. The injustice of it sickened me. But what could Lucas do about it? What could I do about it?

The answer came to me almost immediately, terrifying but inevitable. It took me a second to get out the words: "I'm coming with you."

Dana stared at me. "On a vampire hunt? That's crazy."

"You have no idea"—I sighed—"but I'm going."

Chapter Seven

"THIS IS NO PLACE FOR AMATEURS," SAID EDUARDO. The twin scars on his cheek looked deeper—a trick of the dim lights of the camping lanterns on the walls.

I thought fast. "I've been going to school surrounded by vampires for more than a year now." It was the truth, if not the whole truth. My voice shook, but I hoped desperately that Eduardo would chalk that up to emotion, not fright. The man was an unrepentant killer of vampires; it was hard to look him in the face. "I need to know what I'm really up against."

I'd never seen Eduardo smile before. It wasn't an attractive expression. "Supposedly they behave themselves at Evernight Academy. You're only a kid. You should stick to the ones who pretend to be kids, too."

"I was fighting vampires when I was a lot younger than Bianca is," Lucas retorted. "I think she can handle it." He slung his arm around my shoulders, and at last my fear started to wane. Lucas's support seemed to end the argument; at any rate, Eduardo didn't protest any longer, and if anybody else had objections, they kept them to themselves.

Lucas glanced over at me, questioning why I was dead set on joining them, but we both knew we'd have to talk about it later.

The hunt didn't feel like a hunt at first. It was like any other road trip: People murmuring quietly as they pulled on their jackets, looking at one another with tired eyes and clambering into the beat-up van and Kate's turquoise pickup truck.

I remembered the very first road trip I'd ever taken, when my parents drove me to the beach one summer. They hated the water—both the rivers we had to cross to get there and the ocean that lapped at the shore—but they took me because I wanted to go so badly. They sat under a beach umbrella the whole time. Even though they'd drunk blood before we left, they didn't want to spend so much time in the sun. While I made sand castles, swam, and played with other kids, they watched and waved. It was a sacrifice they had made for me.

When I remembered things like that, I knew that the people of Black Cross were wrong about vampires. If they had seen my parents then, they'd know the truth.

Instead, tonight, they were going to try to kill a vampire girl. Though they didn't know it, I intended to stop them if I could.

I got in the back of the truck along with Dana, Eduardo, a couple of other guys, and Lucas, whose mussed hair hung in his eyes. As Kate backed us out of the parking garage, I whispered in Lucas's ear, "What do we do?"

"We start where we spotted her last, and we track her from there."

The town was all but silent now. Even the hardest-partying college students had gone to bed, or at least taken the festivities back to their dorm rooms. Although the neighborhood had been quiet before, while Lucas and I made our escape, it was now perfectly still, and all the houses were dark.

Once the vehicles were parked near where I'd seen the fair-haired vampire last, everyone started to fan out on foot. Lucas and I stuck together, of course. Kate shot us a look as she went, but she didn't fight it.

Lucas said nothing until we were definitely alone, walking along a side road a few blocks away. "Okay, I'm guessing our plan is to find the vampire and warn her before anybody else gets hold of her. Am I right?"

I felt a wave of tenderness toward him so strong that, for a second, I forgot where we were, the danger that faced us, and the task we had to complete. Instead, I took his hand gently in mine, and he turned to me—first in surprise but then with a small, knowing smile. I felt that deep electric kick, the force driving me toward him. He covered my lips with his hand. "We can't get distracted. We've got a job to do."

"A job." My lips brushed against his fingers as I spoke, and he blinked slowly, relishing the touch. "Let's do it."

Determinedly, Lucas turned from me and led us on our way. "She started going north at first," he said.

"How do you know that?"

"I see what the others don't see." He hesitated. "My night vision is better than it used to be."

There was no need for him to say why. I knew that it was because I'd twice bitten Lucas and drunk his blood. The first bite had had no effect, but the second had given him a few vampire powers. While the rest of Black Cross were off wandering around at random, Lucas was able to pull back the branch from a bush and show me the broken twigs—the ones that would have been broken off by somebody running past. He could find a single footprint in the muddy earth, catch a glimpse of a single curling golden hair that had fallen in the underbrush.

Some of that was his vampire ability, but some of it was Lucas's skill as a tracker. It was a revelation to me. All this time, I'd thought Black Cross only taught him how to fight, but they'd given him skills I hadn't imagined before. That plus vampire power—it was a formidable combination.

He didn't lack for weaponry either. When I saw something glinting at his belt, I said, "What have you got there?"

"My best knife," Lucas said, almost fondly. He tugged back his jean jacket to show me the knife strapped to his side. The blade was nearly as broad as a meat cleaver. "Had it since I was twelve."

"Is that really necessary?"

His dark-green eyes met mine, wary now. "I'd rather have it and not need it than not have it if we do need it. That girl might not actually be trouble, but when she was scared—you remember how it was."

I did remember. We vampires might not be the crazed killers Black Cross imagined us to be, but anybody could be deadly if backed to the wall.

When we turned onto a more commercial street, Lucas started to relax. "Less chance she'd come around here."

"I'm not so sure," I said. He stared at me, and I pointed to the sign I'd just seen, a glowing cross-and-shield insignia that obviously belonged to a hospital. The cross burned in my vision. "Hospitals have blood banks."

"Of course. It's like a snack cart—I can't believe we never thought of this before." Lucas grinned at me like I'd worked a miracle. "Let's go."

Once we reached the hospital, the glass doors slid open automatically to admit us. A guard peered at us—two teenagers sauntering in before dawn—and barked, "What are you kids doing here?"

"It's Grandma," Lucas said, so sincerely and tragically I had to bite my lip to keep from laughing. "There's—there's not much time."

The guard waved us on, and we hurried. It was fairly quiet; hospitals never close, but at this hour, not much was going on. A few nurses and orderlies walked by us in aqua scrubs, and a few glanced at us warily, but as long as Lucas and I walked with purpose, nobody seemed to question that we belonged here.

"Blood bank," Lucas muttered. "Where would a hospital keep a blood bank?"

"Let's check the elevators. Usually they have signs that say what departments are on what floors." Sure enough, the laminated panel next to the elevator bank informed us that blood donations could be given on the lowest level, in the basement.

The basement floor didn't really look different from the main floor, but it felt different. The lighting was slightly more subdued, maybe because a couple of fluorescent bulbs were starting to fade. The smell of disinfectant hung in the air, strong enough to make me wrinkle my nose. And down here it was even quieter. Lucas and I seemed to be the only two people around.

"Isn't the basement where most hospitals put the morgue?" I whispered.

"You're not about to start freaking out about dead people, are you?" Lucas walked down the corridor, peering into each room. "You go to school with them every day."

"I'm not freaking out." I was thinking.

The area for blood donations was closed—not surprising, this early in the morning. The door next to it had been forced open.

"Bingo." Lucas put one hand on the broad knife in his belt.

We stepped inside the blood bank, which basically was mostly a big room full of freezers. A few microscopes and various medical devices lined one wall, maybe to run medical tests, but this place was clearly mostly for storage. In one corner sat a couple of large refrigerators. The door of one fridge was ajar; inside I could see bags and bags of blood—probably the immediate supply, the stuff meant for emergency transfusions. The bags were in disarray, some of them on the floor, and several had been ripped open and drained. Droplets and smudges of blood marked the linoleum and gleamed wetly.

"The blood hasn't dried," I said. "She was here not long ago."

"Well, she's gone now," Lucas said. "Dammit."

"Maybe not. Maybe she wanted to rest afterward."

"Rest?"

"Even humans like to nap after a big meal sometimes. Besides, when I saw her, she was exhausted. Like she'd been on the run for days. If that's true, and she's just gotten a chance to eat—she'll be calm. We can talk to her."

"We need to be absolutely positive she's harmless before we let her go," Lucas said. "It's not that I don't trust your judgment, okay? We should just, well, make sure."

"So we'll talk to her." I was confident that Lucas would quickly see in her what I'd seen—how lost and lonely she really was. "Let's get started."

"You say that like we know where she is."

"I think we do. She's someplace where she can rest undisturbed. Someplace nobody would be surprised to see her, if she were found. Think about it, Lucas."

"Oh, no."

"Oh, yeah."

Okay, I might've spent pretty much my whole life surrounded by dead people, including my own parents, but that doesn't mean I didn't find the morgue a bit creepy. I wasn't panicking or anything, but there's something incredibly sad about the place: all those lives and emotions and hopes reduced to scrawled labels on small steel doors. Lucas and I stood in the doorway for a few seconds, just taking it in.

On three long tables, spread the length of the morgue, were three body bags. I walked toward them slowly. The first was way too big; the person inside must be heavy. The last looked too short. So the one in the middle was our best bet.

Hesitantly, I reached for the zipper. The tab was heavier than I expected, and cold to the touch—they kept the morgue chilly. Lucas took his place beside me, his broad knife at the ready. I tugged the zipper down, feeling each separating tooth like a jolt through my wrist.

Her hand shot out of the bag and grabbed mine, hard. I shrieked; I couldn't help it. Lucas lunged forward, but I threw out my arm to hold him back.

The vampire sat upright, staring at us. She looked less pale than before, and the port-wine mark on her throat was less pronounced; feeding had rejuvenated her. She'd loosened her fair hair for her nap, and the mussed curls framed her face. Her wide eyes remained fixed on Lucas, but it was me she spoke to: "Why did you bring him here?"

"He's with me. We just wanted to find you."

"To kill me."

I shook my head. "We're here to make sure you're safe."

"Safe?" She cocked her head in confusion, as if I'd started speaking in another language. "You're in danger."

"Lucas would never hurt me."

"In more danger than you know," she insisted. "More than you know either, boy."

"You ate here at the blood bank," I said, more for Lucas's benefit. "I can tell you've eaten. It changes our coloring, and makes us stronger."

"I'm stronger now," the vampire girl agreed. She kept glaring at Lucas, her eyes shining with hatred. I had to defuse the situation, and fast.

"Lucas is a friend. He's not here to hurt you."

"I can tell," she said, looking at Lucas's knife.

His motions awkward and unwilling, Lucas tucked his knife back into his belt. When he spoke, his words were clipped. "The family back in Albion—you didn't actually have anything to do with that? We thought you did."

"People make such foolish mistakes." The vampire's voice sounded strangely dreamy. Slowly she kicked the body bag away from her feet, looking for all the world like a little kid wriggling out of a sleeping bag.

"I need to know who did that," he said. "Something deadly is out there, doing a lot of harm. If you know who's been on the prowl in Albion, if you're connected with that gang at all, just tell me. I can get it taken care of, and you can—well, you can go do what you do."

Instead of answering Lucas, she turned her wide, dark eyes on me. "Does he know what you are?"

"He knows everything. Tell us what we need to know, and we can make sure you're safe."

Her fingers slowly relaxed as she let my hand go. The light fixture hanging from the ceiling was almost directly behind her, turning her corn silk hair into a kind of halo. I thought how young she must have been when she died, maybe only fourteen.

Just as she opened her mouth to speak, the morgue door slammed open. We all jumped, and my heart plunged as I saw Dana and Kate standing in the doorway. Dana had her crossbow ready, and Kate held a stake. "Y'all get back!" Dana yelled. "Reinforcements have arrived."

The vampire shrieked, an unearthly sound like a hawk diving for a kill. She leaped past us into the corner behind the autopsy table. "A trap," she whispered. "Always a trap."

I wanted to say that we hadn't meant to do this, but Lucas clutched both my arms as a warning to be silent. He started backing away, pulling me out of range.

Neither Kate nor Dana spoke to the vampire. Kate remained in the doorway as Dana edged forward, her face no longer sweet. I sensed Dana was a good person, but she was about to do a horrible thing, and I had to stop her.

Blindingly fast, the vampire flung one hand forward, and I saw a whirling glitter of metal in the split second before Dana cried out and slumped against the wall. Even as Dana fell, the vampire sprang forward with superhuman strength, tackling Kate and knocking them both sprawling into the corridor.

"Mom!" Lucas yelled, running toward them. But the vampire didn't intend to kill or even fight. She ran off, her shabby shoes thumping against the tiles.

Lucas and Kate took off after her instantly as Lucas yelled, "Stay here! Take care of Dana!"

I knew he'd try to help the vampire get away. But what was I supposed to do for Dana? I didn't know anything about medicine. Yet when I saw the stricken look on Dana's face, I instantly went to her side. "Is it bad?"

"Bad enough." Her face contorted in a grimace. "Must've been an autopsy knife. Don't think—the arm's broken—but—how much blood?"

"A lot, but she didn't hit the artery." I knew enough to realize that if the artery had been cut, blood would be spurting from the wound; instead, a thick red flow oozed downward, coating her shirt to the elbow. "I'm not going to take out the knife. This is more than we can deal with using the first aid kit. We should go to the ER."

"And explain this to the hospital staff how, exactly?" Dana groaned and leaned her head against the wall. I realized she felt faint. "No, we need to get out of here."

"You need medical attention!"

"There are more supplies back at the first aid room. We—we can handle it. Just help me up. Okay?"

"Okay." I slung her good arm around my shoulder and walked her into the hallway. The lights were brighter there, and I saw the vivid red of the bloodstain for the first time. The color seemed almost indescribably beautiful.

Then I felt the hunger.

It wasn't the same as it had been when I bit Lucas—this

was different, more basic and yet equally strong. Dana's blood smelled like steak, like the seashore, like any hundred wonderful things I wanted and hadn't enjoyed for too long. When I breathed in through my mouth, I could almost taste the coppery tang of it, and the hand I held against her shoulder registered every beat of her pulse. My jaw ached as though my fangs were about to emerge. I couldn't think, couldn't speak, couldn't do anything but want to drink.

Stop it.

I turned my head away from Dana and shut my eyes tightly. Dana murmured, "Hang in there. I know it looks bad."

"You don't have to comfort me." I felt so ashamed. "You're the one who's hurt."

"But I know—this kind of thing is scary, especially if you're—not used to it." She swallowed between every gasp for breath. "You never saw—anything—like this before."

I remembered how Lucas had looked after I bit him for the first time, and the boneless way he had fallen at my feet. "I guess I have to learn to deal with it."

We met up with Mr. Watanabe in the parking lot, and he took us back immediately. Dana turned out only to have a flesh wound, but she still needed me to hold her hand while Mr. Watanabe stitched her up. Within a couple of hours, Lucas and the rest returned; I didn't have to ask how the hunt had gone, because Kate looked discouraged. Everybody was completely exhausted, and the sun had only just come up.

When Lucas hugged me, I whispered in his ear, "Did she get away?"

His thumb brushed against my cheek as he nodded. "Always looking out for everybody." He kissed me gently on my forehead, right there in front of the whole group, and that made Dana grin for the first time since the hospital.

After that, the group discipline broke down—or it might be more accurate to say it was suspended. Kate didn't give any more orders, and apparently there wasn't anything else to do until later. Some people shuffled off to an area where several cast-iron cots were lined up. Kate fired up a portable stove and started making breakfast for a few people, and Mr. Watanabe began methodically cataloging all the weapons. Lucas and I helped get Dana comfortable on the cot in the first aid room.

"Sorry about this," she said as she eased her way down. Her braids looked like dark ropes on the white pillowcase.

"Sorry about what?" I asked. "It's not your fault."

"Yeah, but now I'm taking up the only room in this whole place where you and Lucas could've been alone. That's suckiness one, young love zero."

"I'll forgive you this time," Lucas said. "You need some breakfast, Dana?"

"Send somebody up here with some pancakes. If they don't have 'em, make 'em." Dana made a show of putting her good arm lazily behind her head. "What good is getting stabbed if you can't use it for emotional blackmail?"

While Lucas went to tell Kate about Dana's breakfast, I sort of threw myself together in what passed for a bathroom. It was a small cinder block room off the first aid area, one both tinier and grosser than in most gas stations. I couldn't really do much with myself, but I pinned my brooch to my sweater. When I came out, Lucas brightened so much at the sight of it that I felt like I'd had a complete makeover—or maybe he was just that happy to see me.

"Look at you two." Mr. Watanabe chuckled. He was carefully sharpening a small knife with a grindstone, peering at the blade through his bifocals. It was weird to think that anybody so kindly spent his time preparing weapons to attack vampires. "I'm glad to see you with a girl, Lucas. A young man should have a girl."

"No arguments here." Lucas hugged me from behind. "You must've been fighting 'em off with a stick when you were my age, huh?"

"Oh, no. Not me. I had already met my Noriko." The old man's eyes softened as he said her name. "After the first time I saw her, every other girl in the world—for me, it was as if they did not exist. I only wanted to be with Noriko all the time."

"That's really romantic," I said. I wanted to ask where she was, but then I realized that if she were in Black Cross, she would be here. Maybe the reason a gentle man like him joined a group of vampire hunters was because his wife had run into one of the vampires who really was a mad killer. Something like that could blind you to subtleties and leave you with only one wish: revenge.

"Never enough time to be with the ones you love," Mr. Watanabe said as he tested the blade's edge. "You two go out. Explore the town. Don't worry about us here. You should enjoy each other."

"It's early," Eduardo said. He'd come around the tarp behind us when I wasn't looking. "I don't see what you expect to do out there at this hour. It's more secure if you stay here."

"Coffeehouses are open." Lucas took my hand possessively. "We're not in lockdown. I can go if I want to. That's the rule."

Eduardo looked as if he would like to argue, but instead he said, "Go."

We were free, then, and we went outside with no real goal or direction. It was shaping up to be a gorgeous autumn day, the kind where the sun turns all the colors of the leaves into different shades of gold. Because Lucas and I were alone again at last, maybe we should've instantly started discussing all the important secret topics we had to discuss, but we didn't. Instead we talked about anything else. Everything else. As bizarre as our lives were, what we shared was the closest either of us could ever get to "normal." One day just being together, without any worries in the world—it was all we could hope for, and I didn't intend to waste it.

At the local coffeehouse, we debated the brownie cookies versus the peanut butter chip and took turns dunking them into my latte.

In the Amherst square, we sat on a park bench for a couple of hours and made up stories about everyone who passed by—the woman in a red jacket was a secret agent, and that gray-haired man getting into a car nearby had the confidential files she needed to save the world. The old lady across the street had once been a showgirl back in the fifties, dancing around Las Vegas wearing a feathered headdress and sequined bikini. We knew the whole time that our lives were probably stranger than anything we could make up for anybody else, but that didn't make the game less fun.

At the bookstore, we compared notes on our favorite childhood novels. It turned out we both loved the Chronicles of Narnia.

"I never realized that they were Christian," I confessed. "Looking back, it's so totally obvious that I feel stupid for not getting it. But, you know, my parents—it's not like they were taking me to church much."

That was Lucas's cue to laugh. Instead, he studied me gravely, and I thought I detected a slight uncertainty in his eyes. "Does it affect you now? The God stuff in the books, I mean."

"Reading about it? No. It probably never will, either. I can remember Mom reading *Voyage of the Dawn Treader* out loud. It's the visual symbols that are the problem." We were sitting on the floor of the downstairs textbook section, away from most of the customers. As it was the middle of the term, no students seemed likely to interrupt. I risked asking, "Have you felt anything different? You know—your powers?

"I feel stronger. Run faster. A couple people here have commented on it, but not like they're suspicious. They just think

I'm working out. I mean, I'm strong, but it's not like I'm doing anything supernatural. Mrs. Bethany said I'd start feeling some drawbacks as well as some benefits, but nothing."

"Maybe not yet, but someday." Hope flickered inside me like a candle. "You've already said you've thought about leaving Black Cross."

"Yeah, but I don't know what would come after that, for me. Could I just—get a job? This is the only thing I know how to do, and I don't think there's a whole lot of openings in the field." He sighed. "Bianca, I never even went to high school, unless you count that year at Evernight. I've read and studied on my own, but it's not the same. All these college textbooks—this is like a foreign world to me. A place I couldn't ever get to go."

"There are ways to do it without high school. You could earn a diploma, easy."

"Then what? No scholarships for diploma students, and there's no way Mom would ever pay. What money she has is for Black Cross. That's the beginning, middle, and end of the story. Maybe I could work my way through, but—I don't know." He swallowed hard, and I could tell he'd thought about this a lot. "I guess I haven't given up the idea. But it doesn't seem likely."

There was nothing for me to say that was equal to how trapped he felt; I had no information to share, no comfort to give. I simply took his hand. "What would you study? In college, I mean."

"Law, I think."

"Law? I can't see you with a briefcase and three-piece suit."

"I'd wear it if it meant I got to put the bad guys away." Lucas tried to smile. "Wore that stupid Evernight uniform, didn't I?"

"Don't laugh. I still have to wear it."

He brushed a strand of hair from my cheek. "I don't have to ask you. You'd study astronomy." I nodded. "What is it that you love so much about it? You've showed me every single constellation, but you never said why it is you watch the stars."

I put my arms across my knees and rested my chin against them, considering. Although I knew the answer, it was important to tell Lucas in a way that he would understand. "My parents told me what I truly was when I was very small, as soon as they thought I could keep a secret. They made it sound like something special. A big adventure. I thought it was like in the fairy tales, when the girl who sweeps out the cottage finds out that she's really a princess and one day the prince is going to come for her. Like the secret inside me was magic."

Lucas looked as though he wanted to ask a question, but he must have seen that I was struggling for the right words, because he watched me in silence.

"The first time I realized that it wasn't just fun and magic—the first time I knew there was anything bad about being a—" I glanced around. This area of the bookstore was still empty, but I talked around the V word anyway. "—anything bad about it was the first time I realized that I would never die, but all my Arrowwood friends would. Carrie and Tom and Renee—they were all going to die. All of them. They would get old and be gone, and I'd be alone. It scared me, because I realized that of all the people I loved in the world, there would be so few I would ever get to keep."

Softly, Lucas cupped my cheek in one hand. I swallowed the lump in my throat and kept going. "So I tried to think what I could keep. If there was anything that would stay with me always."

"The stars," Lucas said. "You knew you would always have the stars."

I nodded, and I knew he understood everything. He took me in his arms and held me so tightly that I could believe Lucas would be with me forever, too.

In the late afternoon, Lucas drove me back to Evernight Academy in Kate's old pickup truck. We got there at dusk, though the weather was so gloomy that it seemed almost like night. Fog had crept into the hills, obscuring everything more than a few feet away and painting the world milky gray. It wasn't like Lucas could drop me off at the front door, but he pulled up on a side road on the edge of the nearby woods. From there it would be easy for me to hike back—ten minutes' walk, tops. I knew I needed to put in an appearance soon to keep Raquel from asking questions, but I lingered in Lucas's embrace as long as I could. We kissed until the truck windows fogged up inside, and I didn't want it to ever end. But I could feel the nearness of Evernight, as if the building's shadow were falling over us.

"I can't go another six months without seeing you," Lucas murmured into my hair. "We have to meet up soon."

"Anytime. You know that. Just e-mail me—I can give you my Hotmail account, and it's not like Mrs. Bethany has the password to that one."

"Won't work. We aren't allowed to have laptops or anything, not since we got caught out three years ago by a couple of vampires who had learned about hacking." Lucas sighed. "I could try to get to a library sometime, but I never know when we're going to go into lockdown. When that happens, we get stuck in the cell so that we can't go out for any reason."

"Then how are you and I supposed to see each other?"

"We'll set up each meeting as we go. This time, we figure out where to meet next time. Next time, we figure out the time after that. And we get there. No matter what. We just have to do it."

"I know we can. And next month is as good as set up," I said. When Lucas looked at me, uncomprehending, I punched him gently on the shoulder. "Riverton. Evernight has a Riverton weekend coming up. Remember?"

"Of course—that's perfect." Lucas grinned, delighted with the idea. Then he hesitated. "There are going to be a lot of people around who'd recognize me."

"Not if we arrange to meet up someplace where there won't be a crowd. What about the riverbank? Nobody ever walked down that way but Vic, and if Vic sees you, it's not the end of the world."

"I'd rather leave Vic out of this for his own good, but, yeah, we could swing it. Besides, he'll probably hang out at the diner instead anyway."

Delighted with our solution, I kissed him again. Lucas held me close for a few long minutes. If only we could be alone together for longer—was there anywhere in Riverton? I'd have to think of something.

The fog had become even thicker, and I knew nightfall was at hand. "I've got to go," I said. "I should've gone a while ago."

"Go. Hurry. This isn't good-bye. Not for long."

We kissed once more, and he laid his hand against my heart. The touch made me shiver. Somehow I managed to turn from him, get out of the truck, and start running. Behind me I heard the truck's motor rev up, then tires spinning away.

He's gone. My heart ached, and I paused in my run to look back over my shoulder as the truck's red taillights disappeared into the fog.

A deep voice behind me said, "I guess I don't have to ask who that was."

I whirled around to see Balthazar.

Chapter Eight

BUSTED.

Balthazar stood with his hands folded across his chest. With his tall frame and broad shoulders, he seemed as imposing as the oaks in the forest. My stomach seemed to drop to my knees. "I—I can explain."

"You don't have to." Balthazar's eyes darted down to the carved black brooch still pinned to my sweater. I knew he understood it had been a gift from Lucas; I'd worn it nonstop last year. "Has this been going on the whole time?"

"It's none of your business!" Breathing in deeply, I tried to stay calm. "I promise, I haven't told Lucas anything about us he didn't already know. He's not spying for Black Cross anymore."

"Like he did last year?"

That struck uncomfortably close to the truth. "You don't understand. Lucas didn't want to lie to me. They sent him here on a mission—"

"On a mission that he completed, and he didn't care if

he had to use you to do it." Balthazar breathed out sharply, as though he were in physical pain. "I'm not angry at you, Bianca. You're—you're in love for the first time, and you can't see straight."

"Balthazar. Please listen."

He straightened, and his gaze turned inward and became intent. "I'll take care of this. We all will."

My blood turned cold. "What do you mean, *we*?"

"The people who really love you."

He turned toward the school, but I grabbed his arm to hold him back. "You can't tell my parents. You can't tell anyone."

Balthazar put his hands on my shoulders as if he were comforting me instead of destroying me. "Someday you'll understand that this is for your own good."

For my own good. Anytime anyone had ever used those words to me, they hadn't had the slightest clue what "my own good" truly was. I pushed Balthazar so roughly that he stumbled a couple of steps back. "You're jealous. You're just jealous. That's why you're doing this."

Even as I said it, I knew it was a lie. Balthazar's only reply was to start walking toward Evernight.

I ran beside him, my breath catching in my throat. Twigs and branches snapped all around us. Overhead I could hear birds flying away, startled, the flapping of wings heavy and close. "It's not what you think. Lucas loves me. He wants to be with me, and we don't care that we're—that we're different from each other. That doesn't have to matter, not if we love each other enough."

"That's the first stupid thing I ever heard you say. I hope it's the last." Balthazar pushed a low-hanging pine branch out of my way, clearing my path even though he refused to look directly at me. "If he were just any other human, just some kid here at Evernight, do you think I'd care?"

"Yes." Balthazar might not be doing this because he was jealous, but that didn't mean he *wasn't* jealous.

He paused. The fog silhouetted his profile. "Okay. I'd care no matter who you were with. But I wouldn't get in your way, and neither would anyone else. Lucas is not just another kid. He's a Black Cross hunter, which means he's out to destroy us. He can't be trusted."

"You don't know him!" I shouted the words. I almost didn't care if anyone heard me anymore, not with Balthazar about to give everything away. I wanted to punch him in the face. I wanted to cry until he would comfort me. I wished we were back in fencing class so I'd have a sword in my hand. Everything was about to be ruined, ruined forever, and I was so angry and afraid I couldn't think straight. "You don't know what he did last night!"

Balthazar's eyes raked over me, and I became incredibly conscious of my rumpled shirt and hair, still mussed from making out with Lucas. "I can imagine."

"He helped me save a vampire! *Save* her, Balthazar. The others in Black Cross, they would've hurt her, but Lucas didn't. He listened to me. She was the youngest vampire I've ever seen— hardly more than a kid, pale and shabby—you couldn't help but feel sorry for her, and Lucas did feel sorry for her, I know he did!"

Balthazar stopped in his tracks. He turned toward me slowly, and his face was so changed that at first I could hardly recognize him. "The youngest you've ever seen?"

Why was that the part of all this that surprised him? "Yeah."

"What did she look like?"

"Uh—light hair, kind of curly—but the point is that Lucas helped her get away from Black Cross. He understands now, don't you see?"

"Tell me *exactly* what she looked like."

"I just did!"

"Bianca." His voice broke. "Please."

I couldn't ignore his desperation. Slowly I closed my eyes and tried to remember exactly what it had been like as I walked arm in arm with the vampire through the city square. I described her youthful heart-shaped face, her dark eyes, and the wheat color of her hair. Balthazar's face didn't change until I mentioned the port-wine mark on her throat. At that moment, his jaw dropped slightly, and he whispered, "She's back."

"Wait—you know her?"

He nodded, but slowly, and he could no longer meet my eyes. Balthazar looked so dazed and so miserable that my anger at him vanished instantly.

"Balthazar, who was that?"

"Charity."

The name instantly conjured up the memory: last Christmas, Balthazar and I walking through the snow past holly bushes as he told me about the life he'd lost long ago. He had mentioned then the person that he missed the most.

"Charity. You mean—your sister?" I'd thought he was telling me his deepest secrets on that snowy walk, but he had been holding something back. He hadn't hinted that his beloved sister had been turned into a vampire with him. "That was her?"

Balthazar didn't answer me. I thought perhaps he couldn't. As he started to walk away from me, with slow, stumbling steps, he roughly said, "Don't tell anyone."

"Okay. I promise." Belatedly, I remembered that I had a secret, too. "You won't tell either, will you?"

He didn't say yes or no, but I knew he wouldn't talk to anybody about what either of us had learned tonight. For a long time I watched him go, too numbed with astonishment and the sudden ebbing of fear to do anything else. Then I took a deep breath and ran back to school, trying to think of ways to describe to Raquel a meteor shower I hadn't actually seen.

Raquel bought my story hook, line, and sinker. She didn't even ask that many questions, which was a relief but, weirdly, a little disappointing. In fact, I was pretty sure I'd gotten away with it completely until Sunday night dinner with my parents, when Mom idly asked me where I'd been Saturday afternoon—they'd looked for me. I blurted out the first excuse I could think of, which was distantly related to the truth.

It turned out to be the worst excuse I could think of,

because my parents *loved* it.

"Walking in the woods with Balthazar, hm?" Dad made a show of all his questions, which made Mom laugh. He laid on a bit of his long-faded English accent, Sherlock-Holmes style, for comic effect. "Now, what would a young lady be doing speaking to Balthazar More until all hours of the evening?"

"We were hardly out until all hours." I spread butter on my roll, eagerly helping myself to the meal my parents had prepared. The blood was even more welcome than the food. I'd had to go without for half the weekend, so I drank glass after glass. "It's personal, okay? Please don't ask him about it or anything."

"All right," Mom said soothingly. "It's just good to have you home."

When I raised my head from my plate to look at Mom and Dad, they were both smiling at me so warmly—so gratefully— that it was all I could do not to hug them close and apologize for ever, ever lying to them. But I stayed where I was. The memory of Lucas was enough to convince me that some secrets were worth keeping.

Within a few weeks, I'd get to see Lucas again. I'd already worn all our old memories threadbare, imagining myself in them over and over again. Now I had new memories, kisses and laughter I could remember for the first time, and it was like falling in love all over again. During the next few days, I should've been on cloud nine.

But one question loomed overhead as dark and threatening as storm clouds—Would Balthazar tell? I knew he wanted to keep Charity a secret, but Mrs. Bethany would have known Charity back when she attended Evernight Academy. How secret could his sister be? Add how much Balthazar hated Lucas, and I wasn't sure that our pact of secrecy would hold for very long.

I studied Balthazar's face every day: in English, while Mrs. Bethany described Macbeth's motives; in fencing, as he dueled with the professor to show the rest of us how it was really done; or in the halls, as we walked past each other. He never looked back at me. He never seemed to look at anyone any longer. The guy who was always the first to say hello or hold the door open for others was the guy who was now steering his way through the school corridors like a blind man, his path uncertain and his eyes blank.

"That guy is totally cracked out," Vic said one day, as we walked past Balthazar in the great hall.

"I don't think he's on anything."

"I didn't mean, for real. If he was cracked out for real, he'd probably be having more fun, right?" Vic shrugged. "Balty looks like he's not having any fun. He looks like he never had any. Like he wouldn't know fun if it started dancing around yelling 'I'm fun' in his face."

It took me a couple of seconds to process that. "He does look sad, doesn't he?"

"Doesn't look good, that's for sure." Vic brushed his mop of sandy bangs from his forehead, then snapped his fingers. "Hey, I'll invite him to my next classic DVD screener. We're doing a *Matrix/Fight Club* double feature about awesome leather coats and the evils of the corporate hegemony. You think he'd like that?"

"Who wouldn't?" I resolved to look up *hegemony* in the dictionary. Once I'd thought that Vic wasn't a very bright guy, but I'd learned better. Oblivious to details as he often was, he knew more about more subjects than virtually any of my other friends.

I cared about Balthazar as a friend, and that made it hard enough to watch him when he was so obviously miserable. But I would be lying if I claimed that the main reason I was frightened was because I was worried for him. I was too selfish for that. Every time I saw him so lost and strung out, I couldn't help thinking, *He's going to tell.*

Balthazar's funereal gloom, and his silence, lasted for more than a week, until the first day of driver's ed.

The driver's education class at Evernight Academy was split into two sections. There was one for the regular human students, who could be expected to be fairly familiar with modern automobiles and probably drove their parents' cars at home, and one for the vampires, some of whom had been driving regularly since the Model T days, others who had never been behind the wheel of a car before and whose wildly uneven sets of experiences were best kept hidden from human eyes. By rights I should've been put in the human section, but instead I was assigned with the vampires—probably because of my parents' concerns that I wasn't socializing with the "right people."

"I just don't get why every car needs a computer now," Courtney bitched as she fumbled for the blinker. "Seriously, what is the point? I'm not doing math while I drive."

"Please concentrate on the road, Miss Briganti." Mr. Yee sighed heavily as he marked something on his board. We were driving one of the school's official cars—a nondescript gray sedan, several years old—around the gravel paths that stretched through the back grounds. "I'm going to ask you to take this next loop a little faster."

"Speeding is unsafe," Courtney said, then smiled. "See, I read the booklet."

"That's very impressive, Miss Briganti, but you're currently driving approximately twenty miles an hour. I'd like to see how you handle the car at something approaching normal street speed."

Courtney's hands tightened around the steering wheel. She was out of practice, and her nervousness had a tendency to manifest as whiplash-inducing sharp turns. I fumbled around to make sure my seat belt was fastened. It was difficult, because I was squashed into the middle of the backseat, with Ranulf on one side and Balthazar on the other. Ranulf studied the car interior as though he'd never seen one before, and Balthazar stared gloomily out the window.

Ranulf said, "These automobiles have only become popular in the last one hundred years. They might not remain so."

"What, you think we're going back to horses and buggies?" Courtney snorted as she stepped on the gas and the car lurched forward. Mr. Yee braced himself against the dashboard. "Dream on, Prince Valiant."

"Innovations are often forgotten," Ranulf said wistfully.

"I don't think cars are going anywhere." I tried to sound sympathetic and hide my amusement. Poor Ranulf always looked so lost.

"I liked horses. A horse was a friend to you. A companion. This is merely metal, and the countryside goes by too quickly to see." That was about as much as I'd ever heard Ranulf say at once.

"I bet it was kind of nice." I thought about that for a second—about how nobody really had horses and carriages anymore, and how many vampires must have felt more at home in those days—and then I sat up. "Hey, why don't we start an Amish colony?"

That made Balthazar turn toward me, confused. "What?"

"You know. We have Evernight Academy, and we're building that rehab center in Arizona—all the safe places for vampires to go, the ones where nobody else will bother us and where we can control who gets in. So why don't we have an Amish colony? Or town, or whatever Amish people call it." Nobody seemed to be getting it. Maybe I wasn't explaining it right. "People who aren't really caught up with today would be more at home there. They could have horses and carriages, and old-timey lanterns and clothes and stuff, and nobody would care. Come on, that's a good idea!"

Mr. Yee seemed to have become drawn into the conversation

despite himself. "Our gathering places are meant to bring people up-to-date with the modern world, not hide from it. Left turn signal, Miss Briganti."

"It could be a halfway step. People could start there and work up to Evernight or wherever." I really thought it was a pretty great plan. "And people who got homesick for ye olden days could visit sometimes."

"Ooh, would it be like that movie *Witness*?" Courtney laughed, but it was a nicer laugh than usual. She drummed her fingers excitedly on the steering wheel. "Because I totally loved that movie."

"Me, too." I'd seen it on cable a couple of times; that was pretty much the basis for everything I knew about the Amish. "Back when Harrison Ford was hot."

"*So* hot. I would so go to Vampire Amish Town if it was like that— Oh, crap!"

The car swerved sideways, bouncing off the gravel road. Everyone grabbed onto the nearest seat and shouted as we ran into the ditch. It wasn't much of a wreck, but then, it wasn't much of a ditch.

"This brings us back to lesson one," Mr. Yee said. "Watch the road."

"Does that mean I flunk?" Courtney wheeled around to glare at me. "You were distracting me on purpose!"

"I wasn't!"

She didn't stick around to hear my denials. Courtney flung open the car door, let it swing shut behind her, and huffily stalked back toward the school. Mr. Yee opened his door to call after her. "Miss Briganti! We have to get the car back on the road!"

"Do it yourself!" she shouted. Her blond ponytail bobbed behind her, keeping time as she walked away. "I already flunked, remember?"

"You have now," Mr. Yee muttered.

"Her pride is wounded," Ranulf said. "That is why she left."

"Save analysis of Miss Briganti for psychology class," Mr. Yee said tiredly. "For now, we have a car to push."

We took turns trying to steer and floor the gas pedal while the rest attempted to push the car out of the ditch. By the time we finally managed it, all of us were muddy to the knees—not such a big deal for the guys in their uniform trousers, but my legs were filthy and scratched beneath my skirt. We still had about half an hour left in driver's ed, but Mr. Yee gave me permission to head back to the school to clean up. Balthazar said, "I'll walk with her. It's getting late."

Mr. Yee looked like he wanted to argue, but he didn't. It wasn't like I needed protection on the school grounds, but it was Ranulf's turn to drive, and Balthazar was already pretty good behind the wheel. "Sure. Go ahead."

As the car rumbled into life behind us, Balthazar and I began walking back toward the school. It was the first time we'd been alone since the night he caught me sneaking in. The silence lay heavy between us, and I wanted to fill it with nervous chatter, but I held my tongue.

"Vampire Amish." His lopsided smile was only a shadow of its former self. "Only you could have thought of it."

"You're laughing at me."

"Not at you. Never at you." Balthazar took a deep breath. "You haven't told anyone about Charity."

"No. I promise I haven't."

"It wasn't a question. If you'd told anyone, Mrs. Bethany would already have interrogated me about it."

"Why? And what do you mean, interrogated?"

"Charity and Mrs. Bethany never got along."

"So Charity said." I cast him a curious glance. "If you and your sister are so tight, why did you fall out of touch?"

"We've lost track of each other before. It's complicated." He stopped walking. The raw pain in his face hurt to witness. Embarrassed, I dropped my gaze toward the ground. We stood on yellowing fall grass, his heavy-booted feet almost twice as large as mine in their muddy loafers. "She's never forgiven me."

"Forgiven you for what?"

He opened his mouth to answer, then apparently thought better of it. "That's between us. All you have to know is that she needs me. That never changes; for vampires, nothing ever changes. It's always like this—she slips away, and everything goes to hell, but then I find her again and we're all right."

I remembered her unwashed clothes and body, her transparent loneliness. Charity looked like somebody who needed looking after, badly. "How long has it been?"

"We haven't seen each other in thirty-five years." *Thirty-five years*, I thought, recalling a conversation we'd had almost a year ago, just before last Christmas, as we walked together through the snow. *That's when he last "lost touch" with humanity*, I realized. *Losing Charity is what made him give up.* "But she always comes back to Massachusetts eventually. That's where we grew up together; it's *home*, Bianca. Our home. If she's returned, that means she's homesick. I can reach her now. But to reach her," he continued, even more quietly than before, "I have to find her."

Now I understood. "You want me to take you to her. You want me to use Black Cross to figure out where Charity is, so you can get to her first."

"And for you to keep throwing Black Cross off her trail, if you can." He squared his broad shoulders. The sun had begun to set, painting the sky orange behind him. "I know it's a lot to ask. I'm prepared to offer a lot in return."

"You mean, you won't tell about me and Lucas."

"Your secret is safe with me no matter what." Balthazar meant it; when he spoke, it sounded like surrender. My relief turned to amazement as he continued, "If you'll help me with this, I'll help get you off campus so that you can be with Lucas."

"You mean it? You really will?" My head whirled. "But how?"

"Easy." His smile was strained. "We'll tell one simple lie. We'll say that we're together." Together? *Oh.* But I saw the sense of it, even before Balthazar explained the rest. "Older vampires can come and go from Evernight if they get permission, and Mrs. Bethany is pretty free with permissions for the vampires she trusts. She trusts me. Your parents haven't made any secret of the fact that they'd like us to spend more time together. If you and I are supposedly a couple—"

He looked down at the ground, lips pressed together for a second. That *supposedly* had cost him.

"—then I can ask permission to take you off campus sometimes. If your parents okay it, Mrs. Bethany probably will, too. They'll see it as you becoming closer to a 'real vampire.' They'll encourage it. They'll let us go."

It was a good plan. Solid. "You've been thinking about this."

"For a few days now. If you need time to consider, I understand."

"I only have one question. Why do you have to keep Charity a secret? I mean, she went here all those years ago, so Mrs. Bethany knows all about her, right?"

"Like I said, they didn't get along, and that's an understatement. If I bring Charity here, Mrs. Bethany will give her sanctuary—she has to give sanctuary to any vampire who seeks it. That's the most sacred rule here. But Mrs. Bethany would do anything she had to do in order to make sure that I couldn't bring Charity here. She'd try to scare her off, maybe even drive another wedge between us. I can't lose another thirty-five years."

"I understand." I would do what I could to spare Balthazar that pain. Besides—in return, he would make it possible for me to be with Lucas. There was almost nothing I wouldn't have done for that.

"Do we have a deal?" he asked.

❖ 113 ❖

"Yeah. When do we begin?"

"Might as well start now." Balthazar held out his hand.

I took it, and together we walked back toward the school. We remained hand in hand as we walked through the great hall, where a few students were milling around between classes. I could feel their glances on us, hungry and avid, as eager for new gossip as they were for blood. At the bottom of the staircase to the girls' dorm, Balthazar bent and kissed my cheek. His lips were cool against my skin.

The entire way upstairs, I tried to think of how I would explain this to Lucas. *I'm not dating Balthazar. I'm pretend dating him. Which involves some not pretend hand-holding. And maybe some not pretend kissing. But it's all actually pretend, see?*

I groaned. My explanations were making my head hurt already.

Chapter Nine

THAT NIGHT WAS MY SECOND BURGLARY.

Ever since my first break-in at Mrs. Bethany's house had come up empty, I had meant to do more snooping around. But Mrs. Bethany hadn't taken any more trips away from Evernight, which had left me with no opportunity to sneak back to the carriage house. Where else could I look for answers?

There was one possible place—the records room in the north tower—but I had originally disregarded that as a possibility. If Mrs. Bethany had anything up there that suggested the real reason she'd admitted humans to Evernight Academy, surely Lucas would have found it last year. He'd had plenty of time to search.

But as I lay in bed that night, unable to sleep and hungry for blood, I kept trying to imagine how I was going to explain my arrangement with Balthazar to Lucas. I tried out several versions of the speech—jokey, flirty, short, long—and none of them sounded convincing, even to me. I knew Lucas would eventually see the sense of it, but I also knew it would take time.

Sighing, I rolled onto my back and clasped my pillow around my ears, trying to muffle my own confused voice in my head. My stomach growled and my jaw ached. I wanted blood. I'd sneaked a glass around lunchtime, and that should have been enough to hold me for a full day—at least, it always would have been, before. My appetite was growing stronger all the time.

Uncertainties tumbled over and over in my mind, crowding out any hope of sleep. As I put on my slippers and my robe, I cast a quick glance at Raquel, who lay sprawled, facedown, on her bed. She slept soundly—maybe too soundly. Frowning, I remembered the sleeping pills I'd advised her to take last year. I hoped she wasn't still using them and reminded myself to ask later.

The blood in my thermos was lukewarm but welcome. I drank as I walked downstairs, descending the staircase of the south tower. Mostly I was on autopilot, moving just for the sake of movement, but as I reached the classroom level—the bridge to the guys' dorms in the north tower—I remembered seeing Lucas in these hallways. That was the only time Evernight had ever felt like home.

If I could get answers for Lucas—if I could tell him about the compromises I'd made for us to be together *after* I told him that I'd finally learned the secret Black Cross was so desperate to know—everything would be so much easier. He'd be able to throw our success in Eduardo's face, and he'd love that. Afterward, explaining about Balthazar would be a piece of cake.

I slipped my thermos into my robe pocket and sneaked

toward the guys' dorm. The new blood flowing through me sharpened my hearing, so I could discern the footsteps of the monitor—one of the teachers, strolling around, making sure none of the vampire students decided to turn a human student into a midnight snack. I closed my eyes and concentrated on the sound, waiting until the teacher was out of earshot and my path was clear.

Quietly I opened the heavy door and stepped through. It was tempting to let the door go quickly and run for it, but I had to be patient and ease the door back so that it slipped silently back into place. Then I made my way upstairs, ears pricking at every tiny sound: a faucet dripping, somebody snoring, even the click of a desk lamp.

At the top of the spiral staircase sat the records room. I pushed the door open, ducking a fall of spiderwebs and dust. The gargoyle outside the window peered at me suspiciously. Stacks of boxes and trunks loomed in every corner, many of them lettered or labeled with old-fashioned handwriting or stiff, unfamiliar fonts nobody used anymore. Inside those boxes lay facts about countless students who had attended Evernight—most of them vampires.

Think. They want to know why the human students are here, not the vampires. But if you figure out something about the vampires here, maybe it could tell you something about the humans.

An idea occurred to me: What if the humans here had some connection to the vampires? What if these were their family members, or even their descendants?

Energized, I started to open the nearest trunk—then paused.

The last time I'd been in this room, we'd found the remains of a dead vampire in one of these trunks. Surely Mrs. Bethany wouldn't have just left Erich's skull up here to rot. Right?

I carefully pried the lid open a couple of inches and peered inside. Skull free. Breathing a sigh of relief, I opened it all the way and picked up some sheets of paper, pretty much at random. I'd have to read a whole lot of material to figure out if my theory was correct, and no place was better to start than any other.

Then, in the corner of the trunk, I saw a scurry of movement. My eyes caught a glimpse of a tiny dark tail: a mouse, burrowing for cover.

Before thinking about it, almost without even knowing I was doing it, I snatched the mouse up and bit in.

It only squeaked once. If it twitched, I didn't know. All I knew was that blood was filling my mouth—real blood, living blood, blossoming outward against my tongue. It was like biting into juicy grapes on a blazing summer day, except hot, sweeter, and even better than that. The mouse's last heartbeats fluttered against my lips as I took two sips, three, and then I was done.

I pulled the mouse away, looked down at its dead body, and gagged.

Gross, oh, gross! I spat a couple of times, trying to get any fur or mites or mouse cooties off my lips. The little mouse's corpse I hurled into the corner, where it fell limply. Even as I wiped my mouth repeatedly with my sleeve, I couldn't forget the aftertaste of blood—

—and it still tasted great.

At least I didn't do this in front of Lucas, I thought. *From now on, I'm going to have a lot more blood at lunchtime. Like, a gallon, if that's what it takes to keep me from doing this again.*

My loss of control upset me enough that I sort of wanted to go back to my room and hide under the covers. But I didn't; it had been hard enough sneaking up here, and I wasn't going to waste the trip. Doing my best to forget about what I'd just done, I started to read: *Maxine O'Connor, late of Philadelphia—*

My breath fogged the air in front of me, so thick for a moment I could hardly see.

I didn't think it was that cold. Shivering, I hugged myself with both hands, feeling the chill even through my robe. The dry, yellowed paper rattled in my trembling fingers. *No, I know it wasn't this cold a few seconds ago.*

Frost began creeping up the walls.

Transfixed, I watched lines of frost lace their way across the stone, eerie blue crackling streaks that spread and wove and split a thousand times over. The pattern swept up from the floor, covering the wall, even icing the ceiling with something flaky and white. A few small, silvery crystals of snow hung suspended in the air.

I was terrified but in a numb kind of way—I couldn't scream or run or do anything but shiver and try to believe what was happening. I held out my hands, barely noticing that my fingers were red and clumsy with cold; I wanted to touch the snow crystals in the air to convince myself that this was real.

I wish Lucas were here—Mom—Balthazar—somebody,

anybody. Oh, God, what's happening? My breath was coming in thin, quick gasps, and I felt almost dizzy.

Despite my fright, I couldn't help noticing that the scene was beautiful—delicate and ethereal, like finding myself inside the crystal castle at the center of a snowglobe.

The ice cracked so loudly that it made me jump. As I watched, eyes wide, the frost etching its way across the window obscured the view outside, blocking the gargoyle and even the moonlight, but somehow I could still see. The room possessed its own light, now. All the many lines of frost on the window broke this way and that, not at random but in a pattern, creating a shape that I could recognize.

A face.

The frost man was as perfectly illustrated as any picture in a book. His hair flowed long and dark, surrounding his face like a cloud. He reminded me of old pictures I'd seen of sea captains in the eighteenth century. His face carved in the ice was so detailed that it seemed as though he were looking back at me. It was the most vivid image I'd ever seen.

Then the cold stabbed into my heart as I realized: He really *was* looking back at me.

His lips moved, the lines of frost drawing and redrawing his mouth to pronounce something, but I couldn't make it out, and there was no sound. Mute with shock, I shook my head.

He closed his eyes. The air around me instantly became even colder—so cold it hurt—

The ice on the window exploded outward, shards flying

toward me in the shape of his face, three-dimensional now, coming closer and crying in a voice made of the sound of breaking glass, *"Stop!"*

Then the pieces of ice fell to the floor, scattering around me like confetti. It hardly made a sound: The shards were so thin that they melted almost instantly. As the frost lines vanished from the walls and windows, and the room swiftly warmed to its normal temperature, droplets of water began to fall on me from the thawing ice above.

I sat in the middle of it all, so stunned I couldn't move. I'd been too scared even to scream. The only thought my dazed mind could form was, *What the hell was that?*

As soon as I could move again, I scrambled out of the records room, hurried downstairs, and dashed out of the north tower almost without caring if I were caught. I didn't stop running until I got back to my room and dived beneath my covers. There I lay with damp hair and pounding heart, all thought of sleep forgotten, clutching my quilt to my chest as I tried to understand what had just happened.

Could I have been hallucinating? I'd never hallucinated before, so I couldn't be sure what it felt like. But given that I wasn't running a fever or on drugs, I doubted the explanation was that simple.

Had I somehow fallen asleep and started dreaming? No way. As vivid as my dreams had become lately, I'd never dreamed anything like what had happened upstairs. My chilly feet still felt damp from the ice that had melted all around me.

Another explanation came to mind, but I didn't want to accept it. *That can't be right. Those are just old stories my parents told me. Even when I was a little kid, I didn't think the stories could possibly be real.*

I didn't sleep that night. Outside the window of our dorm room, the sky paled slowly into a gray, cloudy dawn. Not long after daybreak, Raquel stirred, groaned, and kicked irritably at the covers.

"Raquel?" I whispered.

She blinked at me. Her short black hair stuck out in all directions, and her oversized white T-shirt hung off one shoulder. "You're up early."

"Yeah, I guess I am." I screwed up my courage. "Hey, if I ask you something that sounds a little bit—well, a little bit crazy—you'll hear me out, right?"

"Of course." She swung her feet out of bed, as if readying herself for action. "You listened to me last year when I was convinced something was creeping around on the roof, remember?"

Something *had* been creeping around on the roof—a vampire intent on hurting her—but I didn't think it would be a good idea to mention that now, or ever. Carefully I began, "Do you believe in—well, in—"

"God? Nope." Raquel's smile told me she was joking around to make this easier for me. "Santa Claus? No again."

"I figured that one out already." I swallowed hard. "I was going to ask if you believe in ghosts."

I was prepared for Raquel to laugh at me. Who could blame

her? I was prepared for her to pepper me with questions about why I was saying such a thing. I thought I was prepared for whatever her reaction might be. But I was wrong.

"Shut up." She scooted backward on the bed, putting distance between us. "Just shut up. Right now."

"Raquel—I just asked—"

"I said shut up!" Her eyes were wide, and her breath was coming fast. "I don't want to hear you say anything about that ever again. Not ever. Do you understand me?"

I nodded, hoping it would reassure her. Instead, she only looked more panicked. Raquel pushed herself out of bed, grabbed her shower bucket, and stalked toward the door, even though it was still hours before our first class. She slammed it shut behind her. From down the hall, I heard Courtney sleepily call, "What is the *damage* down there?"

I wished I knew. All I understood was that I'd just witnessed something inexplicable—and the mere mention of it terrified Raquel even more than the reality had scared me.

The adrenaline rush that started in the records room ran out in the middle of my morning psychology class; one minute I was taking notes on Adler's theories and the next I felt like I was about to dive face-first onto my desk. Exhausted, I propped my head on one hand and did my best to keep writing. By the time class was over, I could tell that the rest of the day would feel like eternity. Normally I would have tried to run up to my room for a quick nap, but Raquel might be there, and things between us were definitely weird right now.

As I trudged down the hallway, jostled by sweater-clad students on every side, I glimpsed a friendly face. "Hi, Balthazar." I meant simply to wave at him as I went.

He smiled at me more warmly than he ever had before. "Hey, you," he murmured as he changed direction and slung his arm possessively around my shoulders. Only then did I remember that Balthazar and I were pretending to be dating. His lips against my ear, he whispered, "At least try to look happy."

"Actually, I'm glad to see you. Is there some place we can talk?"

"Sure. Come on."

Balthazar led me through the hallway and down the stairs to the ground level of the school. Several people saw us along the way, and I noticed a few raised eyebrows and some whispering. Even though our relationship was only a sham, I couldn't help feeling sort of proud that I was being seen with such a gorgeous guy—or being amused when I imagined Courtney's reaction.

But as we walked through the great hall toward the main door, we were seen by someone else.

Vic's ever-present smile faded as he saw me walk by with Balthazar's arm around me, and my heart sank. Vic and Lucas were still good friends, and Vic had already taken risks to smuggle Lucas's letters to me. Looking at me now, he had to think that I was cheating on Lucas—and it wasn't as though I could tell him anything different.

Vic didn't say a word. He just glanced down and pretended

to be incredibly interested in his shoelaces. For my part, I acted as though I didn't notice Vic or anyone else in the world besides Balthazar.

Together we wandered out to the edge of the grounds, near the forest. A few other couples sat together in the shade not very far away. Balthazar sat on the thick carpet of still-soft fallen leaves, orange and red, and rested his broad back against the trunk of a maple tree. As I took my place next to him, I gingerly laid my head upon his shoulder; I thought it would feel awkward, but it didn't.

"You ought to tell your parents about us fairly soon." Balthazar's arm slipped around my waist. "The sooner they're convinced we're together, the sooner I can ask their permission to take you off campus."

"There's no rush. I'll see Lucas in Riverton next month, so—we can get all of this straight then. But I'll make sure Mom and Dad find out soon." One more lie. I was already tired of lies, and the only person who could hear the whole truth—Lucas— felt too far away.

"You sound exhausted. Are you okay?"

"I didn't sleep last night. I saw something that scared me, but I don't know if I even believe it myself. I have to ask you." I took a deep breath. "Are ghosts real?"

"Of course they are," he answered, as easily as if I'd asked him if the stars were in the sky. "Didn't your parents tell you about wraiths?"

"They told me ghost stories when I was little and told me to watch out for them, but I thought they were—you know—*ghost stories*."

Balthazar raised an eyebrow. "You know, for a vampire, you're very skeptical about the supernatural."

"When you put it like that, I feel sort of stupid."

"Hey, you're still new at this. Give it a couple of centuries and you'll be a pro like me."

New possibilities crowded into my mind. "What else is real? Werewolves? Witches? Mummies?"

"No werewolves. No witches. Mummies are only in muse-ums—at least, as far as I know. There are other forces out there, but I'm not sure they have names or faces. Maybe not bodies. They're darker, deeper than that." Balthazar paused and frowned. "Wait, you said you saw something last night that scared you."

"A ghost. A wraith, I guess," I said, trying out the word I'd heard my parents use only a handful of times.

"That's not possible. There wouldn't be wraiths at Evernight Academy."

"Why not? It's creepy enough."

"The way the school is built keeps them out. There are metals and minerals that naturally repel wraiths—the ones in human blood, like iron and copper, work best—and those are laid into every stone of the foundation." He brushed a fingertip along my hairline, a caress so intimate that it made my cheeks flush. Balthazar could apparently concentrate on our conversa-tion and feign romance at the same time. "Besides, wraiths are afraid of us, at least, as afraid as we are of them. I've heard of them making trouble for vampires, hauntings and things like that—but it's rare. Wraiths usually can't get away from vampires fast enough."

"Why are wraiths afraid of us? I see why we scare humans—but vampires can't drink the blood of ghosts. Ghosts don't even have blood, do they?"

"They do when they manifest in corporeal form, but mostly they exist as vapors, frost, cold spaces—an image or shadow, maybe, but no more."

The word *frost* brought back last night's apparition so powerfully that I shivered. Balthazar hugged me closer, as if sheltering me from the autumn breeze. It did help a little. "Okay, if wraiths are afraid of vampires, they'd probably steer clear of this school. And you say the stones and metals in the building should keep them out. But if that's so, then explain what I saw last night."

I went through it all: the crackling sound of ice, the unearthly green-blue glow, the frost man's face and his final, shattered-glass warning. Balthazar stared at me, eyes wide, any thought of romantic playacting apparently forgotten. When I finished, he stared at me for a few moments before he was able to say, "That could only be a wraith."

"Told you."

"It's the most dramatic manifestation I've ever heard of, though. By far. And what could that mean, '*Stop*'? Stop what?"

"Your guess is as good as mine. Hey, is there a difference between wraiths and ghosts? Like, are wraiths superbad ghosts or something?"

"No. Two different names for the same thing." He put one hand on my arm. "We have to tell Mrs. Bethany."

"What? We can't!" I clutched at his sweater, and the Evernight crest—two ravens on either side of a sword—wrinkled beneath my fingers, before I realized how it would look to anyone watching. Quickly I flattened my hands against his chest, the way a girlfriend might. "Balthazar, if we tell her, she's going to ask what I was doing up in the records room."

"What *were* you doing up there?"

"Trying to figure out why she allows humans at Evernight in the first place."

Balthazar considered that question, then pushed it aside to deal with the matter at hand. "We could pretend we were going to meet up. That you saw this vision right before I got there."

"I guess that would work," I admitted. "Lucas and I used to— Well, we went there together once."

Balthazar's dark eyes narrowed slightly at the mention of Lucas's name, and I knew he could sense my reaction to the memory of the hours Lucas and I had spent in that room. Warmth coursed through me as I recalled kissing Lucas, lying in his arms and biting down and drinking deeply of the blood he freely gave me. Did it really show on my face? Whatever it was, it made Balthazar's voice rough as he said, "Good. That makes the story more believable. I'll tell her—you don't have to be there. I'll say you're too embarrassed to come to her yourself."

"This much is true."

"Afterward she'll be on the lookout for the wraith, and she'll probably pass word along to your parents about us. Two birds, one stone."

"I guess that works." Exhausted, I leaned against Balthazar's shoulder again. "I didn't sleep at all after that. I feel like I'm about to drop."

"I wouldn't have been able to sleep either." He stroked my arm. "Why don't you take a nap?"

"Calculus doesn't start for another hour, but—I don't want to go back to my room."

I expected him to ask why, but instead Balthazar patted his leg, offering to serve as a pillow. At first I was uneasy as I lowered myself onto the ground and rested my cheek against his thigh, but his hand on my shoulder steadied me, and I was too tired to fight sleep for long. It was the first time in hours I'd felt safe.

During the next few days, word of my new "romance" spread throughout the school. Balthazar and I met up after our classes and hung out together to study in the library—all of which we'd done before, but add some hand-holding and apparently it looked just like a blazing-hot love affair. I could tell that most people were wondering what a mature, sexy guy like Balthazar was doing with the redheaded astronomy geek, but they didn't seem to doubt the relationship was real. Courtney even started trying to put me down in classes again, which was too ridiculous to be very annoying.

I wondered if Raquel knew about it, but I couldn't really ask. We were speaking, but since that night I saw the wraith, she wanted to be around me as little as possible. When I was in the room, she made an excuse to leave it, and when I tried to start conversation, she'd just say "yes" or "no" or "fine" until I finally gave up. It was funny, but I hadn't realized how much time Raquel had spent skulking around in our room until this—too much, really. I knew she wasn't okay, and something about what I'd said had made matters even worse, but there didn't seem to be any way to reach out to her.

The one person I'd been most worried about turned out not to be a problem at all. One evening, when I went into the great hall, I saw the usual collection of people talking, loafing, and hanging out. Among them, sitting at one of the tables nearest the door, were Ranulf and Vic, who sat on opposite sides of a chessboard. Vic looked as serious as I'd ever seen him, even though he wore a Hawaiian shirt. He moved his knight, smacking it down on a new square with a thunk. "Do you feel the hurt? Oh, yeah, I think you do."

"I feel no hurt from your clumsy play." That was about the best Ranulf could do for trash talk. As Ranulf leaned over the board to consider his next move, Vic stretched in lazy satisfaction, then saw me standing there. I flinched and would've left, but Vic simply rose from the table and came to my side.

"Hey," he began, shifting from foot to foot. "How's it going?"

"Pretty well. I guess—I guess we kind of need to talk." This was even harder than I'd thought it would be. "About Balthazar."

"There's just one thing I want to say, okay?" Vic put his

hand on my shoulder. "You're my friend, too. I want you to be happy."

"Oh, Vic." Too moved to say anything else, I hugged him tightly.

With his voice muffled against my shoulder, Vic said, "I like Balthazar. He's okay."

"Yeah, he is."

"You've told Lucas, right? Or you're gonna tell him soon? Because it's not right, keeping it from him."

"We're supposed to talk before long." I didn't give any more details about our upcoming meeting in Riverton; doing that would only draw Vic in too far. "I thought it would be better if I could speak to him, not just send a letter or e-mail or something."

"I guess it's hard, being apart all the time."

"It really is. If Lucas were still here, everything would be different."

Vic's smile turned smug. "Yeah, I'd have a roommate who could beat me at chess instead of the other way around."

Ranulf never looked up from the chessboard. "I hear your insults and plan to silence them with my victory."

"Keep dreaming," Vic called.

What Vic didn't know was that I'd tell Lucas the full truth about the game Balthazar and I were playing. Everything really would be fine. And now there was only one more hurdle to cross, the most important one of all: my parents.

Chapter Ten

THE CONFRONTATION I'D BEEN WAITING FOR CAME the next day, as I ducked out of the library, already running late. I started to jog down the hall, but her voice stopped me cold.

"What a hurry you're in, Miss Olivier." Mrs. Bethany's sharp gaze took me in, head to foot. She wore a dress of crisp, dark-brown wool that made her appear as though she were carved into the very woodwork of Evernight itself. "You act as though you've seen a ghost."

Was that supposed to be funny? I could only stare at her.

Fortunately, she didn't seem to expect a reply. "We should at some point discuss what you witnessed upstairs."

"I told Balthazar all about it. If he talked to you, then you know as much as I do."

"Have you mentioned this matter to your other classmates? Or your parents?"

"No." That wasn't the whole truth—I'd sort of mentioned it to Raquel, or tried to, anyway—but given that Raquel had refused to hear me out, I figured I'd kept the secret well enough.

"Good. See that you don't. I am certain the event was an aberration. People do behave irrationally when confronted with the supernatural."

For once, I could see Mrs. Bethany's point. Just one question about a ghost had freaked Raquel out pretty badly. The last thing I needed was for my parents to go into overprotective mode. "Yes, ma'am. I won't say another word."

A conspiratorial smile crept across Mrs. Bethany's face. "In recognition of your discretion, we'll forgo any punishment for your infringement of school rules by slipping into the gentlemen's dormitory at night. Despite your lack of self-control, I find this a heartening development. At least this time your romantic attentions have fallen upon a more deserving candidate."

That was a jab at Lucas, but I kept my cool. "Balthazar's great. In fact, I'm supposed to meet him in a few minutes so we can have dinner with my mom and dad."

"Don't let me delay you. And give your parents my regards."

I nodded and hurried down the hall. Even though it was probably my imagination, I could've sworn I felt Mrs. Bethany's eyes on the back of my neck the whole way.

Raquel didn't say anything when I came into our rooom. She simply rolled over to face the wall and kept reading whatever magazine she'd picked up this time. I didn't bother trying to start the conversation myself. If she wanted to be a total jerk to me because of one stupid question, fine.

I started going through the sweater drawer of my dresser. *Periwinkle cowl neck—no, I wore that with Lucas last year, and wearing it with Balthazar just feels wrong. Green cardigan— too thin, because it gets drafty up there this late in the fall. Black V-neck—totally boring, and I have to at least look like I'm getting dressed up for Balthazar.*

"You don't usually bother changing for dinner with your parents," Raquel said. I could tell by the echo that she was still facing the wall.

I paused, unsure how to react. This was the first time she'd started a conversation with me since I mentioned ghosts. I was relieved, but annoyed with myself for being relieved, because Raquel was the one who had been behaving badly. Why should I feel like I was the one getting off the hook?

"I'm taking Balthazar with me." I didn't glance in her direction as I pulled the dark-purple cashmere sweater from the drawer.

"I saw you guys hanging around together the other day. I wondered if something was up."

"Something's up," I said shortly. When I didn't volunteer anything else, Raquel apparently went back to her magazine. Quickly I set about getting ready, putting on the sweater, some dangly earrings, and even a little of the nice perfume my parents had given me for my birthday. It smelled like gardenias.

As I slipped the perfume bottle into the back of my dresser drawer, my fingers brushed against the velveteen scarf that held the brooch Lucas had given me. I didn't think of him buying it for me; instead I remembered the time we had been forced to pawn it, when we had been on the run together, so desperate and totally broke. I'd thought we were in so much trouble, but if I could've traded places with myself and traveled back to that moment, where it was just me and Lucas against the world, I would've done it. It was like I couldn't understand why the world didn't rip in two—just tear apart at the seams—to bring us back together again.

"I'm glad things are going better for you in the romance department." Raquel turned around at last, and there was even a small, hesitant smile on her face. "Not like it couldn't go better than last time, huh?"

She'd never liked Lucas, and hearing her put him down the same way Mrs. Bethany had was the last straw. "It's none of your business," I snapped. "You don't get to ignore me for days and then offer opinions about my love life. You only act like my friend when you're in the mood, and I'm sick of it."

"Excuse me for living." Raquel threw her magazine down and stalked out of the room. I couldn't imagine where she thought she was going in her T-shirt and boxer shorts, and I pretended that I didn't care.

Besides, I didn't have time to worry about it. I had to bring my new "boyfriend" to dinner at my parents'.

"So are you two going to the Autumn Ball again this year?" Mom said as she spooned a hefty dollop of mashed potatoes onto my plate.

Balthazar and I shared glances. We hadn't even thought of the Autumn Ball yet, but Mom's question made sense. "Absolutely," he said quickly. "I hadn't realized it was coming up so soon."

"Time sneaks up on you." Dad shook his head ruefully before drinking blood from his glass. "Seems like the older you get, the faster it goes."

"Tell me about it," Balthazar said. Moments like that reminded me that, even though he looked about eighteen or nineteen, he was actually more than three hundred years old, a vampire as experienced and powerful as my parents.

Of course, I already knew I was the odd one out at the table. It's hard not to know that, when everybody else is drinking blood and you're the only one with turkey and potatoes on a plate.

"We'll need to hurry up and choose a dress, if I'm going to alter it for you." Mom beamed at me like I'd brought home a winning lottery ticket instead of a guy.

"Definitely," I said. "I'd like that."

She squeezed my shoulder, still excited for me, and again I felt guilty. I missed the days when I had been able to tell my parents everything.

The rest of the dinner was marginally less awkward, and afterward, Dad put Dinah Washington on the stereo—one of my favorite singers. It was like he and my mother both were doing everything they could to ensure that I was having a great time. When I said I wanted to walk Balthazar downstairs, they waved us off almost eagerly.

As we headed down the stone steps, I said, "By next week,

they'll have baked and frosted our wedding cake."

"They just want you to be happy."

I could hear in Balthazar's voice how badly he still wanted to be the one to make me happy. "Balthazar—I know it's fun, us hanging out together—and you're great, but it's not like you and I are—" Awkward, I turned it around on him. "What would you ever see in somebody my age?"

"I'm not so different from you. I know I ought to be, but I'm not." He studied me curiously. "Haven't you realized that all the students here act like teenagers? Even the ones older than I am?"

"Well, yeah. I thought that was just—being insecure. Not fitting into the world."

"That's part of it. But maturity isn't a purely emotional thing, Bianca. It's physical, too. Those of us who died young— we'll never wholly be adults. No matter how many centuries of experience we gain, no matter what we live through. We can't change." Balthazar seemed distracted, almost mournful, but then he straightened and gave me a friendly smile. "But don't worry. About you and me, I mean. I'm not confused."

"Good," I said, but I wasn't entirely convinced.

When I got back to my room, it was fairly late, but Raquel wasn't there. Apparently she'd found a really good place to hide. I put on my pajamas and took advantage of the privacy by enjoying a full thermos of blood before bedtime. I'd already had my fill at my parents' house, but I was tired of waking up hungry at 3 A.M. At least I'd sleep through the night this once, I thought.

I didn't, but for an entirely different reason. A couple hours after bedtime, I awoke at the touch of a hand on my shoulder and Raquel whispering, "Bianca?"

"Hmmm?" I rolled over and peered up through the darkness at Raquel. At first I was so sleepy that I didn't remember I was mad at her. "What's going on?"

"We have to talk."

"Oh. Okay." I remembered being angry then, but it didn't seem to matter. Raquel's face was pale, and her eyes held the same intangible fear that I remembered from last year, when Erich had been stalking her. I sat up and brushed my hair from my face. "What's up with you? Why did you freak out so badly when I asked you about ghosts?"

"First you have to tell me the truth." Raquel breathed in so sharply that her nostrils flared. "Did you see a ghost in here?"

"Not in our room. But I saw something upstairs—like, at the top of the tower—I think it was a ghost." I couldn't tell her that I was sure without letting on how I was so sure, which I thought was a bad idea. Raquel was so terrified by ghosts that I didn't think she'd like the revelation that she was also surrounded by vampires.

To my surprise, Raquel seemed relieved. "It wasn't in *here*, though? It didn't come anywhere near me?"

"No. Nowhere close."

"What did it look like?"

I thought that if I described the whole thing, I would just scare Raquel again. So I kept it simple. "It was a man. Middle-aged, I guess. His hair and beard were long and dark, like you see in old paintings. I got the impression he was from a really long time ago. And I know I didn't imagine it. It was real."

"You're sure he wasn't old. Definitely not an old guy, sort of bent over?" When I nodded, she put her fist to her mouth and bit down on her knuckle. I realized that Raquel was trying not to cry.

"What is this about?" At first she didn't say anything; maybe she couldn't. "Raquel, it sounds like you know more about ghosts than you're telling me."

She let her hand drop. A small crescent of blood marked the skin of her thumb. "There's something in my parents' house."

"Something—like a ghost."

"The old man," she said. "Thin and bony. No hair. I've seen him ever since I was little. And I never saw him for very long, back then, and mostly in my dreams. So sometimes I thought I was imagining it."

Raquel sounded reasonable, even calm, but her entire body had begun to shake.

"A couple years ago—when I got older—I started to see him more often, and then I knew I hadn't imagined it. He waited for me late at night, when he could scare me. He liked to scare me. If it even is a he—maybe that's just how it looks, but it might not be a man. Maybe it's just a *thing*. An old, evil thing twisted up with hate. Because it hates me. It always has."

"What did your parents say?" As soon as the words came out of my mouth, I wanted to snatch them back. Ever since I'd known Raquel, she'd told me again and again how her parents blew off her fears. This was one of the things they'd ignored and left her to deal with on her own. "They didn't believe you."

"Neither did my priest. Neither did my teacher. I just had to—be quiet and know that he was there. That he was always going to be there, waiting for me. Looking at me. He has—greedy eyes. Up until this summer, that's all he did. Look. I thought it was all he'd ever do, and I was used to him looking, but then—" A shudder passed through her, so violent that I put my hand on her shoulder to steady her. "This summer—at night sometimes, I would dream that—that he was on top of me, holding me down while he had sex with me. It hurt because I kept trying to get him off me, but I couldn't move. Sometimes it would be every night."

"Oh, my God."

She finally looked me in the eyes, and a tear slipped down her cheek. "Bianca, I don't know if they were dreams. My whole life I've told myself I was imagining it. Last year—the sounds on the roof—the same kind of evil I felt with that thing in my house, I feel here. I've always felt it here. Now you see it, too, and I know it's real."

"It's real. You don't ever have to doubt that again." I wasn't sure how comforting that was. "But it's not the same thing from your house. What I saw wasn't anything like that." What I'd seen had been terrifying, but it clearly seemed to be something else altogether.

"I guess not. It freaked me out, though. Still, I shouldn't

have taken it out on you." Raquel ducked her head. "I'm sorry."

"I'm the one who should apologize." I felt like such an idiot. It wasn't just the past week that Raquel had been acting strangely; she'd been on edge and depressed since the beginning of the school year. I'd been too quick to assume that it was just her prickly personality without ever asking myself if something deeper could be the problem. Okay, there's no way I would ever have guessed that *this* was what was bothering her— but I should've known that something was seriously wrong. I'd been so wrapped up in my own concerns that I'd forgotten to be Raquel's friend. "I should've tried harder to talk to you. I shouldn't have cut you off like that. I'm so sorry."

"It's okay." Raquel sniffled once, then half laughed, wary as ever of showing real emotion. "Didn't mean to get weird on you."

"You can tell me anything. Anytime. I mean it."

"Same goes for you, okay?"

There was so much I couldn't ever tell Raquel, but I nodded anyway.

After Raquel had gone to bed, I lay awake thinking about the horrifying story she had told me. I didn't doubt for a second that she was telling the truth. Balthazar had reassured me about the wraiths by saying that most of them were afraid of vampires, but that reassurance wasn't worth much, now that I knew what they were capable of.

Whatever was upstairs was dangerous, at least to humans and maybe to us all.

Chapter Eleven

"WHY IS LOVE SUCH A COMMON DRAMATIC device?"

Mrs. Bethany walked slowly across her classroom, her pointed boots clicking against the wooden floor. She clasped her hands behind her back. By this point, we had all learned that when she spoke in this tone of voice, she didn't want you to offer answers to her questions. She preferred us to shut up and listen.

"It is, of course, because love is persuasive. Temporary as it so often is, love nonetheless compels otherwise rational creatures to behave in the most extraordinary ways." Her dark eyes gazed out the window for a moment, but then her attention was on us again. "Therefore, it makes sense for Shakespeare to use romantic love as the fundamental motivation for Romeo and Juliet's actions. We ask ourselves if young people would behave this way. We know they would. In this way, the play rings true."

I fidgeted in my seat and glanced at the clock above the door. Only three more minutes to go.

"However, there is more to consider about *Romeo and Juliet* than its portrayal of youthful passions." Strolling to just beside my desk, where I could smell the lavender scent that always seemed to surround her, Mrs. Bethany continued, "Your next assignment, due one week from today, is a three-page paper explaining your view of the dramatic flaws in *Romeo and Juliet*. I shall not lecture on these flaws now; I am more interested in those you can define and defend."

Did she say *flaws*? In *Romeo and Juliet*? My favorite play of all time?

Mrs. Bethany paused, glaring sharply at the entire class-room, and once again I felt as though she'd seen my thoughts and was about to pounce. But for once her irritation had nothing to do with me. "I see that many of you planning to visit Riverton have already let your concentration lapse. Let us hope you've regained your critical faculties by the time your papers are due. Class dismissed."

I wasn't the first one out the door, but I was close. As I ran through the hallway, I could feel my face lighting up with a smile. Even though I knew there was a chance that Lucas might not make it tonight, I knew he would make it if there were any way. And there had to be a way.

Just as I was about to dash into the stairs to the girl's dorms, I saw Balthazar slinging his backpack over one shoulder. A sudden whim made me giggle, and then I thought, *Why not? It fits our cover story.* So I ran straight to Balthazar and basically tackled him, leaping up so that he had to catch me in his arms.

"Whoa!" His arms circled my back so tightly that my feet dangled above the floor. I held on to his neck and grinned. Balthazar laughed. "You're in a good mood."

"Yep."

"I can guess why." He sighed, settling me on my feet again. "See you at the bus."

Balthazar was defying the unspoken rule that the "Evernight type" didn't go on the Riverton trips with the human students. I think most of the human kids believed it was a kind of snobbery, the in-crowd shunning the outsiders. That was partly true. But mostly, the vampires feared revealing their ignorance of the twenty-first century once they were outside the controlled environment of Evernight Academy.

Balthazar would break ranks tonight. Partly this was to go along with the fiction that we were so hot and heavy that we couldn't let each other out of our sight. Also, when the time came for me to slip off on my own, Balthazar had promised to make sure that Raquel was taken care of and having fun.

Until then, she and I were going to stick together, whether she liked it or not.

"There's nothing to do in Riverton," Raquel groused as I linked my arm in hers and drew her toward the waiting bus. She wore Doc Martens, jeans, and a peacoat. "I'd rather hang out in the room, honestly."

"You've done enough of that lately. Come on, at least it's something different, right? We can eat at the diner, and I know you have to want something besides peanut butter and jelly sandwiches for a change."

"Well. When you put it that way." She cast a glance at my outfit—white ruffled shirt, gray jumper that showed off more of my legs than I usually displayed, and the gorgeous high heels I'd only worn twice because they kind of threw me off balance. "Looking good for Balthazar, huh?"

I wondered what Lucas would say when he saw me in this and began to smile crazily again. Raquel laughed, seeing my delight even as she misinterpreted it. We skipped the rest of the way to the bus, me wobbly in my heels, not caring if anyone laughed at us. When Balthazar tugged me onto his lap, it was only to make room for Raquel to sit on the same seat. At least, mostly for that.

We laughed and talked the whole way, Balthazar doing his best to be charming and draw Raquel out. Soon she was telling him about skateboarding, which she'd been into back in middle school, and laughing at how little he knew about it. The whole trip, only one moment jarred us from the fun. As the bus turned onto the bridge to cross the river, I felt Balthazar's body tense, and his hand closed around my shoulder.

Vampires hate to cross running water. They can manage, but usually they need a long time to work up to the crossing. Balthazar had to do it cold, and it was going to be difficult. I took his hand as if I were flirting, really to give him strength. The bus headed over the water. Balthazar shut his eyes tightly.

A wave of nausea hit me. I felt like I'd just had the breath knocked out of me, and I couldn't quite tell which way was up or down anymore. Everything went sparkly and dark, the way it does sometimes when you stand up too quickly. I clutched Balthazar's hand more tightly; his palm was as cold and clammy as my own had become.

Then, as swiftly as it had descended, the sick feeling passed. Sucking a deep breath, I looked around, trying to orient myself. The bus had just finished crossing the river.

The barrier that vampires felt at running water—now I felt it, too.

Balthazar gazed at me curiously, and I wondered if he'd been able to sense my distress. I stared at the window, unwilling to acknowledge to him what I wasn't ready to admit to myself.

We all ate at the diner together, right at the counter. Vic put french fries on his hamburger, between the meat and the bun, which made us all laugh but then turned out to taste pretty good once we tried it. It was strange to see Balthazar eating onion rings and drinking a milkshake; he chewed slowly and deliberately, maybe because he had to remind himself how to do it. But he managed. Nobody else noticed anything strange about how he ate.

Afterward, Balthazar suggested everyone check out the used bookstore. Once Vic and Raquel were on board, I casually said, "I'll catch up with you guys, all right? I think I'm going to run to the theater and say hi to my parents. They always chaperone there."

Raquel shrugged. "We could all go to the movie."

Oh, no, I thought, but this time it was Vic to the rescue. "No way. Did you see what they're showing? *The Philadelphia Story.* Seriously misogynistic take on the causes of marital infidelity."

Raquel blinked at the sound of Vic using so many big words. I wanted to defend any film with my beloved Cary Grant, but I'd have to take the out. "Right. You guys wouldn't want to see that. I'll come by the bookstore later."

Then they were gone, and I was alone. I started walking toward the movie theater, just in case any of them happened to turn and glance behind them, but then I passed the blinking lights of the marquee and kept going.

Almost there. Almost there. My feet had begun to ache from the high heels, but with every step, I felt it less, not more. Every second brought me closer to Lucas.

Within a few minutes I reached the riverbank. Instead of shops, there were houses here, but not all that many. A sidewalk ran along the riverside, one that had been laid down a long time ago; the concrete squares had cracked, and weeds poked their way through the gaps. Here and there, tree roots had pushed the concrete slabs upward at odd angles, so it made for uncertain walking, especially in heels.

I watched the lights of the bridge reflecting on the water. How was it that driving over it today had upset me so badly? Being this close to the water didn't affect me the slightest. The river looked pretty, and that was about it.

Then I heard footsteps on the sidewalk behind me. *Lucas.* My heart leaped, and I spun around with a smile on my face to glimpse a shape coming closer in the night.

All my hopes crashed.

"Hey," Dana said, emerging from the shadows. "I know I'm not who you wanted to see tonight. Sorry about that."

My disappointment vanished, replaced by fear. "Lucas isn't— He's okay, right?"

"He's fine. Absolutely fine. But his cell is on lockdown right now. They got themselves surrounded by a nasty crew of vamps in Boston. For the next few weeks, he's stuck. Can't get out, can't leave. I was somewhere else, so when they told me about the lockdown, he asked me to come find you. I'm supposed to schedule your next secret rendezvous, which, I gotta tell you, makes me feel a little dirty." Though I tried to laugh at Dana's joke, it sort of turned into a sob instead. Dana patted me awkwardly on the shoulder and said, "Hey, hey. You know he would've come if he could, right?"

"I know. I'm just—I really wanted to see him tonight. But thanks for coming to tell me," I said hollowly. It was better to get the bad news quickly instead of waiting by the river all night, wishing that Lucas would come. No matter how kind Dana had been, now I wanted her to leave so I could sit down and have a good cry.

"No big thing." Then Dana's grin faded as she stood up straight. In that instant, when her posture shifted into wariness and readiness to fight, I saw the warrior in her. "Somebody's coming. You sure the vampires aren't on this trip?"

"Only one, and he's not dangerous." Dana gave me a look

that clearly meant, *Are you nuts?* I plowed on like I hadn't said anything about friendly vampires. "It's either a townie or a student. Just act natural."

"You got it."

But I was the one who was going to have trouble acting natural, because the person who came around the river bend was Raquel.

"Hey!" I said, too brightly. "I thought you were at the bookstore!"

"Got bored." Raquel shrugged. "I slipped out."

Great, I thought. *Poor Balthazar's going to spend the rest of the night tearing apart the whole town looking for her.*

"What about you? I thought you were going to the movies to see your parents." Raquel cast a suspicious glance at Dana.

But Dana grinned and held out her hand. "Dana Tryon. Good to meet you. I'm an old friend of Bianca's, and we ran into each other on the street. What are the chances?"

"Oh, okay." Raquel shook hands. "You're from Bianca's hometown?"

"Good old Arrowwood Middle School," I said quickly, grateful for Dana's fast thinking. "Yeah, we used to hang out all the time. So when I saw her, I was like, forget the movies."

Raquel smiled, accepting the story. "Cool. Are you guys just walking around down here?"

"Yeah, basically." Apparently Raquel intended to hang around with us. How were we supposed to fake a big friendship? We'd only met twice before.

Dana didn't seem dismayed. "Actually, I'm headed back up to grab something to eat. Bianca's going to hang out with me for a while. You want to join us?"

"Well—I just ate—" To my astonishment, I could see that Raquel actually wanted to go. Dana's cheerful personality had won a quick convert. "But I skipped dessert. The pie looked pretty good."

"Pie!" Dana grinned. "Everybody loves pie. It's settled."

We talked easily the whole night, and nobody would ever have guessed that Dana and I were nearly strangers. Raquel certainly didn't, mostly because we kept the focus on her, drawing her out about her art projects, her skateboarding, and everything else. When the topic strayed from Raquel's interests, Dana kept making up absurd questions to ask me about the history we supposedly shared: "How's Hubert doing? God, the way you two used to flirt back at good old Arrowwood Middle School! You really never minded those Coke-bottle glasses he used to wear? Or going with him to Star Trek conventions?"

"Oh, you know," I fumbled. "I used to be into the intellectual type."

"You wouldn't know it from the guy she dated last year," Raquel said.

"I can imagine." Dana smirked. I knew she wouldn't be able to resist teasing Lucas about that later.

I jumped in with, "What about you, Dana? Are you still collecting My Little Ponies? You were only two fillies short of a complete set when I moved away."

As Raquel started laughing, Dana shot me a dirty look—but she was grinning. "I might have grown out of that."

About halfway through, Raquel excused herself to go to the bathroom. The second she was out of earshot, Dana said, "So, you and Lucas. When and where?"

"We'd better come back here, to Riverton—say, in front of the movie theater. Let's try the Saturday after Thanksgiving, 8 p.m. " Surely Balthazar would have permission to take me off campus at that point. "The lockdown will be over by then, right?"

"Ought to be." Dana smiled. "Now I've done my part for young love. I feel all virtuous inside."

"Virtuous? Why don't I believe you?"

"Because you're smarter than that, that's why."

Between feigning a lifelong friendship and laughing at Dana's jokes, I didn't have time to get too upset about not seeing Lucas. It didn't really hit me until later, when we were boarding the bus again. Balthazar gave me a questioning look, clearly wanting to know if he and Lucas had a deal; I had to shrug a little and shake my head. He seemed to understand that the meeting hadn't happened, but we didn't have a chance to discuss it. We just had to hang on to each other again as the bus sped across the river.

That night, at bedtime, Raquel was more cheerful than I'd seen her all year. Dana could get almost anybody into a good mood. But I felt like I'd left part of myself standing by that river, waiting for Lucas, who couldn't come. I closed my eyes tightly, willing myself to sleep. The sooner this day was over, the sooner

I could stop thinking about how I should have seen Lucas today. I could start thinking about how we would be together soon. That was how I had to look at it, or else I'd never get through.

But even my dreams conspired against me.

"You have to hide," Charity said.

We stood in the old Quaker meetinghouse where I'd first encountered Black Cross the year before. The chill of consecrated ground crept into my bones and made me shake. Charity clung to a doorjamb, as if she had to hold herself upright.

"We don't have to hide," I told her. "Lucas won't hurt us."

"You don't have to hide from Lucas." She brushed her wheat-colored curls back from her face. Though her coloring was almost entirely different from Balthazar's, I could see the likeness now— the wavy hair, their height, and the intensity of their dark-brown eyes. "But you still have to hide."

What was she talking about? Then I thought I knew. The last time I was in this meetinghouse, it burned to the ground. Was that what the strange shadows were all around us? Was it smoke? "It's burning," I said.

"No. But it's going to burn." Charity reached a hand out toward me. Was she trying to pull me to safety or into danger? "Lucas doesn't know that you're going to burn up."

"He'll save me! He'll come for me!"

She shook her head, and behind her I could see the glow of flame. "He won't. Because he can't."

I woke up breathing hard and lonelier than ever.

Chapter Twelve

"ROMEO AND JULIET DON'T KNOW EACH OTHER very well." The words sounded strange, even though I had written them. "They defy their parents for each other, risk their lives for each other, and finally die for each other, even though they've only met a handful of times. It's a huge love story built on infatuation. Maybe Shakespeare should have let them know each other longer."

"Everything you say is true, Miss Olivier, but I am not convinced that it is a flaw in the play." Mrs. Bethany sat at her desk, tapping her fingers against the wood so that her long, grooved fingernails clicked loudly enough to be heard. "Romeo and Juliet are virtually strangers to each other, even at the play's end. But is it not possible that this is Shakespeare's point? That the kind of mad, self-sacrificing passion Romeo and Juliet share usually belongs only to the first flush of love? That their mistakes should not be made by more mature, informed people?"

I shrank down in my desk. Fortunately, Mrs. Bethany didn't

want to make me her personal piñata for the day. She glanced around the room. "Does anyone else want to suggest a flaw he or she perceived in the play?"

Courtney raised her hand, eager as ever to show me up. "They acted like there was just no way they could have had sex without being married, and, hello, not true."

Mrs. Bethany sighed. "Keep in mind that, despite the bawdy humor in Shakespeare, he generally wrote to suit the morality of the time. Anyone else?"

For the first time I could remember, Vic spoke up in class. "If you ask me, the Bard kind of wussed out by having Tybalt kill Mercutio before Romeo killed Tybalt. They're all supposed to be blood enemies, right? And the Montagues aren't any better than the Capulets, if that prince guy at the end is telling the truth. So it would've been gutsier to have Romeo and Tybalt fight only because they hated each other. Having Tybalt kill Mercutio first lets Romeo off the hook."

I waited for the inevitable smackdown, but it never came. Mrs. Bethany said, "Mr. Woodson makes an excellent point. By framing Romeo's murder of Tybalt as he does, Shakespeare loses a certain amount of moral ambiguity."

As Mrs. Bethany wrote *moral ambiguity* on the chalkboard, I glanced over at Vic, who shrugged with a look on his face that clearly meant, *I just can't help my genius.*

Despite the entertainment value of listening to Vic and Mrs. Bethany discuss literature, I had a strange, hollow feeling all through class and long afterward. In the library, I sat alone in a small chair in one corner, the light orange and gold through the stained-glass window, and kept staring down at my notes. How well did Lucas and I know each other, really? We'd met more than a year ago, and I had sensed the connection between us from the beginning. But the meeting we'd lost in Riverton had reminded me how rarely we'd been able to be together, or to reveal the full truth about ourselves or anything important to us.

What if we were like Romeo and Juliet, risking everything too soon?

Then I remembered sitting with Lucas in this same library, and how the light through the stained glass window had turned his hair to bronze. I remembered him telling me how he'd run away from home when he was only five years old, carrying a bag of Oreos and a slingshot. I remembered us trying on funny old clothes together in the vintage store in Riverton and flirting in the gazebo and the way it felt when we kissed for the first time.

I remembered him saying that he loved me even though I was a vampire, even though he'd been taught to hate vampires his whole life. And I remembered him lying beneath me, arching his neck so that I could bite down, freely offering me his blood.

That wasn't infatuation. That was love. If I knew nothing else, I knew that for sure.

Smiling, I shut my notebook and closed my eyes, the better to get lost in those memories. Even if I had to carry on every day as if I weren't longing for Lucas, I could still be true to him and to what we had together. The time we were spending apart wouldn't matter, not if I could remain strong. I wasn't going to feel sad about all the things our relationship couldn't be, not when I considered all the amazing things it already was. It was time to stop mourning and start celebrating.

My mother didn't have to alter my dress for the Autumn Ball this year, and I handled my makeup myself, so she had more time to fix my hair. As I sat on the corner of my bed upstairs in my strapless bra and panties, I carefully blew onto each clear-polished fingernail and thought of Patrice, who had given herself a manicure and pedicure virtually every day. "Patrice would be proud if she could see me now."

"You should write and tell her." Mom's words were slightly slurred; she was talking despite having a few bobby pins between her lips. "I bet she would love to hear from you."

"I guess." I doubted Patrice spent too much time thinking about anybody but herself. All the same, I owed her a postcard or something.

"I thought maybe you were reaching out a little more," Mom said as another bobby pin nestled itself near the nape of my neck. "Talking to more of our kind. Now that you and Balthazar are a couple, I mean."

"I guess so," I said. "It's a little weird for me, though. He's older than I am." That was an understatement, seeing as how he was practically at the first Thanksgiving.

She shrugged. "Your father has almost six centuries on me. Trust me, after the first hundred years or so, we hardly even noticed."

Mom and Dad made bridging that gap look so easy; I had grown up thinking nothing of it. Only now that I was spending more time with Balthazar did I realize that those years truly made a difference. "Still, it kind of makes you wonder."

"I know. You have to start thinking long-term—the way all vampires learn to think, if they're smart. That's something Balthazar can give you that—well, that Lucas couldn't."

My body tensed, and I felt her hands in my hair go still. We were treading on dangerous ground now, and we both knew it. My parents and I talked about almost everything, but not Lucas. "I'm not with Balthazar because it's a learning experience," I said quietly. "Just like I wasn't with Lucas because I was rebelling."

"Honey, we never thought that. We never blamed you for what happened with that boy. You know that, right?"

I hadn't turned to look at her. Somehow it was easier to have this conversation while we weren't face-to-face. "I know."

She seemed to be more nervous than I was. "Bianca—there might be one subject we should discuss tonight."

"What?" Had she guessed that I was keeping a secret about Lucas? Even that I was slipping out to see him?

I imagined a dozen different possibilities in the few seconds before she said, "Do you and I need to have another talk about sex?"

Oh, my God.

"I know you're aware of the facts of life," Mom plowed ahead, even though I was sure my entire body had just turned beet red with embarrassment. "But when you're getting close to someone, particularly someone more experienced, like Balthazar, it becomes a lot more real. Maybe you have different questions."

"It's kind of early to be thinking about that," I said hastily. Leave it to Mom to share the only information I didn't want to hear. "We just started going out."

"If you say so." She sounded amused, but she patted my shoulder and mercifully didn't mention the subject again while we finished getting me ready for the ball.

I had just slipped my feet into pointy-toed silver shoes when we heard the knock at the door, and then my father and Balthazar greeting each other with loud hellos and a clap on the back, which was how they'd started behaving with each other lately. I'd noticed Dad and Lucas acting that way, too, last year; maybe guys needed to puff up a bit when it came to greeting their daughters' dates—or their dates' fathers. Mom brushed a stray eyelash from my cheek and hugged me. "Go out there and knock 'em dead."

As I stepped into the front room, both Dad and Balthazar fell silent. Dad smiled and rocked back on his heels, clearly proud of me. Balthazar's face didn't change, but there was something in his eyes, an appreciation, that sent a small thrill of feminine power shivering through me.

My dark-green satin dress was strapless and tailored closely to my body, dipping low in the back. It flared slightly at mid-thigh, so I'd be able to dance. My mother's silver-and-opal necklace from the 1920s hung around my neck, and the matching earrings brushed against my throat. Mom had put my hair in a low bun, folding braids over and between each other and finishing it with a single jeweled clip. Last year I had felt beautiful; this year there was more, too. For the first time I felt as if I looked like a woman, not a girl anymore.

My parents shooed us on our way quickly enough, and Balthazar held my arm to steady me as we made our way downstairs. When my new shoe slipped on one of the worn stone steps and I wobbled, he slid his arm around me. "Are you okay?"

"Fine." I glanced up at him and realized how close his face was to mine. His arm was still wrapped tightly around me. I knew I ought to pull away, but I also knew that he wanted me— and I couldn't help liking that he wanted me. It was the first time I'd ever felt that being a woman gave me a unique kind of power.

"Your hair looks beautiful this way," Balthazar said. His dark eyes searched my face. "Women used to wear their hair like that more often. I always liked it."

A small smile played on my lips. "So this is a trip down memory lane?"

For some reason, that broke the spell. He straightened. "I'm happy with the here and now. Come on. Let's dance."

Once again, the great hall had been transformed for the occasion, though in an entirely different style. Candles still burned next to hammered brass mirrors, reflecting mellow, flickering light throughout the room; but this year, the walls and tables had been decorated with thousands and thousands of flowers, all different kinds, but all of them snowy white. Even the dark stone floors were scattered with petals, so that the entire room was soft and bright.

As Balthazar walked me toward the dance floor to the strains of the orchestra tuning up, I saw several girls casting admiring glances in his direction, tall and sophisticated as he was in his evening suit. The thought of them being turned on by him was sort of a turn-on in itself. Maybe everyone wants to arouse some jealousy from time to time. Then I caught sight of someone who was definitely not impressed.

"Satin." Courtney raised an eyebrow as she looked at my gown. Her own was deep gold, low-cut, and stunning—though I still liked mine best. "Brave of you to wear that. It wrinkles like an old garbage bag the second you sit down."

"I'll just have to make sure that we dance the entire night," I said brightly. "That way we won't sit down at all." We swept past her as she sputtered for a retort, without success.

Last year I had enjoyed the ball, but this year I loved it. My heart wasn't breaking for Lucas any longer; I was completely sure of our love for each other. Even though I would've preferred him to be my date, I also realized that he probably wouldn't enjoy this as much as I did. No, I could let go completely and live in the exhilaration of Balthazar whirling me through the steps of all the old-fashioned dances. Violins and pianos and harps played all around us, and the girls' brilliantly colored dresses shifted from pattern to pattern, formation to formation; it was a little like being inside a kaleidoscope that kept spinning every second.

"Your waltzing has improved," Balthazar said about halfway

through the evening. His broad hand splayed against my bare back. "Did you practice?"

"In my room, I gave it a try. And put up with Raquel laughing at me the whole time."

"It was worth it." He leaned closer to me, so that his lips were nearly brushing my ear, and whispered, "Now?"

I glanced around the edges of the room; most of the chaperones were missing, no doubt patrolling the grounds where most couples would sneak off to be together. "Now."

We shifted to the edge of the dance floor and then walked away, laughing together as if we were just taking a quick break. As we started up the stairs of the north tower, a couple of guys in tuxes shifted past us. They stared at me for a very long time, it seemed. Once they were gone, I said, "Do you think they suspect anything?"

"Because of the way that they were looking at you? I think they were envying me." Balthazar sighed. "Little do they know. Come on."

Nobody else was around as we reached the level of the guys' dorms and kept going. Inwardly I cursed the clicking of my high-heeled shoes against the stone stairs, telltale evidence of a girl on the move; but all the same, we made it to the door of the records room. I hesitated, then knocked; Lucas and I couldn't be the only ones who'd figured out this was a good place to be alone, and the last thing I wanted to do was walk in on a couple in a clinch. When no one answered, Balthazar said, "We're clear."

We hurried inside the records room. Someone had definitely

been up there since the time I'd seen the vision—Mrs. Bethany, probably, investigating. Boxes and trunks had been shifted around in every direction; and for the first time in my memory, the room had been cleaned from top to bottom. The windows were so clear that they were invisible, and it looked as though the gargoyle outside the window might hop in at any second. Cobwebs had been expelled from every corner.

"So what are we looking for?" Balthazar said.

"Anything that explains why humans are attending Evernight Academy now. Lucas needs to know. If we can tell him when we're explaining about Charity and—and the rest, it will go better. Besides, don't you want to know?"

"I've always thought Mrs. Bethany did it for the money. People will do a lot of things for money."

"If she wanted money, she could've started admitting human students years ago. Like you said, Mrs. Bethany hates to change the rules. Why did she change this one? Besides, if it was only about making cash for Evernight Academy, she wouldn't offer scholarships to human students, but she does. Raquel's on scholarship, and she's not the only one."

Balthazar nodded, acknowledging that I had a good point, but he didn't look any more thrilled to be there. "The last time you were up here, you awakened a wraith."

"If you want to go back downstairs—"

"I'm not leaving you here alone," he said so firmly that I felt embarrassed for even joking that he might've been afraid.

"I think I've seen wraiths three times now. Three different

places—the great hall, the stairwell, and here. I don't think it had anything to do with this specific room."

Balthazar was obviously not convinced, but he said only, "So, what are we looking for?"

"Any connections between vampire students from long ago and human students today."

"That doesn't narrow it down much, Bianca." That was an understatement; despite Mrs. Bethany's cleaning job, the room was still stacked with crate after crate of documents dating back more than two hundred years. "I guess we'd better begin."

We opened lids and started sifting through yellowing old pages. Dust puffed up from the fragile, yellowing documents, and I had to keep brushing my dress clean; we couldn't go downstairs all dirty. Balthazar called out one series of names while I silently read another: *Tobias Earnshaw. Agatha Browning. Dhiram Patel. Li Xiaoting. Tabitha Isaacs. Noor Al-Eyaf. Jonathan Donahue. Sky Kahurangi. Sumiko Takahara.* The names we found came from different countries and centuries; all they had in common was that they didn't tell us anything. Evernight Academy was a fairly small school, so between Balthazar and me, we knew the names of pretty much all the human students. None of them connected in any obvious way to the vampires we found in the records room.

"So much for that idea," I groaned, brushing filmy dust from my hands.

"We didn't prove your theory, but we didn't disprove it either. The trouble is—there's just too much paper. We can't look through this usefully without knowing more about what we're looking for." Balthazar pulled a pocket watch from his jacket and frowned. "We need to get back soon. They'll notice that we were gone, but if we come back, they'll assume—"

"Right." Thinking of what people would assume made me bashful, and I couldn't quite look Balthazar in the eye.

"We'll keep looking into this. I promise."

"Thanks."

We made the trip downstairs without being seen, and Balthazar sounded relieved. "Good. I don't want to give you a scandalous reputation."

"Vampires can be scandalized?"

"You should know better than anyone." He took my hand as we headed back to the dance floor. "Come on. Let's start a scandal."

This time, when we started dancing, it wasn't just for fun. Balthazar held me closer then he had before, closer than anyone but Lucas had ever held me, so that our bodies were pressed together tightly. We weren't part of the whirling procession of dancers all around us. We moved more slowly, as if pretending that there was nobody else in the world, and that we were all alone. In truth, I was more aware than ever that we were being watched. I could sense the chaperones' amusement, others' interest, and Courtney's glowering jealousy.

It's all a game, I told myself. *It doesn't mean anything to either of us. It's okay to enjoy a game.*

At one point, Balthazar's hand brushed against another girl's gown, and he winced. "What the—"

We fell out of the dance, moving to the side of the room. I took his hand in mine and saw a small red droplet on his index finger. "She must have pinned her dress."

Balthazar shook his hand, then stopped. Slowly he brought his finger close to my lips—offering me his blood.

The vampires around us would recognize that as flirting. Drinking each other's blood was intimate for vampires. The one who drank could sense the other's most secret desires and emotions. Had Balthazar offered his blood to me only to complete the illusion that we were together, or did he mean it?

Either way, I couldn't exactly say no.

My lips closed around his fingertip, and I brushed against the pad of his finger with my tongue. He tasted like salt. Though it was only one drop of blood, that was enough for me to sense a glimmer of what he felt, a strobe-light flash of his mind's eye: me dancing in the green dress, darker and older and a thousand times more beautiful than I really was.

I swallowed, and it was like the world flashed black, then light again.

"Much better," Balthazar said, his voice low, as he slowly pulled his finger from my lips. I realized I'd shut my eyes.

Flustered, I tried to pull myself together. "Okay. Good. I mean—okay." He smiled down at me, and he almost looked proud of himself. Turning toward the dance floor, I said, too brightly, "Let's dance, okay?"

"Let's." Balthazar's hand closed around mine, and at the perfect moment, just on the beat, he pulled us back into the dance. The swirl of people all around us caught me up, as if I could feel the tempo of the music in my own pulse. The taste of blood had made me dizzy with excitement. *Never again*, I thought. *Lucas wouldn't like it. At all.*

I stumbled a little on the slick floor and started to apologize—but then I slipped again. When I grabbed Balthazar's shoulders to steady myself, he frowned, and I realized that he too was having difficulty remaining upright. We both looked down to see that we stood on ice.

All around the room, people began to murmur and shout in dismay as the ice thickened, crackling from a paper-thin sheet into a thick, uneven, blue-white surface. A couple of people fell, and one girl shrieked. I caught sight of a bundle of white flowers tied with ribbons on the wall; each petal was sparkling with frost, rigid, frozen solid.

Balthazar muttered, "Is this—"

"Uh-huh."

The cold, shivery wind I remembered swept through the great hall, and some of the candles flickered out. The orchestra broke off playing, instrument by instrument, moving from melody to cacophony to silence. Some of the chaperones had begun pulling people toward the doors, but as scared as everyone was, nobody wanted to look away. Bluish ice covered the walls and frosted every single window; icicles as thick as stalactites hung from the ceiling rafters and descended lower every second. They were two feet long, five feet long, then ten, and thicker around than I was—all within moments. I could feel flecks of cold against my skin, but it wasn't soft and snowy the way they'd been before. Instead, they were needle pricks like sleet.

"What did we do?" I clung to Balthazar's jacket. "Did we wake up a wraith?"

"Wraith?" Courtney had apparently overheard the last word we wanted anybody to overhear. "This is a wraith?"

People started to panic. Everyone rushed at once for the exits, but people were skidding on the ice, yelling and shouting, falling over one another, and creating a mob. Balthazar grabbed me around the waist and slung his other arm over my head to protect me from the fray. The cold breeze whipped through the room, extinguishing the rest of the candles. Every second, it became darker; every second, I became more afraid.

They'll know what to do, I thought, though now I was trembling all over. *Surely Mrs. Bethany or my parents or somebody knows how to handle this because, oh my God, somebody needs to handle this and make this stop—*

In the frost across the one plain window of the great hall, a few lines suddenly melted clear, and those lines formed a scrawled word: *OURS.*

Then the ice cracked everywhere: walls, ceiling, floor. As we staggered sideways, thrown off balance by the jolt beneath our feet, I heard a terrible groaning above. I looked up and saw the stalactites tremble—and then they fell, ten-foot-long knives of ice stabbing downward toward all of us.

Everyone screamed. Balthazar threw me to the floor and

covered my body with his own. As I gasped from the shock of the cold against my skin and Balthazar's solid weight, I saw one of the stalactites slam down only a foot away. Shards of ice flew in every direction, jabbing into my arms; I heard Balthazar swear and realized he'd felt the impact more than I. The heavy ice toppled next to us, missing crushing Balthazar by only inches.

Then the window shattered, glass tumbling to the floor with a final high-pitched crash.

As soon as it had begun, it was over. All around us, I heard crying and a few scattered screams. Balthazar rolled off me, holding his back and grimacing, and I looked at the ruined scene. Everything was drenched, decorations had been knocked to the floor, and satin shoes and enormous chunks of quickly melting ice lay all around.

"Balthazar, are you okay?"

"Fine." He would have been more convincing if he hadn't remained sprawled on the floor. "You?"

"Yeah." For the first time, it really hit me that I could have died; Balthazar might have saved my life. "Thank you for—"

"It's okay."

I stared at the window where the one ghostly word had already almost vanished. What was it that the ghosts were laying claim to? The records room? The north tower?

Or Evernight Academy itself?

Chapter Thirteen

"YOU WOULD SAY THE EVENTS OF LAST NIGHT WERE similar to what you experienced before?" Mrs. Bethany took notes at her desk without ever looking down at what she was writing. Instead her clear eyes remained fixed on me.

"What I saw in the records room wasn't as scary." I realized that my comment wasn't exactly helpful when Mrs. Bethany frowned. "It was cold, and there was an image in the frost—a man's face, not words. And he spoke to me. He said, 'Stop.'"

"Stop?" My father stood on one side of my chair; on the other, my mother sat next to me. They'd walked me over here for the conference and seemed even more freaked out by the apparition at the ball than I was, which was saying a lot. Dad gripped the arm of the chair so tightly I could see the tensed muscles in his hand. "What does that mean, 'stop'?"

"I don't know," I said. "Honestly, I have no idea."

Mrs. Bethany lifted her pen to her lips, considering. "It wasn't as if you were doing anything much up there. Only waiting for Mr. More. That's correct, isn't it?"

I'd need to tell more of the truth now; obviously, other people's safety depended on it. "I was reading some letters while I was up there."

"Letters?" Mrs. Bethany's eyes narrowed.

"Just to pass the time." Was that convincing? I'd have to hope so. "And—Balthazar and I went back up there last night."

Fortunately, nobody asked why I'd done that. I guess they thought it was obvious; that, or they weren't thinking straight. My parents were even more on edge about this than I would've anticipated. "What letters, honey?" Mom put a hand on my shoulder. "Tell us every detail. Everything you remember. It might all be important."

"There's not a lot to remember! I mean, I looked at some letters. None of them stood out. I don't see why that would make the wraiths angry."

Through gritted teeth, Dad said, "The question here is what set them off. We have to figure that out, and the sooner the better."

"Forgive me, Adrian, but that is not the question." Mrs. Bethany lay down her pen. "The question is how we rid ourselves of this wraith. There are, as you know, constructive ways of dealing with this problem."

My mother's grip tightened on my arm. Her hand shook. I shot her a curious glance, but her expression remained unreadable.

Dad didn't seem to have heard what Mrs. Bethany said.

"The wraiths hate vampires. They're hostile, and they're dangerous. Last night should have proved that beyond any doubt."

"I didn't dispute that," Mrs. Bethany said. "All I meant is that we must remain focused on our own goals instead of worrying overly about the wraiths'."

My father's words reminded me of a question I'd had since I'd first talked about ghosts with Balthazar. "Why do the wraiths hate vampires?"

Mom and Dad glanced at each other, obviously wondering what to say, if anything. Mrs. Bethany folded her hands together, and she was the one who replied. "We none of us know precisely where we come from: vampires, humans, or wraiths. Myths vary, and science has so little to say to those of us who have survived our mortal lives. But there are legends that bear the stamp of truth."

"Legends?"

"Once, there were only humans," Mrs. Bethany said. "Long, long ago. Before history, even before true human consciousness. Therefore, it was also a time before—morality. Intent. Emotion. Man lived as an animal, as united with the joys of the flesh as he was alienated from the knowledge of the soul. What humanity now calls the supernatural—precognition, the hearing of thoughts, and sharing of dreams, powers that go beyond those of the flesh—all of that was part of the natural world then, as simple and evident as gravity. But man evolved. Consciousness developed. And with consciousness came the capacity for sin."

I could only stare at Mrs. Bethany. I'd never heard any of

this before, and judging by my parents' rapt silence, perhaps they hadn't either.

Mrs. Bethany continued, her voice for once free of coldness or disdain. "The day came when the first human being killed another—with foreknowledge, intent, and the understanding of what it is to take another human's life. When that blow was struck, the bonds between the natural and supernatural world were shattered. Even though that first victim's life ended, his existence did not. The supernatural part of the first murdered man split into two—body and spirit. Vampires are the undead body. Wraiths are the undead spirit. Our powers are unlike each other's. Our consciousnesses are different. And we have been divided from them and from humanity ever since."

My head spun from all this new information. "Is that all real?"

"I cannot prove it, but many of us have believed it for a very long time," Mrs. Bethany said. "I tend to believe it myself."

"You mean—every time a vampire is created, a ghost is, too?"

"No. Our 'family tree' split with that first murder. Vampires are capable of creating more of our kind. Wraiths—they have to be more creative." A strange smile played upon Mrs. Bethany's face. "Yet they can be spontaneously created as well. Certain kinds of murders—those involving betrayal and broken promises, in particular—have a tendency to create ghosts. It is rare, but it can occur."

"If vampires and wraiths don't have anything to do with

each other anymore, why do they hate us?"

She studied me carefully before she said, "Most wraiths cannot long maintain any physical form. It must drive them mad in short order—witnessing the world without ever being able to take part in it. Think how you would feel, Miss Olivier, if you were trapped and powerless in that way, and then you saw other undead creatures still able to feel, act, and enjoy their time on earth. Think how much closer we are to the experience of life. Does it seem more clear to you now?"

"Yeah, I guess it does."

"If you witness anything else, of course, report it at once. Adrian, Celia, thank you for bringing her over so promptly."

"That's it?" My mother shook her head. "There's nothing else we can do to protect—to keep the students safe?"

"The students should simply take care not to spend too much time alone." Mrs. Bethany raised an eyebrow. "Particularly in isolated rooms far from the teachers in the hopes that their paramours will soon arrive."

"Next time I'll bring Balthazar with me," I promised. That made Mrs. Bethany scowl, but I could tell my parents were amused.

We walked back across the grounds from Mrs. Bethany's carriage house toward the school. It was a cloudy day, unseasonably cold, and I wished I'd brought a heavier coat. Dad put one arm around me as we went. "You're not worried?"

"No. Are you guys?"

"No," Mom said. When she saw my expression, she sighed.

"Okay. Yes. But not for any good reason. Just because we're your parents and we love you."

"What did Mrs. Bethany mean by 'constructive ways' to get rid of ghosts?" I asked.

"Let's hope the damn thing is gone already," Dad said, which wasn't exactly an answer. Before I could ask anything else, Dad grinned and waved. "Look who's here."

Balthazar came across the grounds toward us, wearing a long coat and a dark blue scarf looped casually around his neck. "How was the inquisition?"

"As much fun as you could imagine," I said.

"Well, as long as this place is haunted, I think we might want to try doing something a little different." Balthazar deployed his most charming smile, which was pretty incredibly charming. "With your permission, of course, Mr. Olivier, Mrs. Olivier."

"What do you mean?" Mom asked.

"If you think it would be all right, I was hoping to take Bianca off campus once in a while. Starting this weekend, maybe. We could go into Riverton or wherever, and she could show me a little bit about twenty-first-century life. I could tell her more about where I've been, what I've seen." Balthazar said it like this was a brand-new idea, not like we'd been plotting this for weeks. "I know she's young to go on dates off campus, but as long as this wraith is here, I'd feel safer somewhere else. I bet Bianca would, too."

"Definitely," I said. "Absolutely."

My parents didn't suspect a thing; in fact, they looked

thrilled. A little too thrilled, really. I mean, I knew they liked Balthazar. Who wouldn't? But they seemed overeager to match us up. Still, as long as it was working for us, I wouldn't argue. Dad spoke to Balthazar first. "You'll have her home by a decent hour."

"Of course."

"And you'll let us know what you're doing and where you'll be," Mom said. She bounced a little on her heels.

"At all times," Balthazar promised. "I'll ask Mrs. Bethany's permission as well."

"I can handle that," Mom said. "She's more likely to say yes if we do the asking."

"This is a big responsibility," Dad said to me. "Are you sure you're ready?"

I was only thinking of the fact that soon I'd be with Lucas again. "I'm very, very ready."

They grinned, so happy and trusting that I felt bad about lying to them—but I knew what I had to do, and I wouldn't back down now.

In the immediate aftermath of the Autumn Ball, people were seriously freaked out. Raquel started packing to run away from school three separate times, and each time it took me more than half an hour to calm her down. We slept with the lights on for a week, and we weren't the only ones in the dorms who did. More teachers took hall monitor duty at night; once I even saw Mrs. Bethany herself striding purposefully down the hall, candle in hand, so watchful she seemed almost eager. Nobody would go near the great hall to study, hang out, or anything else. The tarp covering the one shattered window while the new panes were on order wasn't the best, and it let in drafts of winter-chilled air, but that wasn't the reason why people gave it a wide berth. By the time the weekend rolled around, I was more than ready to get out of school for a few hours for more reasons than seeing Lucas—though, of course, he was still the most important reason of all.

"Do I look okay?" I turned back and forth in front of the mirror, trying to ignore the faint haziness of my reflection. I'd gone too long without blood; I'd have to drink some on the way into town.

"For the nine thousandth time, you look great," Raquel said without looking up from her latest project. She'd immersed herself in her art as a way of hiding from her fears. "Balthazar sees you every day, you know. It's not like he doesn't know what you look like."

"I realize that." I'd dressed fairly casually because of that— jeans and a soft blue button-up sweater—but of course it was Lucas I was going to see.

Raquel laid aside her scissors and magazines. "Mrs. Bethany definitely plays favorites. I mean, I'm happy you get to leave for an evening, but I wish we all could."

"I know it's not fair. But I'm not going to point that out to Mrs. Bethany yet. Besides, you know I'm not on her list of favorites. I'm just lucky Balthazar is."

"Balthazar's crazy about you; anybody can see it."

I pretended to check my makeup in the mirror, so she wouldn't catch the uncertainty in my eyes. "He's great."

"The main thing is that you're in love and that you're happy." It was the most romantic statement I'd ever heard Raquel make, so much so that I would've thought she was joking if not for the tone of her voice. "The rest doesn't matter. Not really. Right?"

Raquel was closer to the truth than she knew. "Right."

"Good." We smiled at each other, and then Raquel rolled her eyes. "It's not like I'm going to hug you or anything."

"Thank *God*."

She threw a wadded-up magazine page at me, and I ducked.

Balthazar had borrowed the gray driver's ed sedan for us to drive into Riverton. We listened to some music on the radio, with me trying to find my favorite artists and Balthazar arguing for the oldies station.

"You have to get with the times," I insisted. "Isn't that why you're at Evernight in the first place?"

"Maybe I'm there for the company," he said with a grin.

Our good mood lasted until we got closer to Riverton and approached the bridge across the river. Balthazar pulled over to the side of the road, steadying himself. "I hate this," he said. "I mean, I *hate* it."

"How did you manage to travel to Europe and the Caribbean and all those places? If crossing a river is this bad, isn't crossing the ocean impossible?"

"Larger bodies of water are actually easier, in some ways. Anytime we're overly stressed like that, if we have to make a long ocean crossing or get stuck on consecrated ground—basically, we fall into a deep sleep. It's like hibernation, I think. The trance protects us. What you have to watch out for are humans finding you while you're unconscious. We don't have pulses, and we can't awaken easily; it's a good way to end up being taken for dead. As in, really dead. Once you're buried in consecrated ground, forget it."

"Or cremated."

"Exactly. But if you're on a ship, you can hide for a few weeks. You'll wake up hungry, but it can be done. On a plane, they assume you're asleep, and you usually come to not long after the plane's above land again. Don't get me wrong—it's no fun. But at least that way you sleep through the worst of it. This— there's nothing but the shock wave."

I thought about all the stupid vampire movies I'd seen on late-night TV, with black-caped Romanian counts making the sea voyage to England as they lay sleeping in coffins. Now I realized that those legends were based in truth; the safest way to ensure that you got where you were going was to ship yourself as a dead body. Who knew that even horror shows could tell me something real?

The river shimmered slightly in the moonlight, and I felt a chill of dread. "Can't we get it over with? It wasn't too bad on the last school weekend, because we took it fast. Maybe that's better."

Balthazar turned toward me, eyes watchful. "You felt it, too, last time?"

"Oh. Uh, yeah."

"You're starting to feel more of what we feel. You're becoming more of a vampire." He sounded sort of excited about the idea.

"I want blood more often, too," I confessed. "And I've started thinking about, well, killing things. Squirrels."

"Have you killed anything?"

I felt so ashamed. "A mouse, once." Still I remembered its pitiful little squeak.

"It's all right. We all want living blood now and then."

"I keep telling myself that it's not really any worse than eating a cheeseburger that used to be a cow."

"It's not." Balthazar paused before he asked, "Have you told Lucas this?"

"Yes," I lied. I hadn't revealed everything, but I'd hardly had a chance. I also wasn't going to tell Balthazar about the vampire-like powers Lucas felt in turn.

"Does he understand that you'll be a true vampire soon? Is he ready to deal with that?"

"I won't be a true vampire until I kill a human being, and it's going to be a while before that happens, okay?"

"I've never met anyone like you, Bianca. Anyone born to be a vampire, I mean. But as I understand it, you can't put it off forever. Sooner or later, you'll have to kill."

"There has to be a choice," I insisted. "Do you know what would happen if I never killed anyone?"

"No." I didn't doubt that he told the truth. "Do you?"

"All I know is that Lucas loves me regardless of what I am."

Balthazar pressed his lips together and put the car back in drive. "Let's get this done," he muttered, and he stomped on the gas.

When we pulled up outside the movie theater, Lucas already stood there, hands in his coat pockets. He lifted his head and smiled—then saw Balthazar. His entire body went still, instantly on guard. I smiled to show him that nothing was wrong. He didn't look reassured.

"Hey," I said, as I ran toward him from the car. "It's okay. Balthazar is helping us."

"And why would he do that?" Lucas's eyes narrowed.

Balthazar folded his arms. "You're welcome."

"You guys stop it," I said. The marquee lights flashed in a pattern, and the poster on the wall showed Bogey and Bacall, *To Have and Have Not*. I kissed Lucas lightly on the cheek, which finally made him stop glaring at Balthazar. "Lucas and I are going to talk for a second. Okay, Balthazar?"

Lucas didn't look thrilled that I'd just asked Balthazar for permission to do anything. I hurriedly took his arm and walked him toward the side of the theater. Balthazar simply leaned against the car, eyebrow raised. As we got to the corner, I whispered, "I can explain."

"Of all the people in the world you could tell about this—"

"I didn't tell him. He found out. Basically, he caught me coming in after the last time you and I saw each other. But he won't give us away, Lucas. He's even willing to help us see each other, as long as we help him with Charity."

"What, like, a fund-raiser or something?"

I'd forgotten he didn't know her name. "The vampire girl in Amherst."

"Wait—Charity? That's her name? You were able to figure out who she is." He smiled so proudly that all the tension of the moment instantly melted. "I fell in love with a genius."

"Not exactly. I only know her name because it turns out that Balthazar is her brother."

"*What?*"

I gave as much of the history as I thought Lucas would understand: their lives together in colonial New England, their slaughter by vampires and Balthazar's insistence that he needed to find Charity and take care of her so that she'd be safe.

"Safe for who?" Lucas asked. "Safe for herself, or safe for the human beings around her?"

"For herself, of course. I told you she wasn't a killer."

"And I trust your call on that. But this girl—Charity— she's hanging around with some vampires who are definitely trouble."

"Well, if she's fallen in with a bad crowd, Balthazar can get her out of it, or at least he thinks so. If we help him do that, he's willing to help us. He'll tell us a lot of what he knows about vampires and ghosts—"

"Whoa, whoa, hold up. Ghosts? Where do they come into it?"

"A ghost is haunting Evernight Academy." The look on

Lucas's face made me smile despite myself. "Yeah, just when you thought it couldn't get more fun."

"Holy crap."

"I'll tell you about it later, okay? The point is, Balthazar can give us a lot of information we couldn't get any other way. He's even willing to help me get off campus to see you. All he wants is a chance to find his sister. We can help him do that, can't we?"

Lucas was silent for a few long seconds before he said, "I thought that guy hated my guts."

"He's not in your fan club. But he'll keep his word."

"So how is he helping you leave Evernight? Does Balthazar know a secret passageway out of there or something?"

Now we'd come to the tricky part. "Well, actually, he's older and pretty responsible, and we've made it sound like he's teaching me about being a vampire, so my parents and Mrs. Bethany let him do it." I took a deep breath and plowed ahead: "We've sort of convinced them that we're dating."

Silence. Lucas stared at me, his eyes wary.

"We're *not* dating. Completely not together. You understand, right? Because I definitely do, and he does, too." At least, I hoped Balthazar understood that.

"Yeah, I get it." Lucas didn't sound convinced. "But he's always had his eye on you. I remember how he was the night of the Autumn Ball. Possessive. Real possessive."

"He actually *was* my date for the Autumn Ball, remember? Because you lost your temper in Riverton and freaked me out?"

"My whole life, I've settled things with my fists, Bianca.

When you're hunting vampires, that's the best way to stay alive."

I stepped closer to Lucas, so close I could smell the scent of his skin. "I understand that. So please try to understand this. It's the only way we could think of."

He took a ragged breath. "I don't mean to overreact. I swear. I'm sorry, Bianca. It's just—I miss you so bad, and we never get any other chance to talk about all this stuff, and the last thing I expected to hear tonight was that some other guy gets to spend lots of time with you when I don't."

"You're the one that matters. The only one." I took his face in my hands and kissed him softly. "Okay?"

"Okay." He squared his shoulders. "Fine, I'll make nice with Balthazar and then we can get out of here together. Right?"

"Right."

We walked back to the front of the theater, arm in arm. Balthazar hadn't moved from the car. When he saw us again, however, he straightened up and came toward us with a swagger in his step. It would've made me snicker at him if Lucas hadn't been doing the exact same thing. "Balthazar," Lucas drawled. "Last time I saw you, you punched me in the gut."

"The last time I saw you, you nearly broke my nose. Lucky thing we're working together on this."

"Lucky for me or lucky for you?" Lucas's cocky grin made it clear that he thought Balthazar was the one getting off easy when they weren't fighting. "By the way, nice wheels there. That ride could take you straight from a meeting with your banker to the

PTA. Makes it crystal clear you're more than a century old."

"It's the driver's ed car." Balthazar's jaw was clenched, like he was biting back a lot of other things he'd rather say.

I gave Lucas a warning look, wishing he'd knock it off, but he still acted like he had something to prove. "What, you haven't owned a horseless carriage since your Studebaker broke down?"

Balthazar smiled, satisfied. "Actually, the last car I owned was a red 1968 Mustang GT 390 Fastback."

I had no idea what that meant, but Lucas did. His expression shifted from disdain into envy, and then to a grudging respect. "Sweet."

"Yeah." Balthazar sighed, all animosity temporarily forgotten.

Guys, I thought. "Okay," I said, hoping to end this before they started sparring again. "We'll meet you back here in, what, two hours?"

"You're not leaving yet." Balthazar had focused his attention on Lucas again. "First you tell me what you know about my sister, and promise me that you're going to call off the Black Cross hunt for her."

"I'm not in charge of Black Cross, okay? They don't do what I say to do. The hunt for that gang is on, and as long as Charity's hanging with the same crew, she's going to be in the line of fire. So we've got to separate her from them, one way or the other."

"There's one way. Only one. Mine." Balthazar stepped closer, using every inch he had on Lucas, who was tall but not that tall. "Charity is a person. The same as you, the same as me."

"You and me aren't the same."

Balthazar cocked his head. "Then let's say the same as Bianca. Will that make you listen?"

"Bianca's no killer! She didn't have a choice about what she is."

"Guys, don't do this," I pleaded, but they paid no attention.

"A choice? You think we all get a choice?" Although Balthazar spoke softly, there was a roughness to his voice I'd never heard before. It sent chills down my spine. "Try being hunted down in the night. Try running as far and as fast as you can and finding out they're faster. Try coming to in a stable, with your parents' dead bodies on the ground in front of you, your hands roped above your head and a dozen hungry vampires arguing with each other about who gets you next. See how much choice you have then."

Lucas just stared at him. Obviously he'd never imagined anything like that; neither had I.

Even more quietly, Balthazar continued, "Try watching your baby sister die, and then tell me that you wouldn't spend the rest of eternity trying to make up for it. When you've done all that, Lucas, then you can talk to me about choices. Until that time, tell me what I need to know and then shut your mouth."

"Back off," Lucas said, but he was calmer now. "I get it, all right? We've all got to do what we've got to do, and it's fine by me." He pulled a small notebook from his coat pocket and handed it over. "That's got some information about her—Charity, I mean—it's just notes about the hunts we've been on lately.

Those 'friends' she's got with her, any ideas who they might be?"

"None." Already Balthazar was flipping through the note-book, scouring the pages for clues.

"Most of the details are probably useless, but maybe there's something. And next time I'll put together some stuff just about her, try to lay it out so you might figure out a pattern." After a few seconds' pause, he added, "Hope it helps."

"Thank you." Balthazar sounded sincere.

In the uncertain silence that followed, I tried to think of what to say after what I had just learned about Balthazar's past, but no words were adequate. So I hugged him quickly. "Are you all right?"

"I'm fine. Just going to the movies, it looks like." He hugged me back, just long enough that I became acutely aware of Lucas watching us. "See you in two hours."

As Lucas and I drove away in his mom's truck, he said, "You all right?"

"Yeah, sure. I'm worried about Balthazar, though. I never knew that was what happened to him. I can't even imagine how terrible that would be."

"I've had vampires after me since I was born. I don't have to imagine."

"I know that a few of us are killers," I said quietly. "I've known that for a while now. But not all of us are."

"Right, I get that. What neither of us knows is the truth behind the party lines our parents taught us—where to strike the balance."

I sighed. "I don't want to talk about this any longer. Okay?"

"You got it."

"Hey, where are we going?" The truck's headlights illuminated the road ahead of us, but it wasn't any place in Riverton I recognized. We were headed sharply uphill.

"Don't worry, gorgeous." Lucas grinned. "You'll be back by curfew. Our ultimate destination is a surprise."

Despite the tense mood that had descended earlier, I had to smile a little. "Hint?"

"You'll know it when you see it."

And I did.

The observatory was an older one, a small pale silo with a copper-green roof that slit open to reveal a telescope's lens. As I began to smile, Lucas said, "They used to have a small college here in town. Been closed for a few decades now. But they've kept the observatory open so the high school kids could come out here once in a while."

"Is it open tonight?" I said eagerly.

"For tonight, it's our private observatory. We'll have to open it ourselves."

This turned out to mean Lucas picking the lock—which he made look easy. Once we stepped inside, we were in a circular room, not terribly wide but about thirty feet high. A spiral metal staircase led up to the telescope. The open dome meant that it was as cold inside as out, but I didn't care. Lucas held my hand as we climbed the stairs, and our footsteps on the metal echoed slightly.

The telescope hadn't looked that large from below, but once we got there, the many wheels and handles made Lucas whistle. "You know how to steer this thing?"

"I think I can figure it out." I'd never worked with a telescope quite this grand, at least not on my own, but I'd been to an observatory at science camp in middle school and read enough books to get the gist. Orienting myself—north, south, east, west—I focused the lens on the nearest constellation. A nebula I'd usually seen as a slightly less defined star was now vivid and detailed, almost like in my books. This was better, though; this was real. "Oh, wow."

"Can I see?"

"The Orion nebula. Look." I stepped aside so that Lucas could peer into the lens, and I put my arms around him, touched and thrilled by the thoughtfulness of his gift. For one moment I remembered Balthazar, whom I'd shown this constellation last year, but from a view so much farther away. I hoped he was okay, alone at the movies.

"That's pretty spectacular."

"Mmm-hmm." Lucas was so warm in my arms, and already I felt his attention shifting from the stars to me. I wanted to revel in the opportunity to see everything in such amazing detail, but it was getting harder to think about anything but how close we were to each other. If only we could always be this close. I would do anything to make that possible; surely Lucas would, too.

Lucas turned from the telescope and kissed me lightly. I took his face in my hands to kiss him again, deeper this time.

It wasn't enough. I kept kissing him, harder and faster, until my breath started to catch in my throat.

"I missed you," Lucas whispered into my hair. "Every night I go to sleep thinking about you, except the nights I can't sleep at all because I want you with me so bad."

"I know." I pulled my coat open and guided his hands inside, bringing them up my sides so that I shivered. "Me, too."

Lucas kept stroking my skin, his fingertips brushing the curve of my breasts, and then I couldn't wait anymore. I couldn't think. I sat down on the metal floor and pulled him with me. Even as he eased himself to my side, I tugged my sweater open, each button popping through its hole just before it might have been torn free. He stared, startled only for a moment, before he opened his coat and lowered himself over me—sheltering me, keeping me warm.

Our kisses were more fevered now, almost desperate. What I was feeling couldn't be said in words. Dizzy and blissful, I let my head loll back. The stars seemed to tilt and spin above the open dome. I wove my fingers into Lucas's hair so I could keep him there as long as he made me feel that way.

He wants this as badly as I do, I thought. *Lucas knows where this is going, and he doesn't want to stop.*

Then he was kissing my open mouth again, and we were both breathing hard, getting crazy. Lucas pushed one of his thighs between my legs. I put my hands on either side of his face. "You and I—do you want me to—is this going to happen?"

"What?" Lucas seemed to be coming back to me from a very great distance. "Oh. Oh. I didn't think—tonight—"

"Me either, but I can tell you want to." I kissed him; he was trembling, maybe with excitement. It was just like it had been at the top of the north tower last year, just as overwhelming and desperate. "Then we'll really be together. Always."

"Are you sure?"

"It changes everything—for both of us—but yeah. I am. Are you?"

He gave me that sexy, lazy grin that always made me warm all over. "Absolutely." When we kissed again, there was a new intensity to it. Purpose. Need. Then he whispered against my cheek, "Do you have, you know—protection?"

"Protection?"

"You know." I didn't. "Well, I didn't bring any condoms. Because I am just. That. Stupid." Lucas thumped his head once against my shoulder. "I didn't think you'd—that we'd get to this. I should've known better. Every time I touch you—"

"Wait, you thought I was talking about *sex?*"

Lucas stared at me. I realized immediately that of course he'd been talking about sex; he was lying on top of me, and I was half undressed. It wasn't like I hadn't been thinking about that, too—maybe even later tonight—but I had been talking about tying us together *forever.*

"Bianca, are you— Did you mean—you were talking about drinking my blood?"

"Yeah."

"But not just drinking my blood." His face was drawn and pale. "Right?"

"I thought you wanted me to—to make you a vampire." The ultimate gift. I lay one hand on Lucas's cheek, loving the touch of him. Old dreams of mine sparkled like new in my mind, and for an instant I dared to hope. "Doing that would make me a vampire, too. And then, Lucas—we'd never have to be apart again."

Lucas went totally still. "I'd die first. I mean, die and stay dead. Bianca, don't ever ask me that again. Because that is the one thing in the world I won't do for you. I'll never be a vampire. Never."

Every word was a blow. He'd come so far in understanding us, and I thought his old resistance to the idea might have vanished. But here it was, as strong as ever. I felt confused; worse, I felt rejected. Lucas didn't want what I'd offered or what I was.

There didn't seem to be anything else to say, and the crazy heat that had goaded us on before had vanished like it had never been. We both sat up, shifting slightly away from each other. My bare skin finally felt the cold, and after a moment I began to button my sweater with shaking fingers. Lucas gently put an arm around my shoulder, but the embrace was awkward now. I'd never thought it could feel weird to be held by him, but it did.

Chapter Fourteen

"YOU OKAY?" LUCAS SAID FOR ABOUT THE TWEN-
tieth time, as he drove me back into Riverton.

"I'm all right. Honestly." Inside I felt torn up and confused,
but I didn't want to admit it—neither to Lucas nor to myself.

We'd pulled ourselves together, looked at the stars, and
talked, but nothing had been the same. The only words I really
heard were Lucas's, ringing in my memory: *I'll never be a vampire.*

He'd said it before. I'd believed him. But this time it had
really hit me: No matter what happened, no matter how much
we loved each other, there would always be a boundary between
me and Lucas. I'd endured our separation this year because I'd
believed it wouldn't be permanent. How could it be, when we
loved each other so much?

But now I found myself wondering if this was all we could
ever have: furtive meetings and smuggled letters, a few moments
of passion stolen amid weeks and weeks of loneliness.

And someday he would grow old—even die—and leave me here alone forever.

Lucas pulled up in front of the movie theater just as patrons started coming out. Amid the older couples and a few laughing teenagers, one shape stood out from the rest—Balthazar, tall and saturnine in his long black coat.

"I should go." I turned back toward Lucas. "Where will we meet up next time?"

"January, I think. There's this one town—Albion—Charity goes there a lot. At least, that's what the reports say. Guess that's where Balthazar would be willing to take you."

"He'll do that, definitely. Second Saturday in January? Eight P.M.?" He nodded. "Where?"

"Center of town. Trust me, it's a small town—we can't miss each other." He cupped my cheek in his hand. "I love you."

I nodded, too choked up to speak.

Lucas drew me closer and kissed my forehead. "Hey. No crying now."

"I won't." I breathed in his scent. If only I could somehow keep him with me all the time, every moment, so that he was never any farther away than this. "Christmas morning, wherever you are, think about me. I'll be thinking about you." We kissed each other tenderly before I reluctantly opened the truck door and climbed out.

On the way home, Balthazar and I didn't say anything to each other at first until we'd driven almost all the way back to Evernight Academy. It wasn't an awkward silence, exactly; I was preoccupied with my own concerns and could tell that Balthazar was, too. Finally I ventured, "Did you learn a lot? From Lucas's notes, I mean."

"Not nearly enough. But I know that Charity's revisiting the towns in this area—the places she remembers. She does that sometimes, but it never makes her happy. It's like she hates those places for having changed while she stays the same."

"You can find her, then." I rubbed my hands together, still chilled from the wintery cold. "You can figure out where she'll be."

Balthazar kept his eyes on the road as he flicked on the car's heater. "I can narrow it down. But there's no pattern—never has been, with Charity."

"Still, it's a place to start."

"Always looking at the bright side." The corner of his mouth lifted in an unwilling smile. "Yeah. It's a place to start."

After we pulled up in the lot on the far edge of the grounds, I opened my car door to get out, but Balthazar didn't move at first. I hesitated. "Thanks," I said. "For tonight. It meant a lot."

Balthazar lifted his hand to my face. He didn't touch me, but his fingertips were close to my mouth. "Your lips are swollen."

"Huh?" Now that he mentioned it, my mouth did feel puffy and sore. I realized it was from the hungry kisses Lucas and I had shared. "Oh. Does it look—is it too—"

"It's fine," Balthazar said lightly. His eyes were shadowed. "Anyone who noticed would assume you'd been kissing me."

* * *

Fortunately, I didn't have much time to brood over the separation between me and Lucas. Finals week approached, and the humdrum tasks of papers and exams demanded their due. In some ways, burying myself in schoolwork was a comfort.

My dark mood lingered, no matter how many essays I wrote for Mrs. Bethany or how many calculus practice exams I took. Nobody really noticed though, because the entire school remained on edge. Though the window in the great hall had been repaired—again with clear glass instead of stained—it remained deserted, even on rainy days when the only alternative was a cramped dorm room. Rumors spread, becoming more absurd by the day.

"I heard that the haunting is part of a voodoo curse," Courtney proclaimed one day from her shower. I was washing my hair a couple of stalls down. "Voodoo is totally and completely real, and some loser dropout from last semester decided to curse this place by ruining the best party of the year for all the cool people."

I would've liked to tell Courtney just how stupid she was being, but I didn't really have a better explanation yet.

As finals week began and the tensions increased, I realized one curious element of the school's fears about the ghost, something I wouldn't have expected: The vampires were the ones who were most afraid. The human kids were on edge, too, but they mostly seemed to take it in stride.

That didn't make sense to me. Okay, vampires might be more likely to understand that the wraiths were real and appreciate the potential danger. But I hadn't heard any of the human students scoffing at the idea of ghosts—not that anybody could doubt something supernatural was going on after what happened at the Autumn Ball.

"Isn't it sort of weird," I ventured one day while Vic and I were studying together in the library, "how more people aren't freaking out?"

"About exams? Trust me, I'm freaking."

"No, not exams. About the—the thing. You know."

"The ghost?" Vic didn't even look up from his anatomy text-book.

"Yeah, the ghost. You're really casual about living in a haunted house."

"I've always lived in a haunted house." Vic shrugged. "I got over the creepy part a long time ago."

"Wait, what?" It had never occurred to me that *Vic* might know more about wraiths than any vampire at Evernight. "Your house is haunted by a wrai—a ghost?"

"Yeah, the cold spot in the attic. Classic spectral activity—lowered temperature, weird sounds, and the way you just *feel* somebody watching you even though nobody else is there. Everybody in my family always knew about it. I had a sleepover every Halloween that was, if I say so myself, the coolest party of the year. Every year." As I gaped at him, Vic started to laugh. "Lots of people here have seen the same thing."

"The ghost in your house?"

"The ghosts in *their* houses. Or their schools, or you know that new girl Clementine? She swears her grandma had a haunted *car*. Like Christine from Stephen King, right? I would love to try driving that thing."

"How did you learn all this?"

Vic sighed. "See, while you spend all your time making out with Balthazar, and Raquel stays holed up with her art projects, and Ranulf's off studying his Norse myths again, I do something else. Something crazy. Something strange. I call it 'talking to other people.' Through this miraculous process, I am sometimes able to learn facts about two or three other human beings in a single day. Scientists plan to study my method."

"Shut up." I gave him a playful shove, and he laughed again, but inwardly I was trying to process all of this. Of course Vic would know more about the human students than anybody else here; he was the most outgoing guy at the whole school. Even some of the vampires who looked down their noses at Vic ended up talking to him once in a while. "Did the ghosts ever, well, hurt anybody?"

"Not that I've heard of. I always kinda liked our attic ghost. When I was a kid, I used to go up there and read stories to it. Show it my new toys. It's just an old spirit stuck between the worlds, right? What's to be scared of?"

"Falling ice?"

"Nobody got hurt at the Autumn Ball. I figure the ghost was just freaking us out. Having fun watching us run around and scream."

"Maybe."

I might have been more reassured if I hadn't heard Raquel's story.

* * *

Most nights, before I went to sleep, I thought about Lucas—sometimes remembering our times together, sometimes fantasizing about it, or sometimes simply wondering where he was and hoping he was happy and well. The night after our last final was different. Exhaustion overwhelmed me, as well as the depression of knowing that our next meeting was still a whole month away.

No, that night I didn't want to think about Lucas. I didn't want to think. I closed my eyes tightly and willed myself to fall asleep as soon as I could.

The storm raged outside the school, and the wind lashed tree branches against the sky. I stood at the broken window, careful of the shattered glass. Droplets of rain spattered against my skin.

"Don't you want to stay inside?" Charity said. She held a torch in her hand, an old-fashioned one out of a horror film. The orange flame flickered close, but she didn't flinch. She was the only vampire I'd ever seen who wasn't afraid of fire. "Warm and dry in here. We can make it even warmer."

"I can't stay here."

"Can't you? Maybe you just don't want to."

I couldn't tell if Charity was right or wrong. All I knew was that I had to get away from her and out of Evernight.

"Bianca!" That was Lucas's voice. I strained for the sound of it, then realized that he was outside in the storm. "Bianca, don't move!"

"I'm sorry, Bianca." Charity's doll-black eyes were as guileless as a child's. She brought the torch closer, and I felt its heat searing my skin. "But it has to burn."

I jumped through the window. Shards of glass jutting from the window frame sliced my legs and arms, and I landed hard in the wet grass. The rain came down so hard and fast that it felt as though I were being pelted with stones. But I started running as swiftly as I could, my bare feet cold in the wet grass. Where was Lucas?

Then the hedge changed, thickening and growing in a way I recognized—but when? When had I seen this happen? I didn't know until I saw the strange, sharp-bladed red flowers begin darkening to black.

My dream—this is a dream—it's not just a dream—
"Lucas?"

I sat upright in bed, breathing hard. Raquel was propped up on her elbows, and she blinked drowsily at me. "Did you say something?"

"I was dreaming." My breath came in gasps. "That's all."

"You sure? Absolutely sure?"

"Yes. I am. I promise." It took me another couple of seconds to collect myself enough to reassure her. "Probably I'm just stressing about how I did on my exams."

She watched me with wide eyes, remembering old night terrors of her own.

I tried again. "It's got nothing to do with whatever the ghost is. Really."

"How can you know for sure?"

"You knew. Didn't you?"

"I guess." Raquel stepped out of bed, her bare feet padding across the hardwood floor. She brushed a few sweaty strands of hair from my face. "Want me to get you some water?"

"That would be good, actually. Thanks."

As soon as I was alone, I thought back on the dream and the flowers I'd seen before—the flowers I had dreamed of the night before I met Lucas for the first time. I'd thought it a coincidence when we found the brooch carved in the exact shape of those strange flowers.

Or so I had always believed. But for the first time, I wondered if maybe my dreams meant something more.

Christmas break was quieter this year than last. Then, several of the vampires had remained, lacking homes to return to. This year, almost all of them had fled the haunted school, and I wondered how many of them would return in the spring.

It was an unpleasant winter, too, without any pretty snow—just gray skies, sleet, and hard ice that made the roads impassable more days than not. Balthazar's frequent solo journeys off campus in search of his sister had to stop for the time being. I could tell he resented not having left Evernight more when it was still possible, so I tried my best to brighten his mood. On Christmas Eve, we hung out in the Modern Technology room as I helped him get a jump start on January's assignment.

"You've got to go faster than that," I said.

"It takes time to figure out what the arrows mean," Balthazar protested, moving stiffly through the steps on the beginner level of Dance Dance Revolution.

"You have to internalize that so your body knows what to do

the second your eye sees the arrow. Your brain can't even come into it." I sat cross-legged on the floor next to the game mat, watching him in dismay. "You're a good dancer, Balthazar. How come you're so bad at this?"

"This isn't dancing. These days, it's merely—rhythmic twitching."

"Well, you'd better get used to it, because the game doesn't have a fox-trot setting."

Balthazar glared at me, but there was some humor behind it. He let me play, too, and took my victory in stride.

Afterward, we went upstairs to my parents' apartment, where I was spending the winter break. When my mother opened the door, the warm scent of cinnamon and apples wafted out to welcome us. "About time you made it." She squeezed Balthazar's shoulder, then gave me a kiss on the cheek. "We've been waiting for you two."

"Look at that tree." Balthazar grinned at the seven-foot-tall fir my parents had set up in the corner. Strewn with tinsel and decorated with the clumsy pipe-cleaner and cardboard ornaments I'd made over the years, the tree looked appropriately festive, but to me it didn't seem any different from any other Christmas. Balthazar was more impressed. "It's been a long time since I opened presents under a tree."

"Since you were alive?" I asked.

"We didn't have Christmas trees then," he said, as Mom helped him out of his jacket. "That was a German tradition that didn't spread worldwide until—oh, two hundred years after I died. It's a good custom, though. I think it'll last a long time."

"Me, too." Dad stood in the door of the kitchen, and the apron wrapped around his waist was promisingly smeared with chocolate. "I'm just relieved nobody decorates them with candles anymore."

"Real candles? Like, with fire?" I couldn't believe it.

Mom mock-shuddered. "Real flame, near real trees that were drying out fast. You wouldn't believe how dangerous Christmas used to be."

We settled in for a cozy night. The chocolate on my father's apron proved to be icing for a cake he'd made as a treat for me. We drank hot cider from mugs and blood from glasses, a Christmas ritual. For the first time in my life, the juxtaposition struck me as strange, but with Mom, Dad, and Balthazar having such a great time, I couldn't dwell on that too much. Christmas music played on Dad's stereo, popping with that peculiarly enjoyable static only vinyl records have. All my blues were forgotten for a while.

Later in the evening, Balthazar got on his knees to inspect the packages under the tree. He'd already promised to bring my gift tomorrow. I'd bought him a sweater—not exactly the most awe-inspiring present ever, I know, but he needed some more up-to-date clothing, and besides, the warm oaky brown of the wool had reminded me of him in some way that was hard to define. But when Balthazar picked up the first package with his name on it, I frowned: It wasn't mine.

"Wait a second," he said. "There are a few for me down here. Several. Bianca, you didn't spend this much money, did you?" I shook my head.

"We plead guilty," Dad said. He hugged my beaming mother around the shoulder. "You're practically part of the family, Balthazar. We wanted you to be as much a part of the celebrations tomorrow as anyone."

"Thanks." Balthazar looked really touched, not because he was going to rack up on the gifts Christmas morning but because they'd taken him in. Maybe I should've felt the same way, once I saw what it meant to him, but I didn't.

Instead, I thought once again how Mom and Dad liked Balthazar almost too much. As good a person as he was, that wasn't what my parents were responding to. No, they liked him because he was my Vampire Boyfriend, i.e., the person who was going to make their daughter into the perfect vampire they'd always planned for me to be.

I'd always planned on fulfilling their hopes. But seeing how badly my parents wanted it—the fine edge of desperation beneath their smiles—made me wonder what it was they were so afraid of.

Afterward, as the evening grew late, not only did my parents let me take Balthazar into my bedroom, but Mom even shut the door behind us—something they'd never done the two times they'd allowed Lucas to come in here with me.

"My parents are nuts about you," I said. "You see that, too, right?"

"They wouldn't be so enthusiastic if they knew the whole truth about where I take you, and why. Let's not disillusion them yet." Balthazar went to the window to study the gargoyle. Icicles dangled from its stone wings. "He looks cold out there."

"I ought to knit him a scarf or something." I curled up on the window seat and touched two fingertips to the cold glass.

"You even take pity on creatures made of stone." Balthazar settled next to me on the window seat, with one arm around my shoulders and his leg alongside mine.

I glanced up at him, uncertain. He said, "If your parents came in—"

"I know. We should look—comfortable."

"Exactly." Balthazar watched me hesitate, a small, knowing smile on his face. "You feel like I'm taking advantage of the situation."

"It's not that. I know you wouldn't."

"You're wrong. I would." He leaned closer to me, so that our faces nearly touched. "You're as much in love with Lucas Ross as you ever were, and there's not a damn thing I can do about it. That doesn't mean I can't enjoy being this close to you."

I couldn't seem to concentrate. For some reason I couldn't look away from his mouth. He had a square jaw and a fine fuzz of stubble. "It just seems risky, I guess."

"The only one taking a risk here is me, if I get too attached to you. It's not risky for you, as long as you're not confused either."

"I'm not."

"Of course you aren't." A small smile played on Balthazar's lips.

I pushed myself up from the window seat. My knees were shaky. Balthazar stayed put, though the smile never left his face. I blathered, "So, I guess you're, uh, in a good mood these days.

Like, you seem cheerful—not goofy cheerful or anything, just cheerful."

"Yeah, I'm good."

I sat on the edge of my bed, so we were a few feet apart. Now I could focus. "You were having a tough time after Riverton," I said. "Have you made more progress than you've told me?"

"No—when I find Charity, I'll tell you immediately. The sooner we can call off Black Cross, the better." He leaned back against the window frame. The gargoyle was visible as a shadow behind him, like a devil on his shoulder. "But I'm learning to accept that it's not going to happen overnight. I've been without her for thirty-five years; I can make it a couple months more."

"You make it sound like you're the one who needs her, instead of the other way around."

Balthazar considered that for a few moments. "I guess I always need someone to take care of."

That came close to dangerous ground. Quickly I changed the subject to something I'd been weighing whether or not to discuss with him for some time. "If I share a confidence that somebody else has told me—something really personal, really private—because I honestly think you might know something helpful, will you promise to keep the secret? And never, ever let on that you know?"

"Of course." He sighed heavily. "Is this about Lucas?"

"No. It's about Raquel." There, on Christmas Eve, whispering so that my parents couldn't possibly overhear a word, I told Balthazar what Raquel had revealed about the wraith that had terrorized her for so long.

He wasn't as shocked as I had been. "What did you think the wraiths were, Bianca? Cute and friendly, like Casper the ghost and his pals?" Then he frowned. "Are there still Casper cartoons?"

"They had a movie," I said absently. "But isn't that—I mean, that ghost isn't just turning things blue or making ice appear. It's a—well, it's a rapist."

"Even human mythology is familiar with the incubi, Bianca. Some female wraiths sexually attack sleeping men; they're called succubi. Wraiths don't have bodies, so they come up with every way they can to violate the bodies of others. Possession, sexual assault, hauntings—all part of the same pattern."

I shuddered. "It's just so scary. There are so many ghosts in the world—I mean, there have to be millions, Balthazar. If they're all capable of that—"

"Wait a second. There aren't millions of wraiths. They're fairly rare. Rarer than vampires, that's for certain."

"That's not possible. Almost all the human kids here grew up in haunted houses."

"What? You're kidding."

"Vic figured it out. Ghosts in almost all their homes. For that to be true, there would have to be hundreds and thousands of haunted houses . . ." My voice trailed off as I realized that wasn't the only possibility.

Either there were tons of haunted houses in the world, so that any group of people my age might have grown up in them—

or it was just a coincidence that so many of them had ended up here—or this was the answer Lucas and I had been seeking all along. *This* was the reason Mrs. Bethany allowed human students to come to Evernight Academy. Not just any human students could attend; only the ones connected to the wraiths got through the doors.

"Mrs. Bethany's looking for wraiths," I whispered.

"What?"

I explained to Balthazar as best I could, my words tumbling over each other in my excitement. "This has to be it. Once the students come here, she has a link to the homes and families that lasts for years. If she needed to get into any of these students' houses, she could probably do it."

"I agree that this can't be random," Balthazar said. Slowly, he started to grin. "This isn't a coincidence. But why would Mrs. Bethany be looking for wraiths? They hate us; we hate them. Normally they give us a wide berth and we return the favor."

"Not these days. Something's changed. The old truce isn't in place anymore." I shivered and tucked my legs against my chest, hugging myself on the foot of my bed. "They're after us. Wraiths are targeting either this school or vampires generally. Mrs. Bethany must have known this was coming, so she let the humans in to—to track the ghosts down or get access to them, maybe."

He drummed his fingers on the windowsill. "You're onto something. Think about it, Bianca—for centuries no ghost dares to enter Evernight, and then tons show up as soon as human students appear?"

"Tons?" I thought about the girl I'd seen early in the year, then the frost man I'd seen in the north tower, and finally whatever it was that had disrupted the Autumn Ball—it didn't seem to have a physical form. "Yeah, more than one. But it wasn't immediate. It took a year for the hauntings to start."

"Given that the incidents started small, the hauntings could have begun last year. We wouldn't necessarily have known."

I'd finally made the breakthrough. At last I understood. The wraiths had come to Evernight, and whatever we'd seen so far was only the beginning.

"Oh, honey, I love it." Mom slid her new bracelet onto her wrist, then kissed my father on the cheek. Given that he'd been shopping for her for more than three hundred Christmases now, I thought he was doing pretty well to still be able to find things that pleased her. Or maybe that was the trick of their long partnership, the fact that they still took pleasure in virtually any gift, gesture, or word.

Dad ruffled my hair. "We'll save the rest of your presents for you to unwrap when Balthazar gets here, but open just one, all right?"

I obediently took a gift bag, which turned out to hold a tearshaped pendant on an antique, green-copper chain. "It's pretty," I said as I tested its weight in my hands. "What is it?"

"Obsidian," Mom said. "Put it on, so we can see."

They beamed at me as I hung it around my neck. I thought obsidian was sort of an odd choice, but the black sheen of the stone really was beautiful.

What was this day like for Lucas? I couldn't imagine Kate or Eduardo telling Lucas stories about Santa when he was a child, or that Black Cross stayed in place long enough for him ever to have a Christmas tree. I imagined him as the little boy he must have been, with sandy hair and big eyes, wishing for toys but never getting them. And he would never have complained. Right now, maybe, he was sleeping in a cot in some other miserable parking garage, without any presents or candy or holiday music. The picture in my mind looked bleak, and I remembered again what he'd once told me about not having any kind of normal life.

The image of Lucas's lonely Christmas morning made me feel hollow inside.

Until our unhappy disagreement at the observatory, I hadn't realized how much I was counting on someday changing the fact that Lucas and I were in different worlds. He needed to be free from Black Cross someday, somehow. I'd hoped he would join me as a vampire—a possibility he had just rejected forever.

If that wasn't in our future, how could Lucas ever be free? And how could we ever be together?

Chapter Fifteen

I FELT RELIEVED WHEN CLASSES STARTED AGAIN. I'd settled into a melancholy mood that only became worse with time and silence to brood. At least when the hallways filled with students and assignments began piling up, I had enough to do. I could stop thinking about my problems for a while.

Apparently most of the Evernight students had spent a great deal of time thinking about their problems, specifically the problem of attending a haunted school. Several of the vampire students hadn't returned; those who had muttered darkly about posting sentries in the halls and sleeping only in shifts while a roommate remained awake. I even heard someone speculating about what it would take to perform an exorcism. *Yeah*, I thought, *I'm sure a priest with his crucifix and Bible would be really welcome here.*

Human students remained relatively calm about the prospect of a ghost. Even Raquel could deal. "It's not the same ghost," she reasoned as she unpacked her trunk, which was mostly crammed with foodstuffs—canned soup, boxes of crackers, and jars of peanut butter. "If it were going to—well, if I were in trouble, I'd know by now. I'd rather deal with this thing than whatever is in my parents' house."

"How do you stand it, living there?"

"This Christmas, I spent the break with my older sister and her husband. Their place is fine. My parents think I'm acting out, but they also think Frida is a 'good influence.'"

I thought about all the stuff my parents would let me do as long as I was with Balthazar. "Hanging around with a good influence helps you get away with murder, doesn't it?"

We cracked up laughing and then split a candy bar.

Soon it became clear that at least one vampire had spent her holiday vacation worrying about something besides the wraiths—and that I now had a brand-new problem.

"I've made it almost thirty years without having to change a flat tire," Courtney huffed as she pumped the car jack. "If you're young, hot, and blond, trust me, you can work around it. There's always some stupid guy happy to help out. Of course, I can see that *you* might need to know how to do it yourself."

"Will you just hand me the lug wrench already? We're not going to get finished any faster if you keep complaining."

"Snappish." Courtney's full lips curved upward into a sneaky sort of smile. "What's the matter, Bianca? Are you, oh, I don't know—having some relationship trouble?"

"Things between me and Balthazar are as good as they've always been." Technically that was true. As I knelt on the cold pavement, my wool gloves getting stained with grease, I tried to pay attention to the task at hand.

"I think you think you're telling me the truth," Courtney said. "I think you don't even know where Balthazar's going without you."

"What are you talking about?"

"Maybe possibly right around New Year's Eve, I happened to see Balthazar in Amherst. Without you."

"What were you doing in Amherst?"

"I happen to be familiar with the town, okay? I go there sometimes. So does Balthazar, but apparently to see someone besides his girlfriend. I'd be suspicious if I were you."

He would have been there looking in vain for Charity. My face fell, and Courtney smirked. She couldn't have guessed why I was actually upset, but it didn't matter. Now that she had identified a weakness, she was sure to exploit it. Quickly, I said, "Balthazar goes all kinds of places. It doesn't mean anything to me. We're not attached at the hip."

"Too bad. Getting attached at the hips is sort of the point." Courtney winked as she thrust the lug wrench toward me. I snatched it and hoped she'd be satisfied with teasing me about the supposed infidelity of my supposed boyfriend. Balthazar and I both needed our masquerade, and we couldn't afford anyone watching us too closely.

I made up my mind that this trip would be different for me and Lucas, but I hadn't realized how different it would be.

"I don't know where exactly we'll meet up with him," I said as Balthazar steered the driver's ed sedan past a small white sign advertising the township of Albion. "He said we'd know it when we saw it, whatever that means."

"Don't worry. Lucas is right. Trust me, there aren't many places he could go."

Soon I realized what he meant. Albion was even tinier than the small town I'd grown up in: only a handful of streets clustered together, marked with a single stoplight in the center. The houses looked old, and except for a grocery, a gas station, and the post office, there didn't seem to be anything like a store around. "Pretty slow, huh?"

"It was nicer a hundred fifty years ago, when we stayed here."

We meant Balthazar and Charity. I watched his face carefully, but he betrayed no emotion.

Balthazar parked the car on a street close to Albion's one stoplight. A fine snow had fallen earlier that day, and our boots crunched as we walked toward the town center. Hungrily I searched in the darkness for some glimpse of Lucas. I badly needed to see him again, to hold him close, and talk for a long time so that we could reconnect. The intimacy between us suffered while we were apart, and that was what I wanted to rebuild.

Just as we stepped to the corner, I heard, "There you are."

I turned around, beaming. "Lucas?"

Lucas jogged toward us, in a heavy parka and knitted hat

that made him almost unrecognizable. He opened his arms for me, and I ran right into them. His nose was cold against my cheek. "Hey, angel," he murmured.

"You always see me first. You sneak up behind me every time."

"And you love it."

"Mmm-hmm, I do." I kissed him on the cheek, then on the mouth. "But someday I'm going to surprise you."

"Good luck trying." Lucas hugged me even more tightly. Despite the layers of clothes between us, the embrace was enough to make me warm inside.

"I have a secret to tell you." My anticipation made my heart leap; I so hoped he'd be happy about this news. "I know why Mrs. Bethany invited human students to Evernight."

"Really? Why?"

I told Lucas about the deduction Balthazar and I had made about Mrs. Bethany's attempt to track ghosts, expecting him to share my satisfaction. Instead, his smile slowly dimmed. Confused, I said, "Come on, Lucas. This is huge. This is what you've been trying to find out for almost two years! Can't you use this to show up Eduardo? Or do you think I'm wrong?"

"No, I'd bet cash money you're right. When I applied to Evernight Academy, we used old Professor Ravenwood's address in Providence, and she always did talk about the ghost in the basement. She was getting pretty senile before she died, though, so I didn't put much stock in it. Guess I owe her an apology at her graveside."

"Then this is it. You can go back to Black Cross and tell them what we've learned. You'll complete your mission. That'll get Eduardo off your back, right?"

Lucas sighed. "I wish. The thing is, Eduardo's not going to like it. Some Black Cross cells deal with ghosts pretty regularly, but we almost never do. So another group of hunters would probably take over the investigation."

"But you still got the answer, and now you know no humans are at risk."

"You don't know Eduardo. The guy doesn't care how well-defended the school is, or how it's the one place vampires never attack humans. He hates it. He wants to wipe it off the map. This looked like his excuse. Now he's just going to have to turn it over to someone else."

"That means—you won't have as many reasons to come back to this area. It's going to be even harder for us to be together." All my efforts had only made things worse. I hung my head.

Lucas took my face in his hands. The coarse wool of his gloves felt scratchy against my cheeks. "We'll find a way. We'll always find a way. You have to believe that."

The lump in my throat kept me from replying except with a nod. Lucas kissed me hard, as if that alone could tie us together.

Balthazar cleared his throat.

I took one step back, belatedly realizing how awkward this had to be for him. Lucas would take this as a cue to be snide, I thought, but he surprised me. "Okay, moving on. Balthazar, I think your sister is here in Albion, right now."

"You've seen Charity." Balthazar lifted his chin, readying himself.

"Earlier today. West side of town. While I was driving in, I saw her walking along the road, out near the woods. Wheeled the truck around right away, but it was like she'd vanished."

Balthazar nodded. "I think I know where to look."

Lucas squeezed my hand. "I'm sorry, but you know we have to get on this."

"I know." I was actually sort of excited about it. If we could finally reunite Balthazar and Charity, they'd both be so happy. My time with Lucas could only be sweeter if I knew that we'd accomplished our goal and helped somebody else.

We ended up taking Lucas's truck, even though it was a tight squeeze with all three of us in the front seat. I felt a little uncomfortable wedged between Lucas and Balthazar, in more ways than one. Balthazar was in the same state of mind that I recognized in Lucas, the kind of determination that demanded action, not reflection. It was strange to see this sameness in them—a hard, driven core that was simultaneously compelling and intimidating.

But I could see the differences between them, too.

"Don't pull a weapon unless I say so," Balthazar said as we rumbled along a winding side road that led into a field. "If she's in Albion, she's probably alone."

Lucas's hands gripped the steering wheel like he was holding it in front of him as a shield. "I'm keeping a stake on me. Sorry, man, but I'm not going in there unarmed."

I saw the angry flash in Balthazar's eyes and quickly asked, "Should Lucas and I even be there? I mean, wouldn't you have better luck talking to her alone?"

"Maybe. Still, I'd like her to see you, so that she knows we're friends. It might help, later on."

Balthazar guided us to a small house on the outskirts of town—if you could even call it part of the town any longer. The old house looked like it would hardly be big enough for two rooms, and the chimney in the center of its ramshackle roof was missing several bricks at the top. Lucas turned off the headlights a couple of minutes before he stopped the truck about a hundred yards away. He walked around to the truck bed and grabbed two stakes, one of which he held out to me. Balthazar said nothing. Though it felt incredibly strange to hold such a thing in my hand, I took it. Lucas's warnings about Charity's gang had gotten to me.

This far out of town, the silence was almost complete. The wind had picked up, blowing small flecks of snow and stinging ice against our faces. Clouds hid the moon and stars, and the night was so dark that I thought I wouldn't even have been able to see the little house if its roof hadn't been gleaming white with snow.

"No tracks," Lucas whispered, his voice so low that it almost didn't carry over the wind and our crunching steps in the ice. "Either she hasn't been here later today, or she got here right after I saw her—"

"—and she hasn't left." Balthazar studied the dark windows, but I doubted even his vampiric vision would allow him to see anything. "We'll find out."

At the front steps we paused. Balthazar took them alone and put one hand on the doorknob. For a long few seconds, he remained completely still, and I realized I was holding my breath.

Then he pushed through and stood inside for only a moment before saying, "She isn't here."

"Dead end." Lucas kicked at the snow, his jaw clenched.

"I didn't say that," Balthazar replied. "Look." He bent to the side, doing something I couldn't glimpse, and then a candle flickered into light.

When Lucas and I walked inside, we saw that somebody had been staying in the house recently—somebody with a very bizarre sense of homemaking. A once-beautiful lace coverlet, stained with dirt and blood, lay atop a mattress on the floor. A perfect, scrollwork brass headboard leaned against the wall above it; spiders had spun cobwebs between the curls of brass. The candle Balthazar had lit sat in a holder atop a small table that was covered in wax of a dozen different colors; incredible amounts had dripped all over the surface, run down the legs, and puddled on the floor. One oval of purple wax surrounded a woman's shoe, a delicate, rhinestone-encrusted pencil heel with long straps that had been caught in the wax when it dried. Empty gin bottles lay on the floor and were stacked in the corners, and the fireplace was filled not with wood but with broken bits of glass, piled so high that it had to have been put there on purpose. The pile glinted in the candlelight, the colors of the glass—brown, clear, blue, green—blazing with their own unearthly form of flame.

"Don't take this the wrong way, Balthazar," Lucas said, "but was your sister always nuts?"

"Tactful as ever." Balthazar knelt by the heap of broken glass. "Honestly, though, there was always something—different about Charity. She isn't insane, and she never was, but she was never contented, either. Never moored to the earth. Once she got upset about something, or with someone, she'd never let it go. It was like she couldn't think about anything else, not while whatever it was still bothered her. I was the only one who could ever talk to her when she got that way."

"Whatever is going on with your sister these days, it's more than her holding a little grudge," Lucas said. "This place does not say 'mental health' to me. Plus, she's hanging out with the wrong crowd, and that's putting it mildly."

I thought about all the strange changes I'd already sensed in myself and how unnerving they could be. How much more frightening would it be to fully change, to be suddenly ripped from life into lifelessness? And I'd been bracing for the change ever since I'd been born, and knew that probably I would be able to choose my time. Charity had been tied up in a stable, watching her brother being tortured, knowing that her parents had been murdered—that would be more than enough to make anyone angry or unstable forever after.

Is this the way it happens for most vampires? I shivered.

"I'm not asking you to excuse the people Charity's spending time with." Balthazar never looked up from the pile of broken glass.

"I bet you want me to let them off scot-free, though," Lucas said.

"Don't pretend you're judge and jury. You're only the executioner, and you decide guilt based on what we are, not what we do."

"How is this about me instead of about Charity's crazy-ass friends?"

At first I wanted to make them stop arguing, but then I realized it might be better for them to hash it out now. The sooner they were done with their bickering, the better. I ignored them and knelt by the side of the mattress. One of the stains on the dingy lace coverlet was in the shape of a hand.

"You don't have a brother or sister, do you, Lucas? If you did, you might not be so dense about understanding this."

"If I had a brother or sister who was hanging around with the Manson family, I think I'd be pissed off at them, not at the cops trying to catch them."

"Still pretending you're a cop?"

I put my hand over the bloodstain. When Charity and I had walked side by side, she had taken my arm. Despite her height, her hands were tinier than my own. This bloodstain was larger, so much so that my fingers looked like a child's by comparison.

"She doesn't stay here alone." When I said that, Lucas and Balthazar stopped arguing and stared, almost as if they'd forgotten I was in the room. "Look at this. Somebody else has been here recently. Somebody a lot bigger. A man, probably."

Balthazar didn't seem convinced, but Lucas smiled. "Leave it to you to see it."

Proud of myself, I eagerly looked around the room for some other proof of the second vampire, but nothing instantly came to mind. The bizarre collection of clutter was more unnerving now, though. Charity on her own was strange, but you'd think someone else—anyone else—would be saner. That he might impose some order. Instead, he lived here in this decay.

Balthazar said, slowly, "Not alone."

"Tell me, Balthazar, what bothers you more?" Lucas started going through the drawers, which seemed to be empty. "That baby sister has a sex life, or that her lover is apparently drinking blood?"

"Think about what I just said." Balthazar rose to his feet. "If Charity brought *anyone* here, then she would've brought *everyone* here. Her entire gang. Her tribe."

"The tribe?" I'd read oblique references to vampire tribes. I didn't know much about them, but they didn't sound good. I should have connected the gang with the idea of a tribe before now. "Like, they're all here in town? Right now. And—and coming back here?"

Lucas and Balthazar shared a look, and then Lucas grabbed my arm. "You're going back into Albion," he said. "Balthazar and I can handle this."

"What? No, I don't want to leave you."

"He's right," Balthazar said. "This is going to be more dangerous than I thought. You're not a fighter, Bianca."

"I've learned a lot." I refused to budge when Lucas tugged at my arm.

Balthazar shook his head. "Fencing class doesn't count."

"Bianca, think," Lucas said. "How often do me and Balthazar agree on anything?"

I hated it, but they were right. My powers wouldn't compare to those of a full vampire. Lucas's wouldn't either, but he had been trained for fighting since he was old enough to walk. If this turned into a full-fledged battle with a group of vampires, I would be out of my depth. That moment, I resolved to learn as much as I could, to become strong; I never wanted to be asked to leave for my own safety again.

But that was for the future. For now, all I could do was go.

"Do you want me to take the truck back into town?" *At least,* I thought sourly, *I've learned how to drive.* "Or I could wait down the road."

"Town's the only place safe," Lucas said.

Balthazar nodded. "Lucas should take you back, then return. And we'd better hide the fact that we're here." He leaned down and blew out the candle. The room went dark.

That's when we realized there was light outside the window.

"What—" I silenced myself instantly. Whatever it was holding the light outside (another candle? a flashlight?) didn't need to hear me, too. None of us moved, and I strained so hard to hear that I could feel all my muscles tensing. Lucas's hand tightened around my forearm. He and Balthazar shared a look. Balthazar put one hand on the doorknob and visibly braced himself; in the dim light I could see both fear and hope in his face.

He opened the door. Instead of twenty crazed killers lunging at us, we were met only by a frigid blast of wind. Squinting into the dark, I saw Charity.

She wore mismatched boots and a long, threadbare coat of gray wool that had been patched and mended in dozens of places. Her fair hair hung loose, blowing in front of her face. In one hand, Charity held a flashlight; her hands were sheltered from the chill only by thin, fingerless gloves. "Balthazar?" she said in a small voice, more childlike than ever.

"Charity." Though he had sought her for so long, Balthazar seemed unable to go to her and unsure of what to say. "Are you all right?"

She shrugged. Her dark eyes alighted upon Lucas. "Strange company you're keeping."

"I'm off duty," Lucas called, a smirk on his face. I didn't think joking was very appropriate and swatted his arm. He glared at me but shut up.

"The girl I understand," Charity said. "She's so much like poor Jane."

Balthazar's face went pale. "Don't say that name."

Who was Jane?

"You've been following me." She took one step backward and let the arm holding the flashlight drop; the illumination now only shone on her feet and the deepening snow on the ground. "I want you to stop it."

"I'll stop if you'll come home."

"Home? Where is home? We lived here once, but that was a long time ago." Charity brushed strands of hair from her face, the kind of confused gesture people make when they're struggling against tears. "Don't even think about asking me to come back to Evernight. You know how I feel about that woman."

Lucas and I shared a look.

Balthazar stepped off the front steps, and Charity skittered back a couple of steps in the snow. If I hadn't known better, I would've thought she was afraid of him. He said, "We could find somewhere else. Something else you and I could do. All that matters is that we're together. Charity, I miss you."

She stared down at the icy ground. "I don't miss you."

It hit Balthazar so hard that he flinched. I put one hand on his shoulder; it was the only comfort I could offer. Lucas watched me but said nothing.

"You remind me of too much," Charity said. "You remind me of what it felt like to be alive. To think of sunlight as something you could enjoy instead of something you could bear. To breathe and have it change you, refresh you, awaken you—instead of just churning on and on, some old useless habit that taunts you with what you used to be. To sigh and feel relief. To cry and let your sadness pass, instead of having it all bottled up inside you, forever and ever, getting more and more jumbled until you don't know who you are any longer."

"I know who I am," Balthazar said.

She shook her head. "No, Balthazar. You don't."

"At least promise me you'll leave the tribe." His voice broke with the strain of surrender, and my heart ached for him. "As long as you're hanging around with them, you're not safe from Black Cross."

Charity glared at Lucas. "While you're hanging around with Black Cross, you're not safe from my tribe. So try taking some advice before you give it, Balthazar. And get out of here now."

"Charity, we can't leave it like this."

Fear hit me so hard I nearly reeled. "She said *now*."

Both of them glanced back at me. Lucas said, "What?"

I knew before I knew, sensed it as deeply as I'd sensed anything. "They're here. Watching us. I think we'd better go."

Charity smiled at me. "You're much too smart to be hanging around with a vampire hunter. You'll probably get out alive."

Lucas turned toward the small grove of trees a couple hundred yards away, and his eyes narrowed. "Get to the truck."

"Not yet." Balthazar's eyes widened in dismay as Charity began walking off in the direction of the grove. "Give me one more chance to get through to her."

"Truck," Lucas repeated. I could see how badly he wanted to fight, but he remained focused on protecting me. "Now."

Instinct told me to run. But other instincts—my vampire instincts—told me that running prey was somehow more inviting. I forced myself to walk slowly toward the truck, and I grabbed Balthazar's arm so that I could pull him along. Lucas kept his stake at the ready as he edged toward the driver's side door.

My belly sank as I glimpsed, behind Charity, the footprints of at least half a dozen people. I knew that somewhere nearby they were watching us. I imagined that I could feel their eyes upon me, and, as the wind rustled through the ice-stiff trees, I thought I could hear faraway laughter.

Balthazar started walking faster. "We'll be all right," he said.

"I'm not so sure," I said, but then we were in the truck. The two doors slammed shut on either side of me, and Balthazar and Lucas shoved down the locks at the same moment. "Let's hurry, okay?"

Lucas turned the key and spun us out of there. As we turned, the headlights washed over Charity, who stood in the field, watching us go. The lights caught her eyes so that they reflected, just like a cat's.

"She thinks I've turned against her." Balthazar's big hands were braced against the truck's dashboard.

"You'll get to talk to Charity again," I said. "You know you will. Once you do, she'll understand."

"Charity will understand why I'm hanging out with a hunter from Black Cross? Then she understands more than I do."

"It's going to be okay," I promised him again. Lucas glanced sideways at us, then stared resolutely at the road.

The snow now was falling faster and thicker. By the time

we had reached the center of Albion, drifts had begun to form around the tires of parked cars. "Maybe you guys shouldn't drive back tonight," Lucas said. "Call the 'rents. Tell them you can't travel on the roads like this."

"We've got another hour or so at this rate. That's enough time for us to get back." Balthazar turned up the collar of his coat as if he could already feel the chill.

I knew that if I asked Balthazar to remain, he would, and I wanted to stay longer so that Lucas and I could have a few minutes alone together. If we managed to convince my parents that we shouldn't drive until the roads were cleared in the morning, then we'd have hours and hours—while poor Balthazar waited nearby. That would be awkward for me and worse for Balthazar, who looked miserable enough already. He needed to go back to Evernight Academy soon.

"We'll go now," I said to Lucas. "It's better this way."

Lucas stared at me, his expression shifting from disappointment into something harder to read. "Maybe it is."

Neither of us knew quite what to say after that.

Balthazar, apparently too dazed to notice the tension between me and Lucas, opened the truck door. A gale of frigid air whipped into the cabin, blowing my hair in my eyes. Lucas already had turned his attention back to the road like a man plotting a getaway. When Balthazar held his hand out to steady me in the snow, I took it. "Good-bye, Lucas," I said in a small voice.

Lucas leaned over to shut the truck door behind me. "See

you one month from tonight. Amherst. Town square. Usual time. Okay?" Then he sighed once and gave me an uneven smile. "Love you."

"I love you, too." But for once, those words didn't make everything okay.

Balthazar and I were both in such a terrible mood in the following days that I suggested we pretend that we were having an argument. Walking around together pretending to be a happy couple—neither of us could do it. But after a week, we could pull ourselves together, pretend to make up.

That left me with more time on my own, though, and anxiety welled up to fill every spare second. Thinking about how Lucas and I had parted made me feel seasick inside, like the ground beneath my feet wasn't steady any longer.

Vic noticed me brooding and tried to soothe my spirit by teaching me chess, but I was too fretful and distracted to keep the rules straight in my head, much less think about strategy.

"You are totally off your game these days," he said to me one afternoon, as the two of us sorted through the weekly shipment of foodstuffs. The human students apparently never noticed that a lot of their classmates didn't ever show up for these; people were too busy gleefully grabbing the stuff they'd ordered—boxes of pasta, packages of cookies. Vic put two bottles of orange soda in his canvas bag. "And I can't help noticing that Balthazar is also one mopey dude right now."

"Yeah. I guess." Feeling awkward, I stared down at Raquel's

list. I'd volunteered to pick up her order along with mine.

"Balty came to our last classic film festival—*Seven* and *The Usual Suspects*. The theme was Kevin Spacey: Before the Fall. Awesome double feature, right? But Balthazar stared at the corner the whole time."

"Vic, I know you mean well, but I don't want to talk about it."

He shrugged as he selected a few cans of soup. "I was only wondering if this had anything to do with Lucas."

"Maybe. Sort of. It's complicated."

"I guess Lucas is the kind of guy girls don't get over. Stormy, broody, all wild and stuff. Me, I can't do that bad-boy thing," Vic said. "Mine is a more mellow path. Lucas, though—"

"He's not doing a *thing*. He is who he is."

Quietly he said, "I know that. And I know you two aren't over. Tough for Balthazar, but I gotta call it like I see it."

I hoped he was right, and that hope lifted my spirits. "You're a lousy matchmaker, Vic."

"Not as lousy as you. Seriously, me and *Raquel*?"

"That was more than a year ago!" Once we were done laughing, we went back to our "shopping" and stocked up. I wasn't exactly in a good mood as I returned to my dorm room with my bags, but I felt better than I had in a long time.

Raquel turned out to be in the middle of one of her larger, messier art projects. This collage covered almost half our dorm room floor and smelled strongly of fresh glue and paint. "What is it?" I said, tiptoeing around damp newspaper and brushes.

"I call it *Ode to Anarchy*. See how the colors are in a constant state of collision?"

"Yeah, you can't miss that."

My halfhearted praise didn't put a dent in Raquel's enthusiasm. Paint striped her forearms, and she'd even gotten some orange in her hair, but she just kept grinning down at her work in progress while munching on a cookie. "You can walk around it, right?"

"Yeah, but I think tonight it might be better if I crashed with my parents."

"Will they let you do that?"

"Not all the time, but I don't think anybody will care about one night."

My parents turned out to be excited to see me. They'd once been very careful about the amount of time they'd let me hang out with them, worried as they had been by my refusal to get to know the other vampires at Evernight Academy. Now they were confident that I was growing up the way they wanted—and their door was open to me whenever I liked.

That had seemed natural to me before, but no longer.

"Dad?" I asked, as we changed the sheets on the bed in my upstairs room. "Did you always know I'd eventually be a vampire? A full vampire, I mean."

"Of course." He kept his eyes on his work, in this case a neat hospital corner. "Once you grow up and take a life—and you know we can find a decent way to handle that—then you'll complete the change."

"I'm not so sure."

"Honey, it's going to be okay." He put one hand on my shoulder, and even his crooked, oft-broken nose couldn't disguise the gentleness in his expression. "You're worried about it, I know. But if we find someone who's already dying, not even conscious anymore—you'd be doing them a favor. Their last act will be giving you immortality. Don't you think they'd want to do that for you?"

"I won't know, because I won't know them at all, will I?" How had I ever found that idea comforting? For the first time, it struck me how presumptuous it was, and how callous it was to assume that I had the right to end a life, even one at its conclusion, for my own convenience. "But that's not what I mean. You keep saying, when I kill. *When* I kill. What happens if I don't?"

"You will."

"But what happens if I don't?" I'd never pressed for this answer before; I'd never felt like I had to. Now all those unasked questions were weighing down on me at once and getting heavier all the time. "I just want to know what the alternative is. Isn't there somebody who would know? Mrs. Bethany, maybe?"

"Mrs. Bethany will tell you exactly what I'm about to tell you, which is that there's really only one choice for you to make. I don't want to hear you talking like this again. And don't say anything to your mother—you'd upset her." Dad took a deep breath, obviously trying to calm himself. "Besides, Bianca, how long can it be? You were eager enough for human blood last year."

That was as close as my father had come to mentioning Lucas in months. I felt my cheeks flush red.

"I'm not naive. I realize you and Balthazar must have drunk each other's blood by now." He said it sort of quickly; maybe he was as embarrassed as I was. "You have to be close to being ready to drink and kill for real. I know you're getting hungrier just from your appetite on Sundays. If you're anxious about it, I don't blame you. Just don't let your anxiety drive you to this kind of crazy talk. Have I made myself clear?"

I couldn't speak, so I just nodded.

Not long afterward, I turned out my lights and tried to talk myself into going to bed. But not only was I confused by my conversation with my father, I was also starving.

The power of suggestion at work, I thought. Dad had mentioned my appetite, and now I was hungrier than I'd been in a very long time— this, despite the fact that I'd drunk a full pint at dinner.

Well, at least I didn't have to sneak a thermos from under the bed. My parents' refrigerator held all the blood I needed.

I tiptoed down the hallway, past my sleeping parents, into the kitchen. My bare feet padded softly against the tile floor. Instead of turning on the lamp, I relied on my night vision and the sliver of illumination that widened as I opened the fridge door. Although some real food for me was on the lowest shelf, mostly the fridge was laden with bottles and jugs and bags of blood. Carefully I took one of the bags in my hand; I usually didn't drink these, because they were hard to get—treats that my parents needed more than I did. They contained human blood.

Maybe my father was right. Maybe my craving for blood had become so acute because I hadn't had any human blood for so long. Maybe that was what I needed now. If Dad tried to yell at me for taking his stash, I'd point out that he'd kind of suggested it.

I squeezed a bag into a large mug, then nuked that in the microwave. Though the timer chimed loudly enough to make me flinch, my parents didn't awaken, and I hurried back into my room.

The heated mug made my fingers sting, but the rich, meaty scent of the blood overwhelmed my discomfort, my worries, and pretty much everything else. Quickly I lifted the mug to my lips and drank.

Yes. That was it—what I'd needed, bone deep. The heat swirled down into the center of me, warming me from within. Human blood did something to me animal blood never did—it made me feel exhilarated, connected, and strong. I clutched the mug with both hands, gulping the blood down so quickly I could hardly breathe. I felt as though I were swimming in the warmth of it. The rest of the world was cold by comparison—

Wait.

I lowered the mug and licked my lips clean as I took stock. The air in my room had suddenly become much chillier. Had one of the windows blown open? No, they were all still shut, and covered with frost. But had they been covered with frost a few minutes ago? Just before I'd gotten up for the blood, I'd looked at the outline of the gargoyle outside the window, but now he was invisible behind a curtain of filmy white.

When I exhaled, my breath made a puff in the air. I began to shake. A bluish glow flickered behind the window, and then I heard a tapping on the glass. Like fingernails. Fear gripped me, but I couldn't turn away.

I went to the window and started rubbing my bare hand across the frost. The cold made my skin sting, but the frost melted into cloudy swirls, through which I could see. A girl stared back at me, about my age, with short, pale dark hair and hollow eyes. She looked completely normal—except for the part where she was almost transparent. And floating outside my tower window.

The wraith had returned.

Chapter Sixteen

THE GHOST SWAM IN SHADES OF WATERY BLUE-green, her hair and skin the palest aqua. Though I could see through her, she was as real as anyone I had ever met. Her eyes bored into mine, not with anger or hatred but with some emotion I couldn't comprehend.

Her lips moved, and I saw small glitters of light upon her lips and cheeks—fragments of ice, I realized. But still there was no sound.

Trembling, I moved closer to the glass. Despite my fear, I wanted to finally understand what was going on. The ghost twitched, and I breathed out sharply. My warm breath made a foggy circle on the glass.

In that circle appeared thin, shaky letters: **We want what's fair.**

"Fair?" That didn't make sense to me, but what about this did? At least I might finally have a chance to find out what they'd been trying to say. I realized that I wasn't afraid—well, at least, not as much afraid as curious. "What do you mean?"

She didn't answer. Her dark eyes were almost mocking now. The foggy spot slowly vanished, taking her words away.

After a long moment, during which it felt like my heart would pound through my chest, I realized what she was waiting for. Shakily I leaned toward the glass again and breathed out once more.

In the foggy spot appeared the words: *You don't belong to them.*

"What?" I had no idea what that could mean. Mostly I wanted to turn and run for my parents. Instead, I exhaled against the glass so the wraith could speak.

You're not like them.

"No, I'm not." It was the only thing I truly knew about myself, the only thing I'd ever known. The wraith was the first one who had ever admitted that truth. "Who am I like?"

Another breath. This time the wraith smiled, and it wasn't reassuring.

You're like me.

Then I heard a terrible gasp behind me and turned to see Mom in my doorway. Her face was whiter than the frost. "Bianca! Come here! Get away from that thing!"

"I—" The word choked off; my throat was too dry for speech. I swallowed hard. "I think it's okay."

"Adrian!" Mom was calling for Dad, running away. Her footsteps echoed down the hall.

The wraith shrank back. "Wait—don't leave!" I pressed my

hands to the glass even as it frosted over, erasing the final words she'd written. Quickly I rubbed it to try to clear my view, so I could see if she was still out there. But all the warmth had been leached from my hands, so the ice didn't melt as quickly. By the time I could see again, the wraith was gone.

Mom and Dad came pounding into the room, their night-clothes disheveled and eyes wide. My father growled, "Where is it?"

"It left. I think it's okay."

Mom looked at me like I had gone insane. "Okay? *Okay?* That thing came here to hurt you, Bianca." Her eyes were wild. "You didn't even know the wraiths were more than children's stories a few months ago. Now you're an expert?"

My father squeezed my shoulders. "It's gone," he said. I'd never valued his steadiness more. "Celia, it's all over."

"It isn't." Mom's voice was muffled, and I realized she was crying. "You know it isn't. They want to take Bianca away from us."

I held one shaky hand out to her. "Mom, that's— It's not— You aren't making any sense. What does that mean?" Then I thought of the letters carved in frost: *Ours.*

"Sweetheart—" She held one hand out to me, but her eyes darted toward my father. I couldn't see his face, so I didn't know what passed between them in that moment. I only knew that my mother sighed and closed her hand around mine. "I'm sorry. The wraith frightened me. That's all."

That wasn't all, and every person in the room knew it. Maybe

I should have pressed them then and there, but Mom looked so shattered. "I'm okay," I said. "Everyone's okay. It wasn't nearly as bad as before."

"Maybe they're going away," Mom said. "Maybe they're giving up."

"Maybe." Dad didn't sound like he believed that, but like he wanted to. "Bianca, did the wraith say anything to you?"

I opened my mouth to reply honestly, but found myself instead saying, "No. There wasn't time. It was quick."

"Please let this be over," Mom whispered. If she hadn't been a vampire, I would've been sure she was praying. I hugged her tightly, and then Dad put his arms around both of us. Our misunderstandings didn't seem to matter as much as the embrace.

At first I thought I would keep the wraith's odd visit secret, but I was too shaken to go it totally alone.

"You saw a ghost outside your room," Raquel repeated as we huddled together in a corner of the great hall. Students had slowly resumed studying and hanging out there, though never alone. "You're sure it was a girl."

"She was as real as you are. And she spoke—well, *wrote* words in frost to me."

"What did she say?"

I'd lied to Raquel since the day we met; I'd have to keep lying to her forever. But it never became any easier. "Just—be careful."

"Be careful? She's the ghost! What *else* is it we're supposed to be scared of?" Raquel fiddled nervously with the tawny leather bracelet on her wrist. "I don't like the sound of this."

"We'll be okay. We have to believe that." I knew I hadn't convinced Raquel, and I wasn't very sure myself.

She said we were alike, I thought. What could that mean? I wasn't a ghost of any kind. First of all, I was alive, and, second, when I died, I'd turn into a vampire. So what had she been talking about?

Balthazar walked into the great hall. When he saw me, he gave me a small, hopeful smile.

"Looks like somebody wants to make up," Raquel said.

I had almost forgotten that Balthazar and I were pretending to be an arguing couple, instead of pretending to be a dating couple. "I ought to talk to him."

"Yeah, do that." Raquel gathered her stuff together. "I'm going online to see if there are any new websites about casting out ghosts or something."

"New websites?"

"You think I haven't looked before? But so far they're useless. Just crackpots making stuff up. The truth is crazier than anything they can imagine."

"I believe it," I said faintly.

Balthazar waited for me at the entrance to the great hall, and I realized that he had both his gym bag and mine looped over one arm. "Did you bring those from the gear room?" I asked.

"I thought we might put in a little fencing practice."

We went upstairs, changed, and entered the fencing room.

The class had progressed slowly, or so it seemed to me; we had only recently started using swords instead of sticks, and the "fighting" we did was more like "knocking swords together about twice before the teacher stopped everything and explained we were doing it wrong." However, I could tell that my arm muscles had become stronger—they hurt less, anyway—and my balance was improving. When Balthazar and I faced each other alone in the fencing room, dressed in white, faces hidden behind steel masks, I realized I was relishing the opportunity to test myself. Not that I stood a chance against Balthazar, but this time I could feel the *rightness* of my moves, the muscles in my body responding to the motion, like they'd known how to do this all along and had been waiting for me to catch up.

For a long time, there was no sound in the room but my panting, the padding of our feet on the mat, and the chirping of steel on steel. After Balthazar disarmed me for the third time, though, we each paused—partly because I was tired, but mostly because I could tell Balthazar was ready to talk.

I wiped my sweaty face on a towel. "You seem better," I said. "Not at fencing—that, too, maybe—but I meant, generally."

"Charity may hate me right now." Balthazar's words were measured, as though he'd repeated them to himself very often. He sat on one of the benches that lined the room and peeled off his mask. "That just makes it more important for me to find her again. It could take me a long time to get through to her, but I can do it."

"Are you sure?"

"Yes."

"Have you thought about what it means if we're wrong?" Remembering her sweet, innocent face made me feel absurd for even suggesting this, but I wanted to be totally sure. "If Charity's tribe is killing people—and she's hanging out with them—"

"I'm sure Charity is safe. I know you're sure, too, really. But Black Cross's idea of being sure is killing her along with her tribe," Balthazar said. "That death counts as much as any other. Maybe Lucas doesn't believe that, but I know you do."

I didn't know what shook me more—Balthazar's absolute faith in his sister or my uncertainty about what I believed. I sat beside him, half noticing that in the mirror across the room, my reflection was sharp and clear, while his was hazy. He must not have eaten in a day or two. "Balthazar, you haven't seen her in more than thirty-five years. She's taken up with an entirely new gang of vampires, apparently dangerous ones. How can you be so sure she hasn't changed?"

His eyes were sad. "We don't change, Bianca. That's the tragedy of what we are. That's part of what it means to be dead."

My heart thumped reassuringly fast and strong in my chest. *I'm alive,* I thought. *I'm not like the others. I'm still alive.*

Chapter Seventeen

"OTHELLO SHOULDN'T KILL HER EVEN IF HE DOES think she's cheating on him." I couldn't believe I had to argue this. Did all vampires take killing so casually? "He's not wrong because Desdemona is innocent. He's wrong because he thinks he has the right to kill his wife."

"That's not what Shakespeare would've thought." Courtney flipped her blond hair over her shoulder. "Back in that day, women had, like, *no* rights. Isn't that so?"

Mrs. Bethany, uncharacteristically, didn't take sides. She wasn't pacing the room today. Instead, she watched us from her desk, distant but amused. "The status of women has changed over the centuries, Miss Briganti, but the murder of a spouse has rarely been taken lightly." She tapped upon the page. "Both of you seem to assume that Desdemona's murder is cold and calculated. Before our next class, I hope you'll both review the sections of the play that deal with Othello's quick temper. We'll also cover how that relates to the question of race in the play. Class dismissed."

Everyone glanced around, all of us making sure we'd heard correctly. Mrs. Bethany letting us out early? Sure, it was only five minutes before the bell, but for her, that was as good as five hours. Slowly, people began gathering their books, like they were waiting for Mrs. Bethany to change her mind, but she didn't.

I shut my notebook and stuffed it inside my backpack, as eager as anyone to escape—until Mrs. Bethany said, "Miss Olivier, please remain a moment." She shut the door behind the last student to leave. "Your parents inform me that you will be taking another trip outside the grounds this weekend with Mr. More."

"That's right."

"I allowed these outings in the belief that Mr. More was helping you to assimilate more completely into our world." She walked toward my desk, her hands clasped in front of her. The thick grooves in her nails seemed darker than usual. "Given your recent behavior regarding the wraith—which your parents reported to me—I doubt that your trips are having the desired effect."

Mom and Dad told Mrs. Bethany about my latest encounter with the wraith? And it sounded like they had told her I'd been talking to the ghost, too—which meant they knew I'd lied and had said nothing to me, only to Mrs. Bethany. I should've expected it, but the betrayed confidence was painful nonetheless. I held my chin high. "I don't see why becoming a vampire means I have to automatically try to hurt things I don't understand."

She cocked her head, studying me with her bright, bird-like eyes. "Becoming a vampire means accepting that you must

✤ 243 ✤

adhere to certain rules. We are stronger than humans, but we have vulnerabilities. We have enemies. The rules that protect you from those enemies are among the most important you will ever learn."

"How do you know the wraith is my enemy?"

"How do you know it's not?"

I couldn't believe I was going to end up telling Mrs. Bethany this, but then again, she already knew most of it—and she was probably the only one with answers. "She tried to communicate. She said that we were alike—she and I."

"How curious."

"What did that mean? Do you know?"

"When I spoke about curiosity, Miss Olivier, I meant that it was odd that a girl such as yourself wouldn't recognize that many adversaries begin their attacks with kindness. What better way to lure an innocent off her guard? After your experiences with Lucas Ross, I would think you'd know better." I stared down at my desk, trying to hide my discomfort, but the amusement in her voice told me I'd failed. "I had also thought that your acquaintance with Mr. More would help you put Mr. Ross more firmly behind you. Perhaps I was wrong."

"Lucas is not a part of my life." The words sounded so final. "Balthazar's been really good to me."

"How little you appreciate what you have." Mrs. Bethany walked away from me, her heels clicking on the floor. "You may leave."

"Balthazar and I—we can still go this weekend, right?"

Her gaze raked sharply over me. "I see no reason to change my earlier decision," she said. "For now."

From this moment on, I realized, any trip I took away from the Evernight campus might be my last.

Amherst seemed unnaturally quiet. Midterms, I guessed, or just a chill keeping the college students in their dorms.

The first time I had come to the town square, the streets had been filled with celebrating kids, the music and lights an echo of the jubilation I'd felt knowing that Lucas was near. Now the streets were still and dark, and uncertainty shadowed my mood.

"Charity just—came up to you here?" Balthazar walked by my side, his long coat billowing slightly in the wind. "Picked you out of a huge crowd?"

"She knew I was a vampire, of course."

"With you it's not that easy to tell, not yet."

I glanced at him. Silhouetted as he was by the streetlights, Balthazar's expression was difficult to read. "Does that mean I'm becoming, well, more *vampire*?"

"It might mean that Charity is becoming more perceptive. That her senses are sharper." After a pause, he continued, "That happens sometimes, when we consume more human blood."

"You think she might have—that she's—"

"It's possible to drink without killing. You know that as well as anyone." He wouldn't meet my eyes. Then Balthazar stopped walking and turned around. When I did the same, I realized that we'd been followed.

"Lucas?" I took a couple of steps toward him. He stood there with his hands in his pockets, wearing an old canvas coat too thin for the weather. His eyes looked both distant and sort of sad—the way he used to look at me at Evernight in the early days before he was willing to risk our being together. I'd forgotten that he had fought our attraction in the beginning. "How long have you been following us?"

"Just long enough to remind Balthazar here what I can do." Lucas smiled, but it didn't reach his eyes.

Balthazar didn't smile at all. "We should split up for this. If Charity sees us together again, I'll never get another chance to talk to her."

Lucas would've liked to protest, I could tell. Quickly I said, "We'll split up. Balthazar can head toward the neighborhoods you've seen her in, I'll stick to the square, and you can keep checking the main roads out of town."

"I'm on my own tonight, huh?" Lucas shrugged. "Sure. Why not? Sounds like a plan."

He walked away from us without another word. We hadn't even touched.

"He's upset," Balthazar said quietly. "Maybe you should go after him."

I wanted to. Something inside me pulled toward Lucas, but I resisted. "We have a plan. We'll stick to it. If we don't find some sign of her tribe in a couple of hours, maybe we can drive to one of the other nearby towns."

Balthazar turned up the collar of his coat. "Thanks. I appreciate it." Within a few seconds, he, too, was gone.

That left me alone. I didn't really expect Charity to seek me out again, not when both her brother and her enemy were available. So while I walked up and down the street, shivering from the cold and casting the occasional wistful glance at a nearby coffeehouse, I had time to evaluate what was going on.

Lucas was angry with me. It couldn't be about Balthazar—could it? There wasn't any reason for him to be jealous. Even as I thought that, I remembered how close together we'd been walking when Lucas called out to us. My cheeks flushed, and I pushed the memory away. No, it couldn't be that, I decided. Lucas had been even more hot-tempered than usual lately. So who knew why he might decide to get upset? It could be anything. And maybe I was tired of him taking out his moods on me.

Just as I was working myself into a real rage, a flash of gold down the street caught my attention. Long, dark blond hair—something familiar in her walk—

Charity?

But it wasn't. It was Courtney.

Courtney was walking along the sidewalk at the far end of the square, headed toward the cozy residential neighborhood I'd seen on my last time here. The clothes she wore seemed very odd, for her: old jeans, a baggy black sweater, and a gray trench coat. I was reminded of the silly way I'd dressed for my own amateurish attempts at burglary just before school started.

Then I realized Courtney was doing the same thing I'd been doing: She was sneaking around. She'd been so catty about Balthazar supposedly straying. Had she followed us here tonight? Did she suspect the truth? We couldn't afford to get caught, especially not with Lucas so close. If Courtney saw him, it would all be over.

Hurriedly I followed her as she walked out of the square. Courtney never glanced back once, so I didn't bother trying to hide. Obviously she hadn't seen me, but could she be following Balthazar? This was the general area he'd gone to search. I kept looking for him as we walked past old wooden houses, each yard filled with the bits and pieces that suggested the lives within—a child's bicycle tipped on one side, a porch swing, or a white bird-bath on a pedestal. Courtney never seemed to pay attention to any of it or even to be looking around for Balthazar or anybody else. Apparently she knew exactly where she was headed.

Her footsteps slowed as she neared a pale-blue house, one with light shining from all the windows. Even half a block away, I could hear music and chatter coming from within, and as I stepped closer, I saw that the house was crowded with people holding plates of food or bottles of beer. A few balloons had floated up to the ceiling.

Courtney crouched in the bushes next to one of the big windows, looking up at the scene within. I couldn't get close enough to be entirely certain what she was doing, other than watching.

Is she stalking someone? There was a time I would have thought that even somebody as mean-spirited as Courtney would never kill a human being. But now I wasn't as sure about vampires as I had been. My skin prickled with dread.

I crept closer. Within the house, I heard people begin to sing happy birthday to someone named Nicole. Courtney didn't make a move; she remained completely still with her upturned face tinted gold in the light from the window. I was only ten feet behind her.

At first I didn't pay any attention to the small room nearest to me—it had emptied out when people started singing. But then, from inside the house, a familiar smile caught my eye. Courtney's smile.

I pressed my face to the glass and realized that Courtney's photo stood among those atop an upright piano. The photograph showed her in a maroon-and-white cheerleader's uniform, her hair in a curly ponytail on one side of her head, the sort of style and makeup people wore back in the 1980s—back when Courtney was alive.

This is her family. This is her home.

The song ended, and everyone cheered and clapped. I looked back at Courtney, who brought her hands together as if she were clapping, but without making any sound. Her eyes gleamed wetly in the reflected light.

People started moving back into the room next to me, and I ducked down beneath the windowsill. I caught a brief glimpse of a woman who looked to be around forty, with her blond hair in a sensible bob and a friendly smile on her face; it was a shock to realize the woman was essentially an older version of Courtney. Her sister, perhaps.

"You!"

I flinched. Courtney had turned around—to follow the party, probably—and had discovered me.

"What are you doing here? You little sneak!" Courtney's face was twisted in a furious grimace, despite the fact that her cheeks still shone with tears. "What makes you think you have the right to follow me around?"

"I wasn't—I didn't mean to—" But I *had* been following her, and I had meant to, and there was no way for me to explain why without saying too much. "How did you even get into town? You're supposed to get Mrs. Bethany's permission before leaving campus!"

"There's a laundry truck you can hitch a ride on, which you might've noticed if you weren't so completely stupid." Grabbing my elbow, Courtney dragged me away from the house. She didn't want us to be seen, I realized. The people inside only knew that Courtney had died a quarter of a century ago, nothing more. If they saw her, risen from the dead, a vampire—I couldn't even imagine how they would react. Probably Courtney couldn't either.

"I'm sorry," I said, more quietly. "I wouldn't have followed you if I'd known."

"Known what? What is it that you think you know?" Courtney grinned at me, though the grin was a terrible fake that made her look sadder than her tears. "All I know is that you're supposed to be with Balthazar tonight, and you're not."

Crap. I should've known Courtney's gossip radar could never go down for very long.

"What's the matter, Bianca? Trouble in paradise?" She folded her arms and tossed her hair, once again the queen of the school, totally in command. "Did you guys have a fight? Another fight, that is?"

"If it's none of my business that you're here, then it's none of your business that I'm here. So you leave me alone, and I'll do the same for you."

Although Courtney clearly wanted to rub in the supposed failure of my supposed relationship, she apparently wanted to hush me up even more. "You say one word about this—one word to *anyone*—I will know."

"Your secret is safe with me."

"I don't have any secrets!"

We could still hear the laughter from the party. I stared at Courtney, hard, and her face fell. She turned to go—and then froze. When I heard the voices, I froze, too. *No, no, no, not now!*

"We don't know that Bianca's in trouble," Lucas said.

Balthazar walked next to him, their paces in stride. "She's not on the square where we arranged to meet. That doesn't spell trouble to you?"

"Bianca has a way of not being where she's supposed to be. If you knew her better, you might realize that," Lucas said. Then he stopped in his tracks. I knew that he had seen Courtney and me, which meant that Courtney had seen him. Lucas. The Black Cross hunter.

"Ohmigod," she breathed. "You've been—Lucas Ross—this is—"

"Courtney, listen to me." Balthazar hurried toward us, hands outstretched. It was the most attention he'd ever paid her, but she shrank back as if repulsed. "I can explain."

"You can explain that you're hanging out with a Black Cross hunter? That ought to be good."

Lucas's jaw was clenched. "I'm not hunting tonight."

"Oh, wow, that's a huge relief. Not out to kill me or my friends *tonight*. Gosh, let's be BFFs until tomorrow when you change your mind." Courtney clutched her trench coat more tightly around herself. "I get you, Lucas. You're a rabid psycho killer, so, that's your motive. I get you, too, Bianca. Still in love with your psycho ex. That's pathetic, and honestly pretty much what I should've expected from a loser like you. But Balthazar? What are you doing? What could you possibly be thinking?"

"I can explain if you'll listen." Balthazar looked unnerved now—even frightened. I'd never seen him frightened before, not even at the Autumn Ball. He knew, as I knew, that Courtney would almost certainly report us to Mrs. Bethany.

Courtney didn't listen. She stomped down the block without another word.

Lucas gestured after her. "What—are you going to just let her go?"

"What do you want us to do?" I protested. "Stake her?"

Courtney, who apparently couldn't tell I was being sarcastic, started to run. Balthazar took off after her, and Lucas and

I followed. I knew that Balthazar and I were trying to catch Courtney to reassure her and explain, but Lucas—I wasn't sure about Lucas.

I hated that I wasn't sure.

"Courtney, wait!" I called.

She only ran faster. Balthazar was quicker, though, and he managed to grab her shoulder and spin her around. Courtney shrieked, but Balthazar pleaded, "We're not going to hurt you."

"Not hurt me? What does the guy from Black Cross say about that?"

Lucas sighed heavily. "You're safe."

Courtney cocked her head, like he'd spoken in some language she didn't understand. "Whatever this bizarro arrangement is, this is totally screwed up."

"Sometimes I agree with you," Balthazar said. "The point is, it's no danger to you or to any other vampire, and we'd appreciate it if you would keep it a secret." Poor Balthazar—he'd try to be calm and reasonable with a rampaging bull.

"If you're in with Black Cross, I can't keep that secret." Courtney backed away from us. She bumped against a parked minivan, then slid around it, her hands pressed flat against the metal like a blind person finding her way. "That's dangerous. You should know better, Balthazar. You're the one Mrs. Bethany will blame."

Then Courtney cried out and clutched at her chest—with the point of a stake sticking between her fingers.

I gasped. For one terrible second, I thought Lucas had

thrown the stake at her, but no—the blow had come from behind. Courtney staggered two steps forward, then fell face down into the street with the stake protruding from her back. Behind her stood Charity.

Balthazar stared at his sister, not in horror but in wonder. Charity wore jeans that had faded to gray and showed the black tights she wore through half a dozen rips and holes. Her dingy sweater had frayed at the neck. She smiled at him sadly. "The girl would have hurt you," she said, nudging Courtney's inert body with her silver-slippered toe. "Couldn't let her do that, could I?"

"Charity. You shouldn't have—but you wanted to help, and for that—thank you." Balthazar reached out one hand, but Charity skipped back a few steps.

"She asked good questions, though." Charity's dark eyes darted toward Lucas. "Why are you spending so much time with Black Cross? Especially while they're hunting me?"

I turned toward Lucas. "You said they weren't hunting her any longer! You promised!"

"We aren't! At least as far as I know, we aren't!" Lucas protested. I was starting to wonder if "as far as I know" wasn't just a dodge, whether Lucas simply chose not to know anything that would inconvenience him. Every bit of the fear and upset I'd felt in the past several minutes was swirling around inside me, desperate for someplace to go, and now it was all being drawn toward Lucas.

"They're trying to kill me," Charity said. "My brother helps them. How would you feel, if you were me?"

Balthazar shook his head. "Lucas promised me they'd stop hunting you if I found you instead."

"So you only meant to be a good big brother? To drag me off kicking and screaming to Evernight again?"

"Charity. Please." Balthazar's voice was only a rasp. "It's been thirty-five years since we've been together."

"Since we lived together, maybe. But I've seen you around long before this, long before Albion. I've been paying attention." Charity hugged herself. "I want the hunter's weapons."

Lucas's jaw set. "Oh, hell, no."

"Lucas," I whispered. "Come on. She doesn't trust you."

"I don't trust her either!"

"We'll all get rid of any weapons we have," Balthazar said, trying to be reasonable.

"You're vampires," Lucas said. "You guys are your own weapons."

Charity held out her hands. "Then keep all your weapons but one. Give me just one. That large knife you held on me in the hospital, maybe. I'd feel safe then."

"I wouldn't," Lucas said.

"I'll be okay," I promised him. Charity looked so young and so cold; she was shaking as she stood there, her little hands outstretched and begging. "Lucas, please."

Lucas gave me the dirtiest look I'd ever seen, but he reached into his coat and pulled out his broad knife. Instead of handing it to Charity, he let the blade clatter onto the pavement. He and

Charity kept their eyes locked as she knelt to retrieve it, and he put one hand to his belt, where I knew he kept a stake.

Maybe we should've turned to Courtney before any of this, but we all knew that a stake through the heart doesn't really kill a vampire—at least, not permanently. Withdraw the stake, and the vampire revives, none the worse for wear. Already I was thinking that eventually we'd have to pull the stake out of Courtney and deal with the fact that she'd be even angrier when she regained consciousness.

Lucas said, "We good?"

"Yeah." Charity gave him a very strange smile. "We are. At least for tonight, hunter, you're safe from me."

For some reason, Lucas took this as a sign that he was now the best person to get through to her. "You need to listen to your brother. I don't run Black Cross, not by a long shot. If you want to be safe from the hunt, you better play by his rules."

"I've learned the rules to play by," Charity said. "And you're the ones who ought to worry about being safe."

"What have you done, Charity?" Balthazar took her arms in his hands—not like he was about to hug her, but instead as though he were going to shake her. "Answer me."

"I've made new friends. They've taught me the way. You should come with us, Balthazar. You'd be so much happier looking toward the future instead of remaining trapped in the past."

"What are you talking about?" I demanded.

Charity wrested herself free from her brother. "I mean that there's only one real way to be a vampire, and it doesn't involve longing for things you don't have or spending time with people you knew when you were alive or ironing your Evernight Academy uniform every morning. It means wanting what you've got. Taking what you can take. Embracing what you have become."

"Killing," Lucas said. "You mean, the only real way to be a vampire is by killing."

Charity smiled at him as she knelt beside Courtney's limp body. "You'd know all about killing, wouldn't you?"

Lucas shook his head. "What I do isn't the same thing."

"Really? Let's see what your weapons are good for." Charity gave Lucas's broad knife a twirl, then brought it down with unbelievable force across Courtney's neck, beheading her.

Beheading kills a vampire forever.

Courtney's body stiffened. Her skin instantly turned gray and dried, shriveling around her bones as her flesh withered. Her detached head lolled from side to side. The corner of Courtney's face that I could see wasn't a face anymore, just something papery and earth-colored stretched over a skull. When vampires die, their bodies decay to the point they would've reached since that first death. The oldest ones turn to dust. Courtney had been dead only twenty-five years, so there was still a lot left of her. Too much.

I gasped. Balthazar turned his head away. Charity smiled up at Lucas. "That's one taken care of for you, hunter. Now your secret is safe, Balthazar. Never say I don't love you."

Immediately she turned from us and ran, vanishing almost instantly into the underbrush. Balthazar took two halting steps after her before he stopped.

Charity killed Courtney. Charity killed. I watched her do it. I'd thought she was so helpless, so frightened, so weak—could I have been completely wrong? I remembered Lucas's distrust of Charity, and my insistence upon protecting her, and shame welled up in me as strongly as horror. How much of this was my fault?

For a few moments, none of us could speak. Finally, I said, "What are we going to do?"

"What?" Balthazar was still staring in the direction Charity had disappeared.

"About the body, she means." Lucas grimaced as he took a closer look. "The neighbors come out in the morning and find this, they're gonna freak out. Run tests. The fact that it's a twenty-five-year-old corpse will only make them ask more questions."

Could they match Courtney's DNA? Her dental records? I felt a wave of pure horror at the thought of that nice family down the block learning that Courtney's body had been found, decayed and dumped on their own street during a birthday party. That was about the worst thing I could imagine.

"We have to get her out of here," I said. "We should bury her somewhere."

"Digging in frozen ground is tough," Lucas said. "Better to burn her."

He didn't say it meanly—just, like, that was reality. But Lucas didn't have a vampire's horror of fire, and he couldn't know how gruesome it sounded to me, burning someone instead of burying them properly.

Maybe it was my disgust at the idea of cremation. Maybe it was my own confused feelings about watching Courtney die—I'd never liked her, but I'd never have wished for her to be murdered. Maybe it was the tension of nearly having our cover blown, then having it saved in the worst possible way. Maybe it was watching Balthazar look so lost. Maybe it was anger at myself for my foolish belief in Charity's goodness. Maybe it was months of separation finally taking their toll.

Whatever it was about that moment, it made something inside me snap.

"Burn her up. Burn her up." I wheeled toward Lucas, so angry that I shook. "You don't even think of her as a person, do you? Because vampires aren't people! Not to you!"

"Whoa, whoa—that's not what I said." Lucas held up his hands. "It's only cremation, Bianca."

"It's not only cremation, not to you. You think vampires aren't like other people, and so you think it's fine to treat them however you want. You could've killed Courtney yourself. You could've killed Balthazar. If we hadn't met at Evernight, you might even have killed me someday. You wouldn't have thought twice about it, would you?"

Lucas couldn't stand being yelled at like that. I could see the last remnants of his self-control incinerate as his temper took over. "Well, you think vampires never, ever hurt anybody, even though every single one of you is hardwired to drink blood and to kill! Even after Erich! Even after this! What the hell is that about, Bianca? I've tried to make you see the truth, but you won't see anything you don't want to see."

Quietly, from beside us, Balthazar said, "I'm going to go get the car, bring it around." We ignored him.

"You're still in Black Cross," I said, shaking with rage. "Still, more than a year after you found out that I'm a vampire, too. You talked about leaving, but that's all it is, isn't it? Just talk! Am I the only one who has to change? The one who has to give everything up?"

"What have you given up, Bianca? You haven't left Evernight. You haven't stopped planning on becoming a vampire. You get to be your parents' perfect daughter and Balthazar's perfect girlfriend and keep me on the side where it's convenient for you."

"Convenient? You think anything about this is convenient?"

"You looked pretty comfortable with the situation earlier tonight."

He was referring to my walking beside Balthazar. Something as simple as a stroll had turned into ammunition to be used against me. Tears had begun to sting my eyes. "I should have known. You never stopped hating vampires. That made it inevitable that someday—someday you'd hate me."

Lucas looked like he'd been punched in the gut. "Bianca—God, please, you know I don't hate you."

"Maybe you don't now, but you will." My throat tightened

so much that it hurt to talk. "I don't know why I ever thought this would work."

"Bianca—"

"Go away. Just go."

"I'm not leaving you alone here."

"Balthazar will be back with the car any second."

Lucas's expression hardened. "I guess Balthazar takes real good care of you. Don't need my help anymore."

"No." My voice broke on the word, but he believed me anyway.

"Fine." Lucas stalked off into the darkness. He walked the opposite direction from Charity, so I knew he wasn't on the hunt, but he vanished into the dark as quickly as she had. I was alone.

Did we just break up? Did I just dump Lucas?

I thought so, but I wasn't sure. Somehow not knowing for absolute sure made it even worse. But we hadn't figured out where or how to see each other again—which meant I might not ever be able to find him again. If he didn't come after me, we'd never see each other after tonight. I leaned against the minivan and started to cry. Then I thought it was incredibly petty of me, crying over my breakup while Courtney was lying dead at my feet, but that only made me sob harder.

It seemed like eternity before Balthazar pulled up in the car, though really it couldn't have been even ten minutes. He saw me crying and said, "It didn't end well, I guess." I shook my head. "It's okay. Get in the car, Bianca. I'll see to Courtney."

Balthazar rolled up Courtney's body in an old blanket that

must have been in the trunk, which was where he put her. I didn't watch; I sat in the passenger seat and bawled. By the time he was done cleaning up the area and locking the trunk, the worst of my sobbing had passed. Tears still rolled down my cheeks, but I felt numb inside.

When he got in the car, I whispered, "What are we going to do?"

"We'll have to drive into the countryside and build a fire." He cast an uncertain glance at me. "Lucas was right about the frozen ground."

"Oh. Okay."

Balthazar started the car. I looked behind us at the house where Courtney's family was still celebrating a birthday party. As we drove away, I could see their silhouettes in the windows. They were dancing.

Chapter Eighteen

"THANK GOD WE'RE FINALLY SEEING SIGNS OF spring," Raquel said, opening our window to let in the breeze. "If I'd woken up one more morning and seen icicles, I swear I would've stabbed somebody with one."

"Can you not talk about stabbing people, please?" I was curled on my bed, in the same pajamas I'd worn all weekend, flipping through one of Raquel's back issues of *Wired*. It wasn't very good reading—by this point she'd cannibalized virtually all the pictures for her art projects—but then, I wasn't really concentrating.

Raquel pushed the magazine down so we were face-to-face. "Remember earlier this year?" she said, more quietly than before. "When I was the one hiding in this room, and you were the one who snapped me out of it? Well, take that and reverse it."

"I don't need to be snapped out of anything."

"Bianca, get real. For the last month, you've been like some kind of zombie."

Vampire, not zombie, I thought. That made me smile just a little. "I just need some time to—get my head together. Okay?"

"A couple of days, sure. A couple of weeks, even. But this? This has been going on for almost a month. Even *your* head should be together by now." Raquel stood up and yanked my blanket off the bed. "Get up. Shower. You smell like funk."

"I only skipped one day," I grumbled.

"I don't care how long it took the funk to get here. I only know there's funk in my room, and it's got to go."

I didn't actually think I smelled bad; Raquel was just desperate to get me to move. So I moved, obediently taking my shower and returning to find Raquel remaking my bed—even though she hardly ever made her own. She'd hidden the magazines. "I made some tuna salad," she said as she snapped one of the sheets. "For lunch, we can have a picnic out on the grounds. Maybe ask Balthazar, Vic, and Ranulf. What do you say?"

"You want to have a *picnic?*" She shrugged. I said, "You are really, really not acting like yourself."

"Neither are you," Raquel pointed out. "Until we get things back to normal, I'm stuck being the perky one. I kind of hate being the perky one. So can you snap out of it already and come to the picnic?"

"Okay." I'd have to eat sometime. Though blood was becoming a bigger part of my diet all the time, I still needed food.

"So, are you ever going to tell me what's bugging you?"

"Probably not." How could I tell her that I was upset over losing Lucas? As far as she knew, I'd lost Lucas almost a year ago—not last month. "Raquel, it's not that I don't trust you. I just—I don't want to say any of it out loud. Like, I don't even want to hear myself speaking the words."

"It's okay," she said. "Let's just get you outside."

The five of us had our picnic lunch (Balthazar and Ranulf both chewing very carefully) on the grounds. One of Vic's tie-dyed blankets served as our tablecloth, and we mostly made small talk about midterms and school gossip. Balthazar sat close by, our arms sometimes touching, and his presence reassured me.

Only once did the conversation swerve into dangerous territory. As Vic shook more potato chips onto his plate, he said, "Hey, nobody ever heard anything else about Courtney?"

"They said she went back home," Balthazar said quickly. He was sticking to the official Evernight cover story for any missing vampire students—which was usually the truth, though not this time. "A few kids leave every year. It happens."

"It's just totally weird," Raquel said. "Last year Erich, this year Courtney. I mean, I get why somebody would ditch Hell High, particularly with the whole ghost situation, but the school administration really doesn't seem to care much. And how come it's the most popular kids who take off? The rest of us manage to stick it out."

"Courtney was not happy," Ranulf said. "She was lonely. I could tell."

Though I'd never thought about that before, I realized that Ranulf was right. I knew I couldn't let anybody see me getting emotional about Courtney, so I leaned my head against Balthazar's shoulder. He patted my back.

For her part, Raquel looked skeptical. "I don't see why the gorgeous popular girl would be any lonelier than the rest of us."

"Everyone is lonely," Ranulf said, but he smiled. "We have to remember that life is to be lived one day at a time. You cannot worry about past or future. Happiness is in the now."

Raquel laughed. "Vic has totally brainwashed you."

Now that I thought about it, Ranulf did seem a whole lot more laid-back these days—and, yes, those were black Chucks on his feet. Instead of looking like a Christian martyr who had wandered out of some illuminated medieval text, Ranulf now dressed and moved almost exactly like a regular kid. He still talked strangely, but not so much that anybody would really notice. Most important, for the first time, he seemed to be happy. A year of rooming with Vic had done him more good than a decade of instruction at Evernight Academy ever could have.

"You should listen to the man, Balty," Vic said, nudging Balthazar's shoe with his own. "Carpe that diem."

"I try." Balthazar tried to sound enthusiastic but didn't do a very good job. He hadn't been much happier this month than I had; he'd taken the confrontation with Charity hard, as had I. I felt like a fool for trusting her because she looked so innocent and helpless—how much worse did that have to be for Balthazar? Not only had she chosen her tribe over him, she had become one of them: violent, ruthless, and cruel. With a single stroke of a knife, Charity had ended Courtney's existence—not to mention my relationship with Lucas.

Maybe Raquel saw something melancholy in my eyes, because she quickly said, "It's a really clear sky. We ought to do some stargazing tonight. Right, everybody?"

"Not tonight," I said. "I promised to help Balthazar with a school project."

"Okay," Raquel said. "But we're going to do it soon."

I remembered how bored she was by astronomy and wanted to hug her for trying so hard.

The "school project" was actually playing video games—pure fun for me, but a difficult subject for Balthazar in Modern Technology. "You should be better at this," I said, as my warrior neatly stabbed Balthazar's on the screen for the dozenth time. "You've fought in some wars, right?"

"Plenty of them." Balthazar scowled down at the controls. "It doesn't make any sense to me, thinking of battle as a game."

"Then think of it as fencing," I suggested. "You know, moves you practice to get right. A role you play."

"That actually makes sense." He grinned and leaned back against the Modern Technology room sofa, and I felt very proud of myself. Then his smile changed, somehow becoming both softer and more intense. "Bianca, why are we still doing this?"

"Doing what?"

"Hanging out all the time. Fibbing to our friends." His dark eyes met mine. "Claiming that we're together."

"Well, because—" I realized I'd never even asked myself

that question. I stared down at the floor, searching for words. "You're still looking for Charity. That means you need an excuse to get off campus."

"I don't need an excuse to leave campus. I can come and go pretty much as I please. Our—whatever it is we're doing, I don't need it for that."

"I guess we can stop if you want to."

"I don't especially want to," Balthazar said. His voice was low.

"I'm—I'm going to get some blood, okay?" I got shakily to my feet and went to the corner of the room that held the twenty-first century kitchenette. Several vampires stored a bit of blood in there for snacks between classes, as this was the only class-room no humans used, and I felt like I could use some blood to strengthen me about now.

I couldn't pretend that I didn't know what he was talking about, or that he had surprised me. Lucas and I—we weren't together anymore, and it seemed impossible that we ever could be again. Balthazar had given me time to handle the loss, and now he wanted to know if things could be different between us.

Always I'd told myself that Balthazar was just a friend. I knew that I didn't love him like I still loved Lucas; I didn't know if I could ever love that completely again.

But I also knew that I'd come to rely on Balthazar this year. To trust him. At this point, he was probably one of my closest friends. And I'd never even pretended that I didn't find him attractive. That would've been impossible.

No, I'd never felt anything for Balthazar that came close to the rush of passion that Lucas awakened in me, every time. But if I gave Balthazar a chance—

I remembered Lucas kissing me beneath the stars at the observatory, the longing for him so sharp it hurt. The memory overcame me at the same moment I reached in the cabinet for a glass and, in my distraction, I dropped it. The glass shattered with a crash, and something sharp jarred into my hand. "Owww," I whined, pulling a shard from my bloodied finger.

Balthazar was at my side in an instant. "Ouch. But it doesn't look too nasty." He quickly collected the broken pieces of the glass and dropped them in the trash.

"No, I just need a bandage." Then I thought—*wait*.

We stood close together, near enough that our bodies almost touched. Instead of turning on the faucet and holding my finger beneath the running water, I hesitantly held my hand up so that I nearly touched Balthazar's face.

I'd caught him off guard; it seemed to take him a second to realize what I was doing. Then Balthazar wrapped his hand around my wrist and took my finger in his mouth, tasting my blood. He closed his eyes. The brush of his tongue against my skin made something inside me turn over, and my breath caught in my throat.

After only a second, Balthazar pulled my hand from his lips. The cut was only a pink line now. "Okay?" he said.

"Yeah." I felt incredibly exposed. My blood had given Balthazar a glimpse into my mind; he would have just felt some of the emotions I was now feeling. I wondered if they were less confusing to him than they were to me. "What did you see?"

Balthazar still held my hand in both of his, his broad fingers enclosing my wrist. "Just some curiosity, that's all. I didn't taste nearly enough blood to really know you." His voice was strangely rough. "When you finally share blood with someone, you'll understand the difference."

I remembered how I'd only gotten a hint of Balthazar's emotions when I licked his finger the night of the Autumn Ball. There was more to it, so much more that I could hardly guess— the true mysteries of being a vampire.

This is what it means to be a vampire.

There had been moments I'd questioned whether I had to ultimately become a vampire, even if it was what I wanted. Now that I'd lost Lucas, I didn't ever want to consider those questions again. I was sick of not knowing exactly what I was, how to behave, what to think. If I could make myself understand what it meant to be a vampire, maybe all those questions would just go away.

I looked up at Balthazar and whispered, "Drink from me."

He didn't move, but I felt the change in him—a kind of tension that electrified the air between us. "You mean, now?"

"Nobody else is coming in here tonight. We're alone. We can do whatever we want."

"That's not what I meant." The eagerness in Balthazar's eyes made me feel weak, sort of scared but in a good way, like the moment before the roller coaster drops. He brushed two fingers against my cheek. "Bianca, are you sure?"

"I already told you. Yes." But then my boldness seemed to desert me, because I didn't have any idea how to go about this. "Do we just—do you—" *Should I pull the neck of my shirt down my shoulder and just let him bite? Would he bite my hand instead?* I didn't know and felt stupid.

"You'll want to lie down. Sometimes it makes you dizzy." Balthazar squeezed my hand. "Couch?"

"Okay," I said, tossing my hair like it was no big deal. Which was stupid, because it was a huge deal—and Balthazar and I both knew it—but I couldn't seem to help myself.

My legs felt wobbly as we went, hand in hand, toward the sofa. Balthazar rummaged around in one of the cabinets and grabbed a couple of dark towels. The computer's screen had gone into holding mode, so it was darker in the room now, but I didn't turn on any lights. It was easier, I thought, having some shadows between us.

"You might want to—I don't want to ruin your shirt," Balthazar said, his voice hard and tight. He was already unbuttoning his cuffs.

"Oh. All right." Fortunately I had a camisole on beneath my lacy blouse. I turned away from Balthazar as I unfastened it and lay it neatly on a nearby chair. Even though the camisole and skirt were more modest than anything I'd have worn to the beach, I felt incredibly undressed.

When I turned around, Balthazar's shirt was off. I'd never seen his body before, and just looking at him—broad chest, sculpted shoulders, muscled waist—made me want to touch. In my nervousness I imagined that he was almost twice as wide as I was, that he could cover me completely.

I didn't touch him; I didn't do anything. Balthazar laid the towels on the couch. "Here. Lie back." I did, adjusting my neck so that the towels would catch any blood, but I felt like I was moving in slow motion. Then Balthazar lay next to me, his body alongside mine. My heart was beating so hard I thought it could burst.

Balthazar brushed one hand through my hair and smiled gently. He sounded more like himself as he said, "Are you nervous?"

"Kind of," I admitted.

"Don't be. I'll take good care of you, I promise."

"The longer we wait, the more nervous I get."

"Shh." Balthazar kissed my forehead, then nuzzled his way down to the curve of my neck. The first brush of his mouth against my skin made me tense up all over. He stroked my arm and stayed there. I realized he was waiting for me to relax and get used to him being so close.

I'd never be used to this. The ceiling overhead seemed lower, like everything was closing in all around me. I knew that this wouldn't turn me into a vampire—only drinking a human's blood until the human died could do that—but all the same I knew I was crossing a line.

I forced my muscles to relax. Balthazar breathed in sharply and bit down.

Oh, oh, it hurts, it hurts! I gripped his shoulders, preparing to push him off me—but then it didn't hurt as much, and I felt this deep, deep pull. It was the tide of my blood flowing into him. Though my body didn't move, it felt as though I was rocking back and forth, back and forth, soothed and dizzy and eager for more.

The world seemed to fall away beneath me. It was like fainting, but wonderful instead of scary. Balthazar's body next to mine was all I could hang onto, the only thing I knew.

His tongue lapped against my neck, the suction tickling me—until he drew back. "Drink," Balthazar whispered. "Bianca, drink from me."

I clutched him closer, buried my face against his shoulder, and felt the familiar ache in my jaw from my fangs. He smelled good, and his skin was smooth, and in one split second, I went from not knowing if I could bite him to knowing that I had to. My teeth sank into him.

The blood rushed into my mouth, burning hot, and instantly I was flooded with everything Balthazar felt, everything he saw. He tasted like longing, like loneliness, and the depthless need for comfort. Everything within me that understood loneliness bent toward him, shaping us together. The images that flickered in my mind were of me—no, not me, but someone so like me that even I could be confused—she had dark hair, and a long, full-skirted dress, and she ran through the autumn woods laughing, spinning in the falling leaves.

He loved her and wanted me to be her. I wanted to be her. I wanted to be anyone but myself.

And I tasted his desire—raw, hard physical need. Within my mind flashed veiled images and sensations, the knowledge of sex that he possessed and I lacked, or had lacked until now. My body responded to it, and then I felt him bite down harder onto my neck as he sensed my arousal in return. That made me want him more, and made him want me more, the feeling doubling in on itself over and over until I couldn't bear it one second longer—

Balthazar pulled away from my neck, far enough that it broke my bite, too. Then he kissed me, not once but half a dozen times, each kiss frantic and sweet with blood. I kissed him back, gulping in breaths every time our lips parted.

"Bianca, say yes," he gasped between kisses. "Say yes, please, say yes."

I wanted to say yes. I was going to.

But as I looked up at him, I breathed out shakily—and realized I could see my breath. The chill in the air hit us both at the same time, and Balthazar's eyes widened as he realized what I realized.

Frost began to streak across the windows and ceiling, and the blue-green glow flooded the room so brightly that I could hardly see. All I could hear was the cracking of ice. But none of that compared to what I felt.

It hates me, Raquel had said. *It hates me. It wants to hurt me.* I hadn't understood what she meant until this moment.

The wraith was angry, and it had come for me.

Chapter Nineteen

"BIANCA, COME ON!"

Balthazar towed me away from the sofa, his hand clamped around my forearm. I stumbled after him but looked back at the startling transformation. Already the room was solid white with frost and ice and colder than anything I'd ever felt before, even at the Autumn Ball. We were sliding on ice, every step unsure, and Balthazar slammed hard against one wall, smearing it with blood from my bite. He winced, but we had to keep going— every second, this became stranger. More dangerous.

We reached the door, and Balthazar tried to pull it open, but it wouldn't budge. The lock was frozen shut. He tugged at it hard, swore, then slammed against the door with his shoulder. The wood cracked deeply, and together we were able to kick it until it broke. Splinters jammed into my legs and hands as we tore the door apart, but even as we worked, the room was growing even colder. Crystals of ice were forming in the air around us, making it so thick it was hard to breathe.

And still I felt it—that deep, implacable anger, swirling around us and as real as the chill.

Balthazar finally destroyed the door by bursting through. Flakes of ice had formed on his bare chest. "Get Mrs. Bethany!" he yelled down the hallway as he reached back to pull me out after him. "Somebody help!"

I got halfway through the door—and froze.

Literally, I mean. My foot was frozen to the floor, I tried to tug it loose, but even as I did, the ice thickened, covering my shoe. I leaned down, trying to pull free, but suddenly it was harder to move at all.

"Somebody help!" Balthazar yelled. He was pulling on my free arm so hard my shoulder hurt, but I didn't budge. I didn't even rock backward when he tugged. I was completely still—completely trapped. Inside I felt as though I were screaming, but I couldn't have made a sound.

Within the Modern Technology room, gravity didn't quite seem to apply anymore. My hair floated around me, as if underwater, and all the books and desks inside were drifting slightly, caught in unseen currents. Everything was the same brilliant shade of aquamarine. I recognized that it was cold, but I had become as cold as the room, so it didn't sting any longer. Balthazar's shouts seemed to be coming from a great distance away.

The glittery snowflakes that filled the room coalesced and took form. To my shock, I recognized the face of the girl who'd appeared in my bedroom. Instead of being a flesh-and-blood person, she was only an image made of snow.

You have to stay. It was my own voice, inside my own mind, saying words that weren't mine. This had to be what going insane felt like, but I knew I wasn't talking to myself—it was her, the wraith, somehow speaking through me. *You're in danger.*

From you! I could still think my own thoughts, at least. *Let me go!*

Her unearthly aquamarine eyes widened. *You'll freeze to death soon. It's the only way to save you.*

They were going to kill me in order to save me? Had the ghosts gone crazy? Was that how they thought all the time? I couldn't bargain with them, couldn't make them see sense. I was trapped here, with her in my mind.

Snow swirled around us, forming blue-green hands that touched my cheeks. Her entire body coalesced and became tangible—her fingernail scraped lightly against my skin. I couldn't flinch. Her thoughts stabbed into my mind again: *This is what was promised.*

Promise? What promise?

Instantly the room changed, screeching with the sound of shearing ice, as terrible as metal being torn in two. The girl screamed, a high, silvery sound that seemed to pierce the air. Colors shifted, aquamarine suddenly deepening to indigo, as the girl clawed at her belly—from which an iron spike protruded. It had been thrown into her like a hunting knife. In an instant, the girl dissolved into sleet and vanished. The spike clattered to the floor.

"Bianca!" Balthazar towed me back through the door as ice

cracked beneath my feet. Sound and sensation returned, and I realized that the hallway was now filled with people, including students, teachers, and my horrified parents. Mrs. Bethany stood next to me, her hand still cocked from where she had thrown the spike, and watched in grim satisfaction as everything icy inside the room began to melt.

Mom hurried to me and embraced me tightly. Only after I felt how warm she was did I realize how cold I'd become, and I started to shake. "You knew—it was iron—iron kills them, b-because iron is in blood—"

"I see you've learned more about the topic than you'd previously suggested. Hopefully, tonight, you've also learned better than to trust the wraiths," Mrs. Bethany said, straightening the starched lace cuffs of her blouse. She turned her sharp gaze onto my father. "Adrian, enough pretense. The girl cannot stay here much longer."

"What's going on?" called a voice from the hallway. I saw Raquel peering through the crowd, obviously panicked. She had to see that I was half frozen and that bloodstains mottled my throat and arm. I wanted to shout something reassuring to her, even if it was a lie, but my teeth were chattering too hard for me to speak.

Mrs. Bethany clapped her hands together. "That is quite enough. Everyone to your rooms." The students obeyed, though I heard murmurings and whispers about *the ghost* and *again*.

"You're okay?" Balthazar asked.

"She's fine," Dad said, his words clipped. For the first time,

❖ 278 ❖

I realized that Balthazar and I were still half undressed. Even though my parents had been incredibly permissive with the two of us—and had no doubt assumed we'd gone farther than this long ago—my father clearly didn't like having the evidence right in his face. "Balthazar, thanks for your help, but you can go."

"You'll all need to leave," Mrs. Bethany said, casting an appraising eye at the Modern Technology lab, which was now soaked with melting ice. "Celia, Adrian, we'll discuss this tomorrow." She then stalked away without another word.

"Sweetheart, are you sure you're all right?" Dad said.

"I'm fine," I mumbled. "I just want to go to my room. Okay?"

Balthazar gave me a crooked smile. The skin of his chest was red and chapped from the cold, and I realized it had hurt him to keep hanging onto me. "You can get out of class tomorrow, I bet. A wraith attack ought to be good for that much."

"I want to go to class. I'll be fine. I just want to sleep."

Finally they believed me and let me leave.

When I opened the door of my dorm room, Raquel was pacing the floor. She opened her mouth to start asking me questions, but apparently one look at my face was enough to silence her. Instead of speaking, she went to my dresser, pulled out my sweats, and tossed them onto the bed.

My sweatshirt and judo pants were cozy, but I still felt chilled to the bone. Raquel crawled into my bed with me and hugged me from behind. "Sleep," she said. "Just sleep."

But Raquel was the one who fell asleep first. I lay awake late into the night, thinking over everything that had happened—not just this evening, not even just this year, but in some ways my whole life. And I saw it all differently than before. For the first time, I thought I saw the awful truth.

In classes the next day, everyone kept casting glances at me and whispering, but nobody dared ask outright what was going on. I ignored the attention. The petty grievances of Evernight Academy had never bothered me less. In driver's ed, Mr. Yee hesitated before allowing me my turn, but he did allow it; for the first time, I parallel parked without any trouble.

"Nice job," Balthazar said, as we strolled away after class. Those were the first words either of us had spoken to each other since the night before.

"Thanks." Even a second's silence between us lengthened and became tense. The awkwardness would only get worse if we didn't deal. "I think we have to talk."

"Yeah, we do."

Students had crowded onto virtually every inch of the grounds to enjoy the spring weather. Even the vampires who shied away from sunlight stretched out in the shade beneath trees with new, pale-green leaves. To get some privacy, Balthazar and I had to retreat to the library. It was all but deserted. We walked to the far corner and sat together on the broad wooden sill of one of the stained-glass windows.

Balthazar said, "You're going to tell me that last night shouldn't have happened."

"No. I'm glad it happened. For too long, I've been telling myself that I could spend all this time with you and flirt with you and not have it mean anything. It does mean something. You mean something to me. But I'm not in love with you."

I'd expected those words to hurt him. Instead, he smiled ruefully. "I've been trying to make this something it's not. To make you someone you're not."

I remembered the image I had glimpsed of a dark-haired girl from centuries ago, laughing in the autumn woods and gazing at Balthazar with depthless adoration. "Charity mentioned somebody named Jane, and I thought I saw—"

"Leave it in the past. That's all it is any longer. The past."

"If we—last night, if we had—I don't think I'd be sorry." The thrill of being so close to him was still too fresh in my mind to deny. "It can't happen again, though."

"No." Balthazar sighed. "You never settle for less than what you really want, Bianca. You'll never be with anybody you don't truly love."

I wished I could love him. Everything in my whole life would be easier if I did. He'd protect me and shelter me forever.

But I was beginning to realize that being sheltered came at a price.

When I changed out of my school uniform that evening, I put on my oldest jeans and a favorite T-shirt. They were so familiar that they were like a part of me—like armor, in a way I couldn't define. Then I went upstairs to face my parents and have a conversation I should've had a long time ago.

My mother opened the door with a smile. "There you are. We were hoping you'd come by tonight—weren't we, Adrian?" As I walked inside, she murmured, "Your father is in an odd mood, and maybe you and I should have a private talk about Balthazar later. Okay?"

Ignoring this, I walked to the center of our living room and demanded, "Why are the wraiths after me?"

Mom and Dad stared. Nobody said anything for a few long seconds. Then Mom began, "Honey, they could just be— This school is probably a target—"

"The school isn't a target. I am. I'm the only one who's seen the wraiths every time they've appeared, and I'm the one they came after. Each appearance came immediately after I drank blood. I don't think that's a coincidence."

"You drink blood all the time," Dad said, trying too hard to sound reasonable. "You've drunk blood since the day you were born."

"Things are different now. Every single one of those times was different, because I was hungrier, or the blood came from a living creature, or—" Well, I wasn't going to get into why it was different with Balthazar. "I'm becoming more of a vampire. And the wraith said I was in danger."

"What?" That genuinely confused Mom, I could tell, but that just went to show how much of this she really did under-stand but wouldn't say. "The wraiths are the ones trying to hurt you!"

"I think she meant that I was getting closer to becoming a vampire. To the wraiths—I think—I think being a vampire is even worse than being dead." I folded my arms. "Then she said that I couldn't break the promise. That whatever the wraiths were doing was what had been promised. What promise is she talking about?"

My parents both went completely still. They glanced at each other, guilty and almost horror-struck, and I felt a queasy kind of dread. Even though I knew I absolutely had to hear this answer, I wanted to run away. The truth, I sensed, was going to hurt.

"You've always known," I said. "Haven't you? That the wraiths were coming after me. But you never told me why."

Dad said, "We knew. And no, we didn't tell you."

It was as if something snapped in two deep inside me. My parents—the people I'd loved the most in the world, the ones I'd always told all my secrets to, the ones I'd wanted to hide with far away from the rest of the world. They had lied, and I couldn't imagine why. It couldn't possibly matter why.

"Honey—" Mom took a couple of steps forward, then stopped when she got a good look at my face. "We didn't want to scare you."

"Tell me why." My voice shook. "Tell me right now."

She wrung her hands. "You know we thought that we could never have you."

"Please, not the 'miracle baby' speech again!"

"We thought we could never have you," Dad repeated. "Vampires can't have children."

In my frustration, I could have thrown something at him. "Except two or three times in a whole century—I know, I get it, okay?"

Mom's face was grave. "Vampires can *never* have children on their own, Bianca. We don't have life to give. Only—half life. The life of the body."

"What is that supposed to mean?" Something horrible occurred to me, and I thought I might throw up. "Am I not really yours?"

Dad shook his head. "Honey, you're ours. You're absolutely ours. But to have you, we needed help."

My first, confused thought was about fertility clinics. I didn't think they took vampire patients. But then I realized the last words my mother had spoken: *half life. The life of the body.* Mrs. Bethany had talked about this before, when she initially spoke to me about the wraiths. The vampires represented the body. The wraiths represented the spirit.

Slowly, I said, "You struck a bargain with the wraiths. They—they made it possible for you to give birth to me."

They actually looked relieved that I'd said it, though relief was about a thousand light-years away from what I was feeling. Mom said, "We found them. We asked for their help. We didn't know what they'd ask—most vampires don't know about this, and we'd only heard whispers, rumors—"

Dad cut in. "The spirits . . . took possession of us, I guess. Only for an instant."

I grimaced. "While you were—"

"No, honey, no!" Mom crisscrossed her hands in front of her like she was trying to erase those words from existence. "It wasn't like that! I don't know what they did, but sure enough, within a few months you were on the way. We went back to thank them." She repeated bitterly, "*Thank* them."

"And they said that you belonged to them." Dad's expression was grim. "They said when you came of age, we had to let you become a wraith instead of a vampire. Now they're trying to kill you—to murder you, because murder creates wraiths. They're trying to steal you, Bianca. But you don't have to be afraid. We won't let them."

My whole life, I had felt so special—so loved—because my parents had told me I was their miracle baby. I had always felt safe with them.

But I wasn't a miracle. I was the result of a dirty, ugly bargain that both sides had betrayed. And the parents I had always trusted with all of myself had been lying to me since the day I was born.

"I'm going," I said. My voice sounded strange. I pulled the pendant they'd given me from my neck and threw it to the floor.

Dad said, "Bianca, you need to stay and work this out."

"I'm going, and don't you dare try to stop me."

I ran through the door, willing myself to make it downstairs before I started to cry.

Chapter Twenty

I'D THOUGHT NOTHING COULD BE WORSE THAN losing Lucas, but I was wrong. The worst was realizing that I'd lost him for nothing because he'd been right about all of it—vampires, my parents, everything.

He told me my parents lied. I yelled at him for it. He forgave me.

He told me vampires were killers. I told him they weren't, even after one stalked Raquel.

He told me Charity was dangerous. I didn't listen, and she killed Courtney.

He told me vampires were treacherous, and did I get the message? Not until all my illusions had been destroyed by my parents' confession.

I decided that the only vampire who had never lied to me was Balthazar, but after seeing what Charity was capable of, I thought he probably did most of his lying to himself. Every other vampire—including my parents—was deceitful and manipulative.

Well, maybe not Ranulf. But the rest of them.

And Lucas? Lucas had told me only one lie, ever; he'd kept the secret of Black Cross because it wasn't his secret to tell. In every other way, he'd been honest with me and shared the hard truths nobody else thought I deserved to hear.

I wasn't only mourning losing Lucas, of course. Too many other things had gone horribly wrong. But the grief was worse for my realizing that, if I'd only listened to him, everything might have been different. Better. Happy. Instead of this.

April was almost the worst month of my life. My parents tried to talk to me a couple of times, but I didn't want to hear it; after about a week, they gave up. Probably they thought I was sulking, that I'd just "get over" learning my whole life was a lie and come crawling back for dinner some Sunday. I knew I'd never do that again. They'd figure it out soon enough.

The second Sunday I skipped, Raquel said, "Not going upstairs?"

"Nope."

"Last week I thought—you know, maybe you guys were just taking a week off."

"I'm not going up there."

"I thought your parents were better than mine," she said quietly.

How often had my parents discouraged me from hanging out with Raquel, just because she was a human? She had given them more credit than they'd given her. I could've hugged her, but she would've hated it. "Maybe I'd rather hang out with you."

"I've got homework."

"So we'll do homework."

That was fine with me. Even researching boring psychology papers was preferable to facing my parents again.

Balthazar and I were officially "broken up," so far as the student body knew. Vic had made a few half-baked attempts to mediate so we'd be friends and hang out again; I hadn't had the heart to discourage him, but after he backed off suddenly, I realized Balthazar hadn't taken the suggestion kindly. Balthazar wasn't angry with me, exactly, but he was kind of angry at the world in general, and he wanted to be alone for a while.

It was probably good for us to spend some time apart. I understood that, but I'd spent more time with him this last year than anyone else, even Raquel. I hadn't realized how much I'd grown to rely on him cheering me up after a rough day, or simply giving me a smile when I walked out of class, until he wasn't there anymore.

I still had Vic and Raquel, but if Mrs. Bethany had her way, I wouldn't even have them much longer.

"Your regrettable refusal to discuss this with your parents compels me to deal with you personally," Mrs. Bethany said, watering the line of violets along her windowsill. I sat in one of the uncomfortable, high-backed chairs in her carriage house. "You realize by now that you are a specific target of the wraiths."

"Yes."

"Do you know why that's so?" She seemed almost cheerful at the thought of my illusions having been dashed.

I gritted my teeth. "Yes."

"The fact that you are a target, in turn, endangers the other students. We have managed to hold the wraiths at bay with the stones so far, but there are limits to what we can accomplish. The wraiths are more determined than I thought they would be."

"That's flattering."

She set the watering can down. "Please reserve your sarcasm for your friends, Miss Olivier. You are here today to discuss what is to be done about the situation. I am not so heartless as to drive you out of Evernight Academy altogether. In the outside world, you would lack any protection whatsoever."

"I left campus a lot this year with Balthazar, but the wraiths never came after me anywhere else."

"I expect they simply did not know where you were. Given enough time—eventually, the wraiths would find you, any place in the world."

I'd never thought of that. "Why do they want me so badly? Aren't there enough ghosts in the world?"

"I imagine the broken promise matters to them more than any individual. When they consider themselves betrayed, they are relentless." Mrs. Bethany's heels clicked against her wooden floor as she walked toward me with her hands clasped behind her back. "There are empty faculty apartments within Evernight. I will move into one for the duration of the school year. You are welcome to stay here."

"Here?" I couldn't have understood that right. "Like, in your house?"

"Yes. I believe that you can still attend classes, if you'll wear this." She held out a pendant—the obsidian one my parents had given me for Christmas, the one I'd thrown at their feet. "It's protection for you, though you must not have realized it. Its protection is not fail-safe, however, which is why you are safer remaining in my home at night."

"Wait, I don't understand. If I'm in danger at the school, why am I safe here?"

"You may have noticed the copper roof," she said. "As you have apparently learned, wraiths are especially vulnerable to the metals and minerals found in human blood, such as iron and copper. My residence cannot be haunted. No wraith can enter."

"Then why don't you do that to the school, so it would be totally secure?"

It was an automatic question; I expected her to have a good answer. Copper is expensive, maybe. Instead, she cocked her head, on her guard. "There are reasons," she said, like that was an answer.

But I realized the answer almost instantly. Maybe it was because I was in the same room where I'd committed my first burglary in an effort to understand why Mrs. Bethany had admitted human students to Evernight. I remembered figuring it out with Balthazar: The humans were connected to the ghosts. I'd thought that she wanted to learn more about the vampires' enemies somehow. Since then, I'd seen her attack a wraith, devastating it almost instantly. I'd seen that she knew how to shut them down cold, yet hadn't done it. Mrs. Bethany wanted something else.

"You're hunting the wraiths," I said. "You need them to come into Evernight so you can catch them."

Strangely, her eyes lit up, like she was almost excited someone had caught on. But she said only, "Your theories are irrelevant, Miss Olivier. The wraiths are a danger to you and to others of our kind. You will be best protected here."

"You're not going to tell me why you're hunting them." She hadn't denied it either, I noticed.

"Do you accept my offer or not?"

"Do I really have a choice?"

"No, not really."

I'd have liked to tell Mrs. Bethany where she could stick her offer. But she was right about my being a danger to the other students. For their safety, as well as my own, I'd have to move to the enemy camp.

Mrs. Bethany's carriage house was actually sort of pretty once you got used to it, but staying there unnerved me. No matter how many times I opened the windows or sprayed a bit of my perfume in the air, the house always smelled of lavender, reminding me of its true owner.

I noticed that every desk drawer and closet had been thoroughly cleaned out before I moved in. She hadn't left me any more chances to snoop.

My human friends didn't understand why Mrs. Bethany's place was safer than Evernight Academy, but after I'd given them an (edited) account of the wraith's most recent attack, they didn't question that something had to be done. Raquel helped me pack my clothes, and Vic helped me haul them to the carriage house while she toted the telescope. I didn't bring everything; no point in even pretending I could ever get comfortable there. Yet I managed to sneak in the carved jet brooch Lucas had given me last year. I thought of it as my own stone with its own power—my talisman, my shield against the gloom of the place.

Late at night, I'd lie in Mrs. Bethany's massive canopy bed and imagine that the shadows in the corner of the room were starting to move, or that the air was colder than it ought to be, or any other number of crazy things. Then I'd reach for the brooch on the bedside table and clasp it in my hand, willing all my fear and loneliness to go away. It didn't matter that I'd lost him. Remembering Lucas would always give me strength.

As April drew to a close, the school became very quiet. Even more of the students had fled in the wake of the most recent event with the wraith; probably only two thirds of the student body remained. The vampires had been far more likely to depart, meaning that humans made up almost half the students at the school. The mood was friendlier overall, and because so many of the humans considered ghosts no big deal, the atmosphere became almost relaxed. I might have enjoyed it, if I hadn't been an exile.

The next-to-last night in April offered one small treat, though—a blue moon.

It's not like a blue moon is some incredible astronomical event. All it means is that it's the second full moon in a single month. But I always sort of liked to make a celebration of them, to be sure and look up at the sky and remember that nights like that didn't come along very often.

I waited until late at night before I slipped outside in my jeans and T-shirt. I wanted to be alone. The sky was too overcast for real stargazing, but the moon shone brightly, tinting the clouds nearest it pale with light.

Quickly I walked across the grounds to the gazebo, so I could sit down and watch the moon through the cast-iron lattices. I had other memories of the gazebo—memories of Lucas. This was the first place we'd ever kissed.

"You still love a blue moon."

I whirled around to see Lucas standing on the grounds behind me.

At first I honestly thought I had to be imagining things. But he stepped into the gazebo, his battered boots making the floor creak, and I realized he had to be real.

"Lucas? What—what are you doing here?" I cast a hurried glance around us. "It's dangerous. If they find you—"

"They're not going to find me."

"They will if you just stand here!" Now that I had finally accepted that Lucas had come back to Evernight, I was even more astonished than I'd been before; this was reckless to the point of being suicidal. "Anybody could walk out here at any second!"

"I won't stay much longer." Lucas put his hands in the pockets of his corduroys. He wore an old flannel shirt over a T, and his body was hunched and tense, ready to fight at a moment's notice. But none of that wild energy was directed at me. When Lucas looked at me, his eyes were only sad. "I thought I'd have a good chance of catching you outside tonight, what with the blue moon and all."

"Yeah. You caught me." I couldn't think what to say. My longing for him wouldn't come out in words, and I was too startled to know what to do. "How long have you been waiting out here?"

"Since sundown."

It was almost midnight. He'd been on the Evernight grounds for hours, and anyone could've seen him. If somebody had reported Lucas to Mrs. Bethany, by now he could've been a prisoner, even dead. He was as reckless as ever, but this time I couldn't be angry. "Why did you come?"

"Because I couldn't leave things between us like that."

"I was ugly to you," I whispered. "Lucas, I'm so sorry."

"You were angry, and you had a right to be angry."

"We ended up cremating Courtney after all."

"Okay, you didn't have a right to be angry about *that*." The hint of a smile played upon his face, but only briefly. His hair had grown out, scruffy again. I thought he'd lost some weight. Wasn't he taking care of himself anymore? "You said I didn't accept you being a vampire, Bianca. I guess—maybe you were right."

Even though I had realized that for myself, it stung to hear him say it. "You said once you loved me no matter what I was."

"I do," Lucas said, taking a ragged breath. "But when I said that—it was as if, what I felt for you, it was in spite of you being a vampire. Inside, it was like—like I was forgiving you just for being what you are. That's probably the crappiest thing I ever did to anybody, not figuring out what a jackass I was being. If I'd figured it out faster, I could've been to you—what I should've been to you. What I wanted to be."

"Lucas—"

"Let me finish, all right? You know I suck at the emotional stuff. So I just—" His foot scuffed the gazebo floor. "Whatever it is that makes you the person you are—that's what I love. All of it. Including you being a vampire. You shouldn't ever have had to defend that; I should've accepted it a long time ago. If I had, maybe I wouldn't have lost you. That's on me, and I know it."

He was staring down at his boots. I thought if he'd been looking at my face in that instant, Lucas could never have fooled himself that he'd lost me.

More quietly, he continued, "I saw the thing with Balthazar coming. It made me pretty crazy. But—you know, for a—for *anybody*, he's a decent guy, and I guess he never asked you to pretend you weren't the person you really are. So maybe you made the right call. I just wanted to say— Bianca, if you're happy, I'm glad. You ought to be happy. You deserve that."

"I'm not with Balthazar."

Lucas lifted his head, his expression disbelieving. "You aren't?"

"No. We were never together, not really."

"Oh. Okay." Lucas shifted from foot to foot, obviously torn

between hope and uncertainty. "Listen, I—I know I screwed up, but if I could—"

I jumped from my seat and flung my arms around him. Lucas hugged me tightly as I buried my face in the curve of his neck. At first neither of us said anything; I don't think we could speak. It felt so incredibly good to hold him again, to feel him next to me, when I thought I'd lost him forever. Hadn't I told him to believe that we'd always find each other again? I should have listened to my own advice.

"I love you so much," I finally whispered.

"I love you, too. I swear to God, I'll never screw up like this again."

"But you were right about everything."

Lucas's hands combed through my hair. "Hardly."

"Lucas, I mean it. You knew my parents were lying. You knew what vampires really were. If I'd only listened to you, none of this would have happened."

"Whoa." Lucas took my hands and pulled me down onto the gazebo bench. The blue moon shone down on us through the ivy leaves. "What are you talking about?"

I spilled out the whole story—the truth about how I was born, about how the wraiths were coming after me, about how I was apparently a pawn in a battle between wraiths and vampires in which both sides were evil. I didn't even skip over what nearly happened with Balthazar and me, because I was sick of secrets. That part made Lucas press his lips together into a thin line, but he listened without a word.

When I was finished, my head leaning against his broad shoulder and his arms around me, he said only, "We have to get you out of here."

"Are you asking me to run away with you again?"

"Yeah. This time forever."

"The wraiths will still be coming after me."

"There are people in Black Cross who know more about wraiths. We should be able to get you help, even if you don't come with me—but I wish you would."

"I'll come with you." I knew I could do it. There was no future for me anywhere in the vampire world. "I just wish I knew what I'll become."

"What do you mean?"

"I'm not going to become a full vampire. Not ever." I turned my face up to his. "But if I'm not going to be a vampire, what becomes of someone like me?"

Lucas gave me an uneven smile. "I don't know. But I'm guessing it's whatever you want to be."

We kissed each other tenderly, then simply gazed at each other for a few moments. There were times during the past year when we'd hardly been able to keep our hands off each other, but this night was different, quieter. I think we both knew how important this moment would be.

Finally I said, "The last Friday in May."

"Is that the last day of exams?"

"Yeah. That means it's also the day tons of cars will be pulling up to take students back home. I can slip away easily in the crowd. My parents—they'll assume I went home with Raquel or somebody. That will buy us a few days while they call around looking for me." Despite everything, I didn't doubt they'd search. "I could leave tonight—I wish I could—but they'd know right away something was wrong. If we wait for the last Friday in May, it's our best chance to get a head start."

"Only one more month, then."

"Until we're together all the time."

"I meant, one more month for me to figure out what we're going to do afterward," Lucas said. "But I'll figure it out. I promise, Bianca, I'll take care of you."

I pushed his scruffy hair back from his face. "I'll take care of you, too."

Far away, something snapped with a sharp pop. Lucas and I both jerked upright, but to my relief, it turned out to be nothing—a tree branch, probably. Still, the moment had reminded us both how dangerous it was for Lucas to be here.

"You have to go," I said. "Right away."

"I'm going. Love you." Lucas kissed me roughly, bruising my mouth. His hands gripped my hips, and I wished I could keep him close. But when he pulled away, I let him leave. He ran into the underbrush without looking back. I knew why he had the strength to do that. It was easier to say good-bye when it wasn't for long.

May was just about the best month of my life, at least at first.

Every single day was just a box on the calendar that I could put a red X through; each one brought me closer to Lucas and to liberty. I daydreamed through classes and was spoken to sharply—not just by Mrs. Bethany but by my other teachers, too. What did I care? If I flunked all my exams, it wasn't like I'd be around to pick up my report card. It was easier to stare out the window and fantasize about Lucas, fiddling with the obsidian pendant around my neck, than it was to concentrate on *Henry V.*

Sometimes I felt weird tremors of uncertainty—*I won't go to college now. How will I keep in touch with Vic and Raquel? Will I ever see Balthazar again? How will I protect myself from the wraiths? Can I bring my telescope?* But nothing was as important as escaping Evernight or the "destiny" my parents and teachers had decided on for me. I had only one chance to be free and to be with the guy I loved. I intended to take it.

I even started packing the few clothes I had in Mrs. Bethany's carriage house. That's what I was doing one night in mid-May when a rap on the door startled me.

Who could it be? I quickly stowed my half-packed bag under the bed, hurried into her living room, and called, "Come in!"

Mrs. Bethany entered, imposing in a long black skirt and gray, high-necked blouse. "What a nuisance," she said, apparently to herself. "Knocking on one's own door."

"Hey, Mrs. Bethany. Is there something you need?" If I was helpful, I reasoned, she'd get out faster.

She didn't pause as she swept past me into her bedroom. "I require some of my things and wanted to ensure that you hadn't failed to water the violets."

"They're doing great, actually."

"So I see." Mrs. Bethany froze and stared at the wall. "What on earth is that monstrosity?"

"Oh, you mean the art project? That's one of Raquel's collages. She calls it *Those Lips Will Lie to You*." It was a huge mural with all different kinds of mouths, magenta and peach and orange with lipstick, intercut with jagged black streaks and bolts. There were knives and guns, too, because Raquel said no artwork about the deception of love would be complete without some hostile phallic symbols. "Do you like it?"

Mrs. Bethany held one hand to her throat. "You do intend to remove this when you leave?"

I hadn't considered it before, but now I thought I'd leave it behind as a souvenir for Mrs. Bethany. "When do you think I can move back into the school, Mrs. Bethany?" I asked, just like I really wasn't going to run away.

"We will inform you when the time is right."

Then there was another rap at the door. I'd become very popular all of a sudden. I went to the door and opened it, saying, "Hello?"

The danger occurred to me even as I started pulling it open—*What if it's Lucas? What if he came back and Mrs. Bethany sees him?* But it wasn't Lucas.

Charity stood on the step, hair pulled back into a neat chignon and a dark red cloak around her. With her youthful face and guileless eyes, she looked almost like Little Red Riding

Hood—even though I knew she was really the wolf.

"You aren't the one I expected to find," she said with a smile. Perversely, there was still something about her that made me feel protective. "Has there been a mutiny?"

"Who is it?" Mrs. Bethany demanded as she came back into the room. Then she drew herself up to her full height. "My word. Miss More."

I could feel the hatred in the air between them. But Charity opened up her arms like a beseeching child. She said, "I call upon the sanctuary of Evernight."

Chapter Twenty-one

WITHIN A FEW HOURS, THE WHOLE FACULTY shared my dismay.

"Do you understand the rules of conduct at this school?" Even from my place outside the carriage house, where I crouched in the shrubs to eavesdrop, Mrs. Bethany's voice rang sharply. "You have chosen to ignore them in the past."

"The first rule of Evernight is that any vampire who seeks sanctuary must be given a place." Charity sounded completely unruffled. "I'll obey the rules if you will."

The teachers, who were gathered around, muttered among themselves. I didn't dare peek above the windowsill to see what was going on, but it basically sounded like Charity wanted to join the school as a student and they were going to have to let her in. But they didn't like it.

Mr. Yee said, "There's a certain wraith situation going on."

"Because of the little baby. But that will be taken care of soon enough, won't it? One way or another." Charity obviously didn't care if I lived or died; the feeling was rapidly becoming mutual.

I winced as I recognized my mother's voice. "There are human students here now, and we have to protect them from harm. Your track record in that area leaves a lot to be desired."

"I swear," Charity said, as sincere and sweet as a child. "I swear upon my own grave that I will not be the one to break the peace at Evernight Academy."

After a moment's silence, Mrs. Bethany said, "Very well. How long do you intend to remain?"

"Not long. Cross my heart, I'll be out of here before June."

"Then we will find you a place in the faculty apartments. You should remain there as much as possible until the end of the semester. It would be difficult to explain a new pupil arriving so close to the end of term, and the fewer questions asked, the better," Mrs. Bethany said. "We should review the new rules about blood consumption that have been instituted following the new admissions policy."

"Hey." The whisper was close to my ear, and I jumped in fright, then breathed a sigh of relief as I realized it was Balthazar. "What's going on in there?"

"You nearly scared me to death." We stepped away from the building together. "Why did you sneak up on me like that?"

"I didn't sneak up on you. I sneaked up to the carriage house, and you were already there, doing the spying for me."

I smiled a little at that. Only then did I realize that we were talking to each other again, and it wasn't nearly as awkward as I'd feared. That might have been only because he was so focused on the carriage house. Balthazar's eyes remained fixed on it like he had X-ray vision and could watch his sister through the walls.

"They're going to let her stay," I said. "She has to hide up in the tower, though, so nobody asks why there's a new student coming only for finals. Mrs. Bethany's ticked off about it, but apparently you were right about the sanctuary thing."

"Sanctuary." His face lit up with hope. "Sanctuary means she's running from someone. It's got to mean she's running from the tribe. She's turned away from them."

"Maybe."

"It's got to be."

He wanted to believe in her so badly. I didn't trust Charity as far as I could throw her, but I didn't say anything. For Balthazar's sake, I hoped Charity behaved herself for a while, so at least he could visit her again. "Are you going to go in and see her?"

"Mrs. Bethany wouldn't want me to interrupt. I'll find Charity later tonight." Balthazar tentatively put a hand on my shoulder. "Have you been okay?"

"Yeah." I couldn't share either my disappointments or my excitement about my impending escape. I could only ask, "How about you?"

"Everything's going to be all right now," he said, and he grinned.

"Maybe." I thought about Lucas and returned his smile "Maybe for both of us."

The next day, as we all met up in the hallway, Vic said, "Is it just me, or has time slowed to a standstill? It's like summer is getting farther away, not closer."

"I know what you mean," I said. "Where is your family headed this summer?"

"Looks like we're renting a villa in Tuscany," Vic replied, with the kind of carefree boredom that only somebody super rich could ever use to announce news like that. Next to him, Raquel's eyes became wide. "Me, if I'm in Italy, I'd rather be in Rome, right? See all the ruins, like, where the gladiators fought, stuff like that? Not just sitting in some fancy-schmancy house in the middle of wine country while I'm still not legal to drink."

"I always heard the drinking age was lower in Europe," Raquel said.

"It is, but try telling that to my mom." Vic stopped as we reached the entrance to the north tower where the boys' dorms were. I figured he would tell us good-bye, but instead he peered up the spiral stairs. "Something weird is going on up there."

"Weird?" Raquel pulled her books closer to her chest. "Like, ghost weird?"

"I don't think so. Some other kind of weird. Normally they don't really care if people sit on the stairs in the evening—you know, just to hang out without annoying your roommate, or every once in a while Balthazar has a cigarette up there and blows the smoke out the window. But last night, Ranulf and I made, like, one move toward the stairwell, and all of a sudden

Professor Iwerebon appeared out of thin air and read us the riot act for even thinking about going up that way."

"I bet it has something to do with that," Raquel said. "With ghosts, I mean. That's the main reason people have acted strange this year."

I knew that really they were trying to keep the students away from Charity—or vice versa. "I wouldn't worry about it," I said. "Whatever it is, in two weeks we'll all be out of here."

"Unless that time-stretching thing keeps up." Vic grinned and flipped us a wave as he loped into the dormitory wing.

As Raquel and I headed back down the main corridor toward our own tower, she said, "Here comes trouble." I glanced to my right and saw my father walking purposefully toward us.

"Oh, no." There was nowhere for me to run. "Stay here with me?"

"I would, but you know he's going to make me go eventually. The sooner I leave, the sooner you get it over with."

She was right. I sighed. "Okay, talk to you later."

Raquel headed in the direction of the room we'd once shared, which left me alone as my father walked up. "I want to speak with you," he said.

"That makes one of us."

Dad didn't appreciate backtalk, but I saw him resist an angry response. "You're upset. I understand that you're upset. I suppose you have a right to be."

"You *suppose*?"

"You need to be mad at someone? Be mad at me. Ultimately

it was my decision to handle things this way, and if I made a mistake, I'm sorry." Before I could ask him what he meant by *if*, Dad continued, "But how long are you going to do this to your mother?"

"I'm not doing anything to her!"

"You've shut her out. You ignore her. You think that doesn't hurt her feelings? That you're the only person in this family who can be hurt? Because this is tearing her up inside. I can't stand to see her suffer, and I can't believe you could stand it either, much less be responsible."

A memory flashed in my mind—Mom with bobby pins in her mouth, braiding my hair for the Autumn Ball. I refused to dwell on it. "I can't have a relationship with people who can't be honest with me."

"You're looking at this situation in its most extreme light. You're a teenager; I guess it comes with the territory—"

"It's not because I'm a teenager!" Quickly I glanced around—no students in sight, human or vampire. "Tell me what happens if I refuse to ever take a human life."

"That's not an option for you."

"I think it is." Still, he couldn't tell me the truth. So much for my having a right to be upset, or Dad admitting he made a mistake. "What if that's my choice?"

"Bianca, that is not something you can choose. Not ever. Don't let your temper get in the way of reason."

"We're done," I said, walking off. I wondered if he'd follow me, but he didn't.

That night, I lay in Mrs. Bethany's bed. My brooch sat upon the nightstand, Raquel's artwork was almost as bright as a nightlight upon the wall, and I tried to take as much pleasure in the colors, and in my plans, as I had before. But I kept thinking about my mother. *This is tearing her apart.*

As long as I was angry with Mom and Dad—and I was still furious—the separation from them didn't have to hurt. In other moments, I remembered how close we had always been, and then I missed them so badly I ached.

What I had lost was lost forever. Wasn't it? I didn't know how to look at the lies they'd told any other way.

The door of the carriage house banged open, and I jumped out of bed. "Who's there?" I cried, before thinking that if it were an intruder, I might have done better to stay quiet.

The intruder proved to be Mrs. Bethany, which wasn't that reassuring. Though it was late, she wore the same dress she'd had on in class today, as if she'd been at work a very long time. Her eyes blazed. "Come with me."

"Where are we going?"

"To face your accuser and hopefully discredit her."

What was that supposed to mean? My stomach sank with dread. "I—well—just let me get dressed."

"A robe will be sufficient. We must settle this question immediately."

Obviously no further explanation would be coming. With shaky hands, I put on my bathrobe and knotted the belt. I managed to slip the brooch into my pocket without Mrs. Bethany noticing; I felt like I needed it near.

Once I put the obsidian pendant around my neck, Mrs. Bethany led me across the grounds toward the school. High atop the north tower, several windows burned brightly—including the one that I'd guessed was Charity's. "Are my parents up there?"

"I wasn't under the impression you would be interested in their company any longer," Mrs. Bethany said, her long skirts trailing in the grass. She never looked back, taking it for granted that where she led, I would follow. "You can manage perfectly well on your own, I'm sure."

I wasn't sure she really wanted me to manage. Mrs. Bethany was clearly furious, but I couldn't yet determine whether she was angry at me or someone else. Given that we were headed for Charity's room, I suspected it was someone else.

We ascended the winding stone steps in silence, as I nervously fiddled with the belt of my robe. I knew that my "accuser" had to be Charity, but what could *she* possibly accuse *me* of?

Then I knew. Fear clamped me in its hold like a fist. I stopped in front of the door, unwilling to go inside. "Mrs. Bethany—if you and I could just talk—"

She reached past me to open the door, then pushed me within.

Charity sat in a high-backed chair in the very center of the room, wearing an Evernight uniform, the only intact clothes I'd ever seen her in. Primly she folded her hands in her lap. She looked so deceptively—ordinary. I realized with a shock that somebody else was in the room, too: Balthazar, who sat on a small bench in the corner. Judging from his slumped posture and the sick expression on his face, I knew that Balthazar hadn't joined her in accusing me. He, too, was one of the accused.

I sat beside him on the bench without being prompted. Balthazar gave me the most desolate look I had ever seen.

Mrs. Bethany demanded, "Miss More, please repeat what you told me earlier this evening."

"I'm so glad you and I were able to catch up, Mrs. Bethany." Charity smiled. "It reminded me that we had some good times— before we really knew each other."

Unsurprisingly, Mrs. Bethany didn't want to revel in the good times they'd had. "Repeat your accusation."

"These two have been chasing me throughout the school year." Charity smiled at us like she was greeting old friends. "But not alone. They had a friend with them. Someone named—*Lucas*, was it?—whom I'm fairly sure is a member of Black Cross."

We thought we'd done such a great job sneaking around, keeping the secret; we'd never asked ourselves if Charity would show up and ruin it all.

"Then it's true." Mrs. Bethany drew herself up. Until this, I saw, she'd been hoping that Charity was telling lies and that she'd have an excuse to expel her from Evernight Academy. Once Charity had spoken Lucas's name—or maybe once Mrs. Bethany had seen the guilt on our faces—that hope was gone.

Balthazar nodded. "It's true."

"Consorting with a member of Black Cross. A grave crime

indeed." Mrs. Bethany folded her arms as she stood before Balthazar and me. "Last year, Miss Olivier, your connection with Mr. Ross was unknowing, and I forgave it. This year, I cannot be so lenient. And you, Mr. More! Of all people, I would expect better from you."

"I wanted to find my sister," Balthazar said dully. His shoulders were hunched like those of someone in pain. "I'd think you'd understand that. Or she would."

"Black Cross hunters—they're terrible." Charity swung her feet back and forth beneath her chair, like a little kid having fun. "Violent. Vicious."

"Both of you have lied and abused the hospitality of this school. You have broken every rule we have and committed some errors so foolish that we never even thought to make a rule against them. I cannot stand for this."

"Fine. Expel me." I rose to my feet. What was the worst she could do? Throw me out of Evernight? I didn't need a school to teach me to be a vampire when I didn't intend to be one any longer. "If you want me to sign something you can show my parents later, then I will. If you don't even want to give me a chance to pack, that's fine, too. I don't care."

"Vicious," Charity repeated. "Though of course Black Cross hunters think they're doing the right thing. Just like you, Mrs. Bethany."

Mrs. Bethany whirled around, even angrier than she had been before. She disliked me, but she hated Charity. "How dare you compare me to those vermin?"

"Everyone hunts." Charity stood up, taller than anyone in the room but her brother, and she didn't look like a child any longer. "I hunt humans. Black Cross hunts vampires. You hunt ghosts. The ghosts hunt Bianca. And Bianca's been hunting me. It's a perfect chain, and you're a part of it."

How did Charity know about hunting ghosts? It took me months to figure it out—did somebody tell her? What does she know?

Charity stepped closer to Mrs. Bethany. She could look down at her. "I think everyone should go on hunting. My brother and his girlfriend used Black Cross to hunt me, so I think I should do the same to them."

Mrs. Bethany snapped, "You think you're using me?"

"No. I'm using Black Cross."

Balthazar stood. Something of his strength and purpose had returned to him in that moment. "Charity, what are you talking about? *Tell me.*"

His tone of voice resounded in the room, making me shiver; it affected Charity even more strongly, because she turned to him, childlike and obedient once more. Her voice broke as she said, "Why did you do it? Why?"

"I was out of my head with hunger. They'd tortured us for days— You were there, you know, don't you know?"

"You didn't have to do what they wanted. You didn't have to kill me."

My entire body turned to ice. *Balthazar* was the one who had turned Charity into a vampire? It couldn't be true. It couldn't. Yet—

"Punish me later," Balthazar said. Shadows lined his face and obscured his eyes. "Tell me about Black Cross."

"I hate this place. You know I've always hated it, and I hate *her*," Charity said, glaring at Mrs. Bethany, who looked on the verge of attacking any one of us, if not all. "I hate the way she pretends to be the supreme authority on what it means to be a vampire, when she ignores what it means. She doesn't kill humans. She doesn't understand that it's *what we do*."

Balthazar shook his head. "Don't say that."

Charity never stopped staring malevolently at Mrs. Bethany. "She'd undo us all, if she could. She pretends to protect vampires, but she'll be the end of our kind if she gets her way."

"You wretched girl." Mrs. Bethany was now so furious at Charity that she'd forgotten all about Balthazar and me. I wondered if I could run for the door, whether anybody would notice. "You never could learn."

"I've learned more than you think." Charity glanced at the delicate wristwatch she wore. "Midnight."

"Black Cross," Balthazar repeated. "What did you mean about using Black Cross?"

"They always leave Evernight alone, because they think all the vampires here behave so well," Charity said. She was right; Lucas had told me so. "But lately they've begun to doubt that. You see, in the past two weeks, they've found so many bodies in the nearby woods that they're sure something terrible has been happening. Something they have to stop."

Downstairs, I heard something—shouting, perhaps.

Charity's face shifted into a broad smile of pure delight. I'd never seen her totally happy before. "The hour has come."

Balthazar said, "Charity, you'd better say it."

Somebody else was shouting in the stairwell—closer now, louder—and then another person screamed. All of us turned toward the doorway in horror.

"I had to get myself cornered to do it," Charity said. "I could've been killed. But finally I made that scarred man believe me."

Eduardo. Lucas's stepfather. The most hard-core member of Black Cross that there was. "What did you make him believe?" I said.

Charity triumphantly lifted her head. "That Evernight's vampires would massacre the human students tonight. So Black Cross has come to massacre you instead."

Chapter Twenty-Two

MRS. BETHANY FLUNG OPEN THE DOOR. THE screens instantly doubled in volume, and every hair on my arms stood on end.

"Balthazar, come with me." Charity held out her hand. "We can leave this place. You can stop pretending to be something you aren't. We can be together if you'll only stop pretending."

"Go." He turned from her. "I have to do what I can here."

Charity stood there a few moments longer, hand open wide, and for a moment she was the one desperate for her brother's return; he was now the one who didn't need her. "You're on the wrong side!" she cried. Balthazar still refused to budge; Charity shuddered, and I thought maybe she was crying. She staggered toward the window, pulled it open, and whispered, "I really thought you'd come."

Balthazar ran into the hallway, ignoring her. Charity threw herself from the window, which made me gasp—until I realized I was being stupid. Charity was the safest of any of us. We were many stories up, but a long fall couldn't hurt an immortal.

"How do we get everyone out of here?" I said.

"Even we have to fulfill state regulations." Mrs. Bethany hurried down the hallway to pull something so routine I'd never thought about it before: an ordinary fire alarm. Instantly a siren began to shriek, deafeningly loud as it echoed off the stones. I grimaced and covered my ears.

"Get to the girls' dorms!" Balthazar shouted to me over the din. He was at the end of the hallway, almost out of sight. "I'm going to help the guys!"

For her part, Mrs. Bethany was already running down the stairwell. Even though she was unarmed, I didn't want to be the first Black Cross hunter she encountered.

But what if that hunter was Lucas?

I ran behind Mrs. Bethany, but I couldn't make it downstairs as fast as she could. The uneven stones made me stumble, and I had the shakes. *Everyone's in danger. Everyone. Lucas. Balthazar. Mom. Dad. Raquel. Ranulf. Dana. Vic.* What I felt went beyond fear. It was a blank, wrenching need to survive and to save—fight and flight—but who was I supposed to fight?

Someone screamed, and then there was a wet crunch and thud. I ran downstairs and saw the crumpled form of a man on the floor, a stake still gripped in one of his hands. Blood spattered the wall behind him, and Mrs. Bethany stood there, admiring her handiwork—but only for an instant. Then she ran toward the din.

I thought I recognized the man from the Black Cross cell in

Amherst, but I couldn't tell. Blood covered his face. The shouting all around me was only getting louder, and I could hear more and more footsteps on the stairwell as students started to flee. I ran after Mrs. Bethany—

—and into the battle.

The main corridor of classrooms was packed with Black Cross hunters—I recognized little Mr. Watanabe, a crossbow steady in his hands, and Kate, who was fighting hand to hand with Professor Iwerebon down the hall. Next to me, Mrs. Bethany deftly dodged an arrow, swung around, and slammed her fist into a hunter's throat. As he stumbled back and gagged, she got his neck in a headlock, then twisted it sharply. I heard a terrible crack just before he slumped to the floor. Instantly Mrs. Bethany whirled toward the next Black Cross hunter, kicking his knees out from under him as she grabbed his crossbow. When he fell, she shot him with his own weapon. Two deaths in ten seconds—and she was still going, still fighting, while I could only stare in horror.

"Bianca!" That was Dana, farther down the hall. "Get the hell out of here!"

"Go!" That was my mother squaring off against Dana. "Honey, go!" She and Dana looked at each other in a second of confused recognition, but then Mom leaped at Dana and took her down to the floor.

I ran. Somebody had to stop this, but I couldn't; I didn't know how. If I could only find Lucas, surely he could do it. Surely he could call off Black Cross. But where was he?

"Everybody outside!" That was Balthazar. I turned around to see him hustling students down the stairwell, and I caught a glimpse of Vic in boxers and an undershirt, staring at the mayhem in dismay, but running as fast as he could. Even though he never seemed to turn toward me, Balthazar must have sensed that I was there, because he yelled, "Get to the girls' dorms!"

"I can't! There's fighting in the main building—we're cut off!"

"We'll figure something out!"

Then a voice down the hall, audible even over the screams and the wail of the fire alarm, said, "Don't listen to him, Bianca. You need to leave this school immediately."

I turned to see Eduardo, weapons strapped to bandoliers across his chest and a smear of blood on his scarred cheek. Why did it have to be him? Quickly I held up my hands. "You don't have to go after Balthazar. He's safe, I promise."

"You don't know how to tell a vampire from a human yet," Eduardo said. His smile twisted the scars on his cheeks. "Let me let you in on a secret. Only vampires would remain in this building to defend it now. Which means we can finish the job."

"Please, you've been lied to. Charity—the vampire you caught, the one who told you something terrible was happening here—she wasn't telling the truth!"

"You're not the best at knowing when you've been lied to, Bianca. I suggest you trust me. Get downstairs. If you don't, it's on your head." Then he held up the walkie-talkie that dangled from his belt and said, "Torch it."

Fire. One of the only ways to truly kill a vampire. The Black Cross hunters were burning Evernight.

Balthazar grabbed me and towed me into the stairwell, but when he tried to pull me downstairs after him, I tugged myself free. "Bianca, we have to go!" he shouted.

"I have to get to the girls' dorms!"

"You said you couldn't make it! *Bianca!*"

I ignored him and ran up the stairs, two flights, until I ran into the guys' dorms—the level that looked out over the roof of the main building. Already firelight was flickering down a couple of the hallways, but I didn't look too closely. I just jumped out onto the roof.

A few other people had had the same idea—I could see students running over the many angles and gables of the enormous roof of the main building. Some were vampires, others human; Eduardo had given the order much too soon. All the people I saw were probably only trying to save themselves, and I couldn't blame them. But I was the one who understood what was going on, and that meant it was my responsibility to reach the girls' dorm and make sure everybody got out. I ran over the roof, up and down, slipping on the shingles but somehow remaining upright. My robe had come untied and rippled behind me; the heat of the nearby fire seemed to sear through the T-shirt and pajama bottoms I wore. A loud crackling behind me made me look back; part of the roof glowed orange with flame, then gave way with a crash of timber and soot. Sparks shot up in the air, and I started to cough, but I kept running. *Faster, you've got to go faster!—No!*

I lost my balance and fell, rolling over and over toward the edge of the building. Though I scrambled to grab hold of something, there was nothing to grab, until the roof suddenly wasn't beneath me any longer and I was falling—

Something made of stone smashed against my back, and I blindly clutched for it. My grip held. I dangled off the side of the building for a moment while I tried to keep from passing out from pain and shock. As soon as my vision cleared, I could see what had broken my fall: one of the gargoyles, identical to the one I'd always hated outside my window. My hands were locked around his neck.

"Thank you," I whispered as I hooked one of my feet against his claws and pushed myself back up again. When I resumed running, I could feel how badly my body ached, but smoke was now thick in the air, and there was no time to hesitate.

Finally I got to the south tower and clambered inside, only to realize the blaze was much worse here. My big rescue effort didn't seem that important, either—so far as I could tell, everyone was gone. Then I saw a figure moving through the smoke. "Hello?" I called.

"Bianca!" It was Lucas. He ran to me and hugged me; my aching back protested, but I didn't care. "I've been looking for you everywhere—carriage house, here—"

"You have to call them off, Lucas. You have to tell them Charity lied!"

"Wait—the vampire Eduardo got that info from was *Charity*?" Lucas swore. "I knew some student massacre didn't sound like

Mrs. Bethany's game, and I told them so, but Eduardo wouldn't listen. The bastard never listens."

"Mom—Dana—everybody—they're in danger, and we have to end this!"

"We can't." Lucas held my face in his hands. His features were hazy through the thickening veil of smoke. "We can't end this. We can only get you out of here."

I hated it, but I knew he was right.

Together we ran into the stairwell, shouting for anyone else who might somehow have failed to flee, then hurried back down toward the ground floor. By now the smell of ash was thick in the air, and I had to tug the collar of my robe over my mouth to keep from choking. I imagined the print of Klimt's *Kiss* in my bedroom above us slowly curling up and blackening, fire consuming the lovers forever. Lucas held his forearm across his face. "We're almost there," he yelled. "Come on!"

As we ran out onto the grounds, we ran almost instantly into a fight—one of the Black Cross hunters, a woman I didn't know, was circling Mrs. Bethany. By now Mrs. Bethany's bun had shaken completely loose; her dark hair tumbled down her back, and her haughty face was smudged and dirty. Firelight outlined her high cheekbones, and despite the destruction all around us, she was smiling. For the first time, I saw her fangs.

Lucas pulled me away from the fight, but we both kept looking back at them, transfixed. Somebody nearby called my name, but I couldn't recognize the voice or turn away.

Mrs. Bethany shifted to one side, then the other, then sprang forward. The hunter tried to dodge her, but she was too slow. I could do nothing as Mrs. Bethany twisted the hunter's body around and then sank her fangs into the woman's neck.

The scream behind me was one of pure horror. I turned to see Raquel, in a tank top and underwear, shrieking as she watched Mrs. Bethany drink the hunter's blood. There was no mistaking what was happening, especially if you understood that the supernatural actually existed, as Raquel did. Now she knew that vampires were real.

"Oh, my God, oh, my God!" she yelled. "Bianca, did you—Mrs. Bethany—she—" Then Raquel stopped short. "*Lucas?*"

Lucas said, "Run now, explain later."

We all ran. I cast one more look behind me as we headed toward the forest. Most of Evernight still stood, seemingly as impregnable as ever, but the south tower and the roof both blazed orange. Gargoyles were silhouetted against the flame. It seemed like the end of the world. Then I heard the sirens.

"What's that?" Raquel cried, still panicked.

I realized the answer almost instantly. "Fire engines! The fire alarm Mrs. Bethany pulled—they're coming!"

"We can't have the authorities find us here," Lucas insisted. "There's a transport close by. Let's move." We did what he said, going as fast as we could into the forest—but as we ducked into the trees, I saw a shadowy figure ahead, and I gasped out loud as we all skidded to a halt. Charity blocked our way.

"Leaving so soon?" She cocked her head. If her fall from the north tower had injured her, she gave no sign. "You hate

Evernight nearly as much as I do, Bianca. I thought you'd like my surprise."

"People could be killed," I said. "Balthazar might not have made it out."

"You doubt my brother." Her eyes were dark. "I believe in him. He's too strong for any Black Cross scum."

"I believed in you," I said. "I won't make that mistake again."

Raquel said, "Uh, guys? Who is this kid? Is she Balthazar's sister or something?"

Charity glared at Raquel, then smiled. "You brought me a snack."

"Like hell." Lucas swung a fist at Charity's face, which she dodged easily—but she hadn't counted on his vampirelike speed. Almost faster than I could see, Lucas spun around, grabbing one of Charity's arms and twisting it behind her back.

"Stupid boy," she hissed, trying to get out of his grip. Strong as she was, I knew she could do it in a second. Raquel tried to rush forward, but I prevented her.

"I've cut you slack for Bianca's sake," Lucas said. He and Charity were struggling in the underbrush; he was managing to hold her arm back, but only barely. "No more. We're through."

With that he pushed her forward, full strength, into a tree. Charity smashed into it face-first. At first I expected her to scream in outrage, but instead she slumped into unconsciousness. Lucas was still holding her against the tree—and, I realized, against the broken-off branch that jutted from the trunk and had acted as a stake.

"You killed her!" Raquel gasped.

"Can't do that for real." Lucas looked chagrined. "She stole my knife."

"Just let her fall," I said. "I know that's going to, well, 'unstake' her, but it'll take a few minutes before she can pursue us. In that time, we can reach the transport, right?"

Lucas didn't like the plan, but he knew it was our only choice. He took off running, and as Raquel and I followed, I saw Charity slump to the forest floor.

The "transport" turned out to be the van I'd seen before. When we jumped inside, a few people were already waiting— Kate, who was in the driver's seat, and Dana, who had a black eye and a cut lip. The sight of her made me queasy inside; Mom would have been the person who did this to Dana, but if they were fighting and Dana was still here . . . "What happened?" I whispered. "What happened to the vampire you were fighting?"

"Lady jumped out a window." Dana's words were thick because of her swollen lip. "You ask me, that's cheating."

Mom had made it. I slumped against Lucas in relief. Vic and Balthazar were probably safe as well. But what about my father? Or the teachers I knew or Ranulf or so many people—the humans, too, because fire didn't discriminate when it killed.

Lucas put his arm around me as he asked, "Where's Mr. Watanabe?"

"They got him," Dana said.

A terrible silence fell in the van. Raquel was looking from

Dana to Lucas to me, clearly incredibly confused, but she must have understood this wasn't the moment for questions. Lucas put his forehead on my shoulder, and I held him tightly.

Enjoy each other, Mr. Watanabe had said. He'd had a sweet smile. I wondered if he was with Noriko now, if there was anything after death for humans that didn't involve being a vampire or a wraith. I'd never asked myself that before.

Kate started the van. As we pulled away, I watched the fire-haloed silhouette of Evernight Academy shrink in the rearview mirror until it disappeared entirely.

The rendezvous point turned out to be a warehouse in the middle of nowhere, one half filled with enormous crates. I had no idea what was inside them, and I thought Black Cross didn't either. It was just a place the hunters could use to regroup.

Dana held an ice pack to her face, and Eduardo was at work bandaging a cut on Kate's shin. As they cleaned and repaired their weapons, most of the hunters remained silent, either from grief or exhaustion. But I could tell that they all thought they'd done what they had to do. I wanted to tell them they were wrong—that they'd been lied to—but I knew they wouldn't listen.

Lucas and I sat on one of the crates, leaning our backs against each other. Raquel stood next to us, wrapped in a blanket one of the hunters had given her. Slowly she repeated, "The whole school was full of vampires. The entire time."

"Basically," I said. "There were human students, too—you

weren't the only one. Vic, for instance."

"And Ranulf," she said. I shook my head, and Raquel gaped at me. "*Ranulf?* But—was Balthazar—was he a vampire, too?"

I nodded. Lucas said, "And all the teachers. Used to be nothing but vampires until a couple of years ago."

"Wait, wait, wait. That can't be right. Bianca, your parents are teachers."

In my weariness, I think I would have blurted out the truth if Lucas hadn't put a warning hand over mine. Revealing that I was part vampire in the middle of a group of Black Cross hunters could have been the last thing I ever did.

Eduardo answered the question for me. "We believe Bianca was kidnapped as an infant. Probably her real parents were murdered, so two vampires could play house."

Raquel covered her mouth with her hands. "When did you find this out? Oh, Bianca, I'm sorry. I'm so sorry."

Lucas cut in so I wouldn't have to reveal how long I'd known. "I came to Evernight last year to investigate why they were letting humans in as students."

"That's why you got into all those fights!" Raquel said. "God, I always thought you were this total hothead creep."

"Wow," Lucas said. "I'm touched." I could hear the smile in his voice.

"I'm honestly sorry I thought that about you. Obviously I'm not such a great judge of people." Raquel sat down on a nearby crate, shaking her head in bewilderment. Then her expression shifted from confusion to awareness, and she met my eyes with new comprehension. "The vampire thing explains Erich, doesn't it?"

"Yeah."

She slumped over. "I *knew* that school wasn't right."

"I doubt they'll have any more human students for a good long while," Kate said. "Or any students, given the damage we did. Which means we can cross Evernight Academy off our list of concerns."

Maybe they could. I couldn't. I knew I had to get back there, to find out who had lived and who had died, how my parents were—so many things. But how could I go back, now that Mrs. Bethany knew I'd been seeing Lucas all year? For all I knew, she might blame me for the part I'd played in attracting Charity's attention and bringing all this to pass. I knew better than ever how lethal Mrs. Bethany could be. No, I'd have to wait.

"Mrs. Bethany made it." Kate winced as Eduardo smoothed the last bandage over the cut on her leg. "That means she's going to want revenge. And that means we've all got to get on the move. This cell is in lockdown, effective immediately. We'll have to be underground a long while, after this one. Raquel, if you want to go home, we can give you some money to get you started. After that, it's up to you."

"Go home?" Raquel was on her feet again immediately. "Are you crazy?"

"Raquel?" I asked. "What do you mean?"

"All this evil in the world—the ghosts and the vampires, all this crap that's been ruining our lives forever—there's a way to fight it! These people fight!" She gestured toward the room, the blanket over her shoulders flowing behind her like a superhero's cape. "Am I supposed to go back to Boston and sleep on my sister's couch and ignore what's in my own home? Ignore the evil out there? No way. I want to be a part of this."

Eduardo shook his head. "We don't take amateurs."

"Everyone's an amateur before they start," Kate pointed out. "You said yourself we needed fresh blood."

My stomach rumbled. When would I ever be able to drink blood again?

Raquel looked from person to person, hope in her face. "I didn't want to go home this summer anyway. It's not like you're breaking up some big happy family—trust me. I need somewhere else to go. And the things you're up against—I've been waiting my whole life for this battle. Just give me a chance. I'll prove myself to you."

Dana grinned. "I believe Black Cross just got itself another fighter."

Most people looked satisfied, but Eduardo's face remained stern. "You'll have to train hard. It's difficult, and it's dangerous. Most people in Black Cross don't live as long as Hideo Watanabe; most of them don't even make it as long as I have. You'll be giving up everything. Nothing less than total commitment is acceptable."

Raquel said, "I'm in. Absolutely. From this second on." Then she turned to me. "Bianca?"

Me? Join Black Cross? I couldn't be a vampire hunter; I was

a vampire. Kind of a vampire, at least—enough for virtually everybody in this room to turn on me instantaneously if they knew the truth.

I glanced over at Lucas, thinking surely he would know a way out of this. Instead I saw only his dismay. Obviously he realized the problem, but just as obviously, Black Cross was about to go into lockdown—foiling whatever plans he might have had to run away with me. We were trapped.

"I know it's tough for you, Bianca," Kate said. "You really thought they were your parents for a long time, and I can imagine what kind of lies they must have told you about Black Cross. But you see the truth now. You've showed courage. And frankly, I'm tired of Lucas running off all the time. We need him to stay put." She tried to smile. "That means we need you."

"Come on, Bianca!" Raquel could hardly contain her excitement. To her this was a great adventure, a way out of all her problems. "Are you with us?"

I had nowhere else to go. But at least I would be with Lucas—and while we were together, there was always hope.

"Yeah." I looked at Lucas as I took his hand in mine. "I'm with you."

THE ROMANCE AND DANGER CONTINUES WITH

THE THIRD BOOK IN THE EVERNIGHT SERIES
COMING SOON IN JULY 2010

"Once I picked *Evernight* up, I couldn't put it down! I can't wait for Claudia Gray's next book!"
L. J. Smith, bestselling author of *The Vampire Diaries*

CLAUDIA GRAY